HUNTER'S TRAP

a novel by

C.W. Smith

Texas Christian University Press

Fort Worth

Library of Congress Cataloging-in Publication Data

Smith, C. W. (Charles William), 1940-
Hunter's Trap: a novel / by C. W. Smith.
p. cm.
ISBN 0-87565-162-3 (alk. paper)
I. Title.
PS3569.M516H86 1996
813'.54—dc20

96-5770
CIP

DESIGN BY *Barbara Whitehead*

Books by C. W. Smith

NOVELS

Thin Men of Haddam
Country Music
The Vestal Virgin Room
Buffalo Nickel

SHORT FICTION

Letters from the Horse Latitudes

NONFICTION

Uncle Dad

The dark road is before me; I must take it,
Doomed by my father and his avenging Furies
—POLYNEICES, *Oedipus at Colonus*

We cannot escape the savage human origins,
the savage human nature, the savage human body.
—ORMUTH

1

1930　On the vernal equinox, two men sat in straightback chairs on the roof of an El Paso hotel admiring how the sunset fell on barren, suede-colored hills to the south. One, who called himself John Bliss, had a pale burn scar on his cheek shaped like a spider. He was drinking mescal; from time to time, he hoisted the bottle from beside his boot and poured a double-shot jigger, momentar-

1

ily resurrecting the pickled caterpillar. The other man, known as Will Hunter, watched it sink in the clear liquor and rest on the bottom like a laboratory specimen. Although Hunter was not drinking, he was extremely thirsty, and he kept picturing a clean glass sitting on the marble top of the washstand in his room below; beside it stood a white enamel pitcher of water, and if he lowered his face over the pitcher's dark mouth, it would give off a faint cool breath. He saw himself pouring the glass full and drinking the water slowly. Accustomed to ignoring such thirsts, Hunter merely sat smoking one Camel after another and watching the light ooze like butter down the slopes of the spiny hills. A pebble pinched his left sole, but he made no effort to remove it from his shoe because he had put it there.

"I should've stayed down there." Bliss was staring fixedly at the hills. An indistinct band of gray hovered over the far horizon. Hunter imagined the ancient city of the Aztecs steeped in darkness. "Why?"

"Because we lived like kings, I tell you. *El jefes*. A few of us, we'd go off on our own and come riding through those little villages scattering chickens and pigs and dogs. We'd shoot a greaser or two just to get everybody's undivided attention, then we'd have our pick of the *señoritas*. We'd stay sometimes a week, then we'd get restless and move on. Stay any longer than that and we'd start squabbling, and the peons'd start laying plans to get rid of us." Bliss chuckled. "I bet I got little bastard sons and daughters all over the state of Sonora."

Hunter slowly ground his cigarette out in the asphalt with his heel. Around his shoes lay a litter of crushed butts. He wasn't interested in Bliss' stories about riding with Pancho Villa—or, rather, riding on the periphery of the revolution like a nasty little tornado spawned by a hurricane. However, he did want to hear Bliss describe his modus operandi.

"So the Mexicans gave you trouble?"

"Oh, sure. Spics are like sheep, but you always got one wants to be a hero. Touchy about their women."

Hunter lit another cigarette. His hands were sweating from the nicotine in his blood. "So what'd you do?"

Bliss shrugged. "Squashed 'em like bugs, whatta you think?" Bliss described how he was set upon while sleeping by the father of a girl he'd raped, but Hunter could hardly bear to listen: Bliss had put a knife under his pillow in the story's expository overture, so the outcome of the yarn could easily be predicted, and the *mano-a-mano* struggle across the room—overturning a cookstove, fire spilling everywhere, exchanging blows, knife thrusts—was the stuff of a Tom Mix movie. While Bliss went on, animated, pleased to have an audience, Hunter wondered if the name Bliss was real; if so, it represented a dark, reverse twist on that irony occurring when Bones or Hart became a surgeon, and God had a hangman's wit. Probably the name was false, and Bliss—who also went by the surname Shingle—had chosen the alias for the perverse delight it provided. It was hard to judge which was worse: that the name was real or invented.

"Had to choke the daughter," Bliss said, jolting Hunter back to the moment. "Jumped me after I gutted the beaner." Bliss smiled, moved by nostalgia. "You might say I took utmost advantage of her spasms."

Hunter told himself he hadn't understood; he changed the subject abruptly by asking, "You ever do a fire?"

Bliss turned to regard him thoughtfully. "See this?" He touched his scarred cheek with the rim of the glass.

"Burn scar?"

Bliss shook his head. "Acid. Girl who did it burnt up

in a house fire after, though." Bliss sounded satisfied with the result, though apparently the revenge had afforded him only professional gratification. Or perhaps the lack of triumph in his voice was his way of expressing sorrow, Hunter couldn't tell. "Paper said 'burnt beyond recognition,'" Bliss added, and Hunter involuntarily shuddered. He licked his dry lips.

"Dynamite?"

Bliss chuckled. "You gonna write my memoirs?"

Hunter shrugged. "Always room to learn something."

"Did some road and bridge work down in Morelia. That's how I was in Mexico to begin with. I tell you, there's something in it, you know, to just stand there and push down on a little handle and a whole damn mountain just goes ka-blooey! right up into the clouds. I do love that de-construction work!"

"Let's say somebody wanted you to do some blasting on the Q.T."

Bliss eyed him with a new curiosity. "You know somebody?"

"Maybe."

"You want me to teach you, that it?"

"Not exactly. Maybe I'm a de-construction contractor."

Bliss smiled. "Sure, if the money's right."

"How do I know you can get it done?"

"I'm experienced."

"You do a remote?"

"That's tricky."

"But you know how?"

Bliss nodded. "It's not hard to do; it's hard to hide it's been done."

Hunter couldn't probe too much without arousing suspicion. "It's not me wants it. Another party."

"I understand."

"You have satisfied customers?"

Bliss nodded.

"You sure?"

Bliss grinned as if he knew a tantilizing secret Hunter might be astonished to learn. "Once I worked for a fellow—maybe you know him—" Bliss squinted at Hunter and leaned closer. "Fact is, you look a bit like him. You got kin around here?" Hunter shook his head. "Well, anyway, this fellow, he had a certain flotation device out in California obstructing his plans."

Hunter got to his feet, maybe too quickly, for Bliss' head snapped about and he lurched as if to rise from his chair, so Hunter froze, smiled to reassure him, and patted his empty coat pockets.

"Need some smokes," he said.

"Got any stogies down there?"

Hunter detected a yearning for celebration in the question; it was wholly out of keeping with his own grim mood.

"No. Sorry."

Bliss shrugged, poured himself another shot, and the pickled green worm tried to swim again.

The pebble pinched the arch of his foot as Hunter went down the steps to the hall and into his room. He had left the door open for ventilation, but now he closed it behind him. He went to the washstand, and, with his hands shaking violently, poured a glass full of water, spilling some across the marble. He drank it down in one long series of gasping swallows, poured another more carefully, steadily; this he drank slowly, resting and breathing deeply between sips. Several months of agonized, obsessive searching had brought him to this moment: he had to go on from here; he was afraid his rage would show, but having to damp it back made him swoon with dizziness. Bilious mescal boiled up from his gut, and he felt he might puke.

He jammed his palm flat to the wall, then he set the glass down. The washstand mirror framed his face, a stranger's beard. On the marble top next to a wash bowl lay a pair of spectacles and a folded straight-razor. He gingerly held the gold wire temples of the spectacles and hooked them over his ears. He picked up the razor, thumbed the metal moon to unsheath the silver blade, inspected it, snapped it shut.

He was on his way out of the room when the telephone rang. He hesitated, then answered it.

"Will?"

"Yes."

"I didn't recognize you."

Hunter coughed. "Frog in my throat."

The girl giggled. "I'm alone now. Mother and Dad went to a musicale, and I think they're going to Juarez afterward with some people. They'll be out late."

"I'll be there in a bit." The window framed a chunk of violet sky in which a quarter moon lay on its back, slowly levitating, pincers aimed at Venus hovering above it.

"You sound so strange."

"I was napping, Sissy."

"Lazybones!" When he failed to respond, she added softly, "I missed you all day. Did you miss me?"

He could picture the girl standing in the salon amidst her mother's heavy Victorian furniture, playing with the cord to the telephone as she spoke, putting her hand through its loops so it wound around her arm like a bracelet. A wave of nausea forced him down onto the bed. "Yes."

6

"Oh, really, Will!" she scoffed. "Your enthusiasm is overwhelming."

"Sorry." He looked about the room. The dry wash bowl, the empty glass, the blank mirror stood oddly expectant in the twilight dimness. "Like I say, I'm not awake."

"Well, please hurry. Please? I've been waiting all day." Now she sounded like a peevish child. "And bring me something to drink, will you?"

"What?"

"I don't know. Surprise me!"

"Tequila?"

"Ugh! No, bring stuff to make those, oh, what Daddy drinks?"

"Manhattans."

"Yes! And we'll be oh so so-phis-ti-cated! I'll wear a trayz chick negligee."

"I'll shave my beard," he uttered, surprising himself.

"Really?" she said, then fell silent, and Hunter thought he detected a faint uneasiness about seeing him beardless for the first time. "Oh, that's exciting, we can dance cheek-to-cheek!" Then she said, "How come?"

"No reason."

Hunter returned to the roof, and the sounds of his shoes crunching gravel startled Bliss from a reverie. Bliss twisted about to watch Hunter move toward him. Hunter didn't take his former seat; he stood behind and between the chairs, placing his left hand on the shoulder of the vacant one. His right hand propped the unfolded razor up his coat sleeve. Both men looked off toward Mexico, as if posing for a family portrait.

With his spectacles on, to Hunter everything observed from the roof now looked more real, therefore less real. He traced the sharp outlines of the craggy mountains to the south, their crenelations and folds holding the darkness, their ribs catching the ruddy last lumens of a sunset lurid enough to advertise the Apocalypse. The air was teeming with red and purple highlights like colored smoke, as if Hunter were seeing through a filter or had ascended from the hallway to find himself unexpectedly on Mars. White stars glimmered on the grid of Juarez across the border; on the outskirts, in the *colonias*, there were flickering orange lights from the cooking fires of the landless hordes who lived in shacks fashioned from crates and oil drums.

"I heard a phone."

Hunter nodded. "The aforementioned other party."

Bliss grunted. "What'd he say?"

"He wanted to know if the so-called 'flotation device' was a sailboat."

"Well, he *is* an inquisitive fellow."

"He doesn't want to waste his money."

"He's asking for too much and giving too little. Besides, I can't talk business on an empty stomach. I've been sitting here thinking about skedaddling across the bridge and getting some enchiladas and some poontang—you game for that? It's Friday night. You probably know some good pussy palaces. I haven't been over there in a while."

Hunter couldn't picture himself and Bliss carousing in a bordertown bordello, but he could see the two of them staggering with arms about each other's shoulders down a Juarez street, singing, then himself steering the groggy Bliss into a dark alley, and, suddenly sober, he'd stick his middle fingers in Bliss' ears and both thumbs in the man's eyes and squeeze until they all met in the middle of his brain. Such sudden death left much to be desired, though—Bliss would not suffer enough nor would he learn why he was to die—but it would be far safer than doing it here on the roof where they'd been sitting for the past hour and no doubt could have been observed. Poor planning, or too much planning, really—he'd played this out a thousand times in a thousand ways; consequently, the present reality seemed so much less satisfactory than his fantasies that it robbed him of the will to move decisively.

He stared at the nape of Bliss' neck and let the handle of the razor slip down into the nest of his grip. He started trembling. He'd longed for this moment; over and over he'd imagined thrusting his rage into a black hole of opportunity. He clenched his jaw. Where was that speech? Nothing had occurred cleanly enough—no clear-cut confession, only teasing probabilities: a "flotation device"—could that be anything but Copperfield's boat? *You scum! You killed my wife!*

"I say what do you think about—" Bliss began, obviously about to repeat his invitation, but he'd also turned slightly in his chair to look up at Hunter and had seen that thunderstorm on Hunter's face, his shaking limbs, the razor. "Say, fella!" he barked. He bolted from the chair and tried to stand clear, but Hunter grabbed his lapel in one fist and, with a wide fierce swipe of his right hand like a haymaker, slashed at Bliss' throat. The swing went wide and only nicked him, and Bliss, astonished, the whites of his eyes showing like those of a spooked horse, frantically snatched at the razor. They fell to the roof and wrestled for it, breath heaving, grunting; Hunter wound up on top, his left hand in Bliss' mouth, and Bliss savagely clamped down on it with his teeth. Hunter howled in pain but managed to wrench the other man's head up and back and sliced him deep across the jugular with the razor.

While Bliss jerked and flopped like a huge, landed fish, Hunter lay on him with one hand jammed in his mouth and the other pressed against the man's nose. Bliss pounded his head and ears with his fists, but Hunter rode him without being bucked until, at last, Bliss lost consciousness.

Hunter snatched his hand from the slackened jaws. He rose and stood over Bliss, trembling violently. He kicked the man ferociously in the ribs, as if to wake him. Blood was spurting, a red ejaculate, from the gash in his neck.

"You fucker! You got off too easy!"

Hunter was so furious he began to bawl, and he squelched an urge to fling the corpse off the roof. He sank into the chair Bliss had occupied and fought to control himself, holding his bloody left hand in a fist on his lap and rocking, cooing from the pain. He bent over suddenly to the side and splattered the gravelled asphalt with vomit. He couldn't stop crying, like someone who has crawled from the wreckage of a home flattened by a tornado.

After a while, his breathing evened, and he sat up. He felt drained. The razor lay in the other chair as if it had been placed there, but he couldn't recall having done that. He took out his handkerchief—it was an awkward reach with his right hand to his left hip pocket—and wrapped it around the razor. The moon had a hazy shape; he'd lost his glasses in the fight. He slid off the chair and duck-walked about, squinting at the asphalt, until one moon-white lens winked at him.

When he put his glasses on and looked about, panic shot through him; dusk still hung faintly in the sky, and the rising moon would soon cover the roof with a wan light. So much left to do. He needed to move Bliss' body so it wouldn't be spotted at least until morning. He tried to consider his next moves with the calm rationality of playing chess, but his thoughts were fuzzy, electrified, wouldn't stay put. He saw himself driving to Sissy's house, her talking on the phone, the cord around her arm, then around her neck, tightening.

⧉ ⧉ ⧉

His glasses had been bent in the fight so that the stairs down to the hall were framed in his gaze like a Cubist's vision; he tripped but caught the bannister with his right hand so fast it astonished him.

The hall was empty, though a radio was playing "My Blue Heaven." Hunter shut his door and tiptoed to the washstand. The furniture was draped in darkness. The spectacles pinched his nose; he removed them. He poured a drink; the pitcher's lip went *tink tink tink* against the shaking glass. Light dim as grey silk lay across the bed, the window open for exit or entry. Swallowing, he saw a swift dark movement on his right, and he spun, gasped, choked on the water, coughed it into the empty washbowl. Only his mirrored twin. Trembling, he groped the air over his head for the knotted cord, studying his dark reflected form. When the light popped on, he shuddered and gave an involuntary yelp: the man in the glass was bathed in blood. For an instant, Hunter wondered if he'd been cut then realized the blood was the dead man's.

He shivered out of his coat in a great panic. "Ohhh!" he groaned. He ripped off his shirt, then, nude to the waist, hurriedly scanned the room, grabbed a white towel, poured water into the bowl and swabbed at the blood on his arms and neck. His left hand ached. Bliss' bite had broken the skin, and it hurt so much he guessed a bone was cracked or broken. He tried to ignore the pain, relying on his right hand. He doused the towel, squeezed it over the bowl, and soon the water turned pink. He grimaced, picked up the pitcher, set it down, picked it up, scurried to the door, peeked into the hall. The radio music was louder, and he heard talking, but, seeing no one, Hunter slipped out, filled the pitcher in the bathroom down the hall and brought it back. He sopped a clean towel and scrubbed hard at his neck and shoulders; soon that towel was pink, also. He dropped it with disgust onto the blood-stained shirt and coat. He'd have to do something with the towels and the clothes. But he couldn't stash them here, had to take them. What to put them in, wrap them in something? Wouldn't that get bloody, too?

What about this pink water? Couldn't leave it for the maid. Have to flush it down the hall toilet, wash out the basin, hope no one sees. The razor? Get rid of it! But he'd wanted to shave his beard, part of the plan, now it seemed impossible, given his trembling and having to make so many trips down the hall for warm clean water. Plan? Yes, he'd "planned" to kill Bliss, but it seemed now he'd not thought of what would happen after the knife gun hammer hatchet cut pierced punched or bludgeoned the man. Now, his heart thundered and a thousand simple questions hummed like wasps in his brain. Someone on the roof? Was Bliss groaning or shouting? The razor was wrapped in his handkerchief in the coat pocket. What—

He licked his lips. His bloody clothes might stain the carpet. He bent, scooped them up, flung them down as something wet and cold brushed his arm. He removed a case from a pillow and stuffed the bloody shirt and coat into it. Jam the bundle into his valise? Blood might leak onto his clean clothing. Maybe wrap them in a blanket. But the blanket would prove he'd been here. Never get it into the valise.

His mind hopped nimbly away from whatever resisted it. He wondered suddenly if his trousers were clean. He ran his hands down his legs, felt nothing wet. They were dark and would hide a smudge, but Bliss' blood, on him, that was horrid!

He had to move fast.

No, don't hurry! He needed to take care that panic didn't cause a mistake, make him overlook a step that needed to be taken before he left this room.

First do the clothes.

No, first shave? because he'd need to put on fresh clothes after, then pack. Gather up the photograph of Bobette and Pearl, his ivory-handled toilet set from Bobette. Then the papers from under the bed, check that everything's there for presenting the evidence. Letter from Pearl in the desk drawer, don't forget it. Calm down, breathe deeply, slowly.

He turned out the light and sat on the bed for several minutes, forcing his mind to empty and his pulse to slow to normal. He told himself he had to go about the next few minutes—and the next few hours—with the same cool, unhurried economy that he'd practice had he not slashed a man's throat for the first time in his life only moments ago and on the roof hardly fifty feet away.

Yes, he would shave; it would give him a reason to go to and from the bath and allow him to dispose of the bloody water. Testing his procedures, he pictured himself packing and checking systematically to make sure all signs of his presence were removed.

The telephone jangled; he lurched but didn't pick up the receiver. It would be Sissy, impatient.

●   ●   ●

To avoid having a porter in his room, Hunter carried his bags to the desk. His left hand hurt from gripping the valise handle. The bite was no longer bleeding, but the heel of his hand was swollen and tender. Using his good hand, he'd awkwardly swathed his wound in a handkerchief.

The clerk was reading a newspaper spread on the counter.

"Where's Fairfield?"

"Uh, I don't know," said Hunter.

The clerk tsked, tapped the paper, noted Hunter's bags and drew a ledger from a drawer. While the clerk leafed through it, Hunter read that Wilma Jones of Fairfield was tied to a bed in her hotel room and the bed set afire. He shuddered. A New York man ate forty raw eggs. Proposed name for new planet—Minerva. Mrs. Dugan to hang. First blonde Virgin Mary at Oberammergau.

"Leaving us for good, Mr. Hunter? Or just taking a business trip?"

"Yes. I mean I'll be back in a few days. On Wednesday. I've got business up in Santa Fe."

"Very good. Shall I—"

"Yes," Hunter put in quickly. "Same room, if you would."

The clerk said, while writing Hunter's receipt, "Burn your hand?"

"What?" The woman tied to the bed—

"Did you burn that hand?"

"Yes. No, I mean no. Car door. I shut the car door on it."

"Ouch."

The clerk slapped the bell; waiting, they both watched Hunter's bandaged hand resting on the counter as if it might suddenly commence some extraordinary activity, then Hunter held it against his chest and looked out the window onto San Jacinto Plaza. He could hear the clerk breathing. Every second they waited it seemed more possible that Bliss would stumble down the stairs to the lobby, severed head tucked under his arm. Hunter was sweating across his brow. He'd reshaped his glasses, but the right lens was low, the other high, giving him the sensation of standing at a list. The bridge pads pinched his nose. He was thirsty again.

"Warm tonight," he said.

"Think so? Seems cooler to me."

At last the old porter shuffled in from the hotel's kitchen, wiping his mouth daintily with his handkerchief. Both men were outside standing on the curb before Hunter recalled that when he had returned to the hotel this afternoon, traffic had forced him to park across the plaza. His heart skipped—another surprise, another decision: he could either let Sanchez walk with him and risk having the contents of the valise exposed by blood dripping from it or by the latches popping open—*Oh, this is crazy! Calm down!*—or let him—

"Only take a minute, Sanchez. My car's over on Main." He gestured with the bandaged hand. He started to say, "*Just leave the bags here,*" then knew that would be strange. "If you'd just watch the bags."

"*Bueno.*"

Hunter set off across Mills, darting through the traffic. It was fully dark now, but on the Oregon side of the plaza the theatre's marquee showered light onto the walk and the crowd milling underneath. Like sheep, bleating. He resisted the compulsion to read the feature's title and plunged into the plaza. Under the arbor of cottonwoods and elms, old Mexican dueñas sat crocheting while their young charges strolled about arm in arm. Hunter looked back to the hotel. Sanchez, now smoking, had one foot propped on the suitcase.

Hunter hurried past the pond where, by day, charcoal-colored alligators dozed in the sun, oblivious to the pebbles children tossed onto their backs. From inside the pit came a grunt, a splash. He strode on quickly, thinking of Sanchez standing over the bags, and a fleeting image beseiged him: Bliss, on the roof, throwing his voice like a ventriloquist into the valise, breathing the bloody clothes to life. *Help me!*

He dashed in front of a trolley on Main, trotted to his Ford, jumped in, cocked the gas and spark and jammed the starter plunger. The engine's sudden bang jolted him; he pulled away and was almost rear-ended by a truck, came round the corner onto Mills, skidded to where Sanchez stood looking worried or surprised—*I mustn't seem to be in such a hurry*—leaned over to open the door, took the bags Sanchez handed in, and roared off.

Three blocks away, he pulled to the curb. He hadn't tipped Sanchez. He breathed deeply, raggedly. He needed to feel secure, safe; he wanted to appear normal, but lapses in his behavior were undermining his confidence.

To calm himself, he catechized his revenge like a man running a check before a vacation. Had he stripped the room of all his belongings? Did he put the razor in his jacket pocket? Had he been careful not to let the clerk know where he'd come from or who he worked for? Or who he knew in El Paso?

The shot glass! Where... no, the last thing he'd done before leaving the roof was to pitch it like a stone high over the adjoining building because the maid had probably seen it in his room.

He let out a long, slow breath. No need to panic. Even if the body were discovered in the next few seconds, Hunter was safe now. It might be days before Bliss stank enough to draw attention, and you couldn't see the body behind the chimney if you only looked out the doorway to the roof.

I am not running from the law. I am simply a man like any other young bachelor out on a Friday night in his car, on his way to court his girl. Officer, I am just on my way to Kern Place to pick up my girl. I am not a fugitive. I am a bachelor....

Coaching helped. He pulled the rod into first, set his good hand firmly on the wheel, and inhaled. On to the hard part. The justice. He slipped into the traffic and felt safely inconspicuous until he realized he was going the wrong way and had to make a block to get himself headed back toward Mesa and northwest into the hills. It shook him for a moment, but then he told himself it was just as well that Sanchez last saw him heading toward the rail yard. He could picture Sanchez being questioned, pointing east.

Heading out of downtown, he tended his speed like a clergyman. In his rearview mirror, across the Rio Grande, stood the Sierra Juarez and the Mexican town lying at its skirt. The lighted bridge over the river thrust nightly into willing Juarez, where the streets glowed with gin joints and whorehouses for scum like Bliss and his boss. The city sprawled for miles but shrank at night to the eye: electrification ran like a hot finger up Avenida Juarez and onto Avenida 16th of Septiembre, but a few blocks off to either side the city had only sporadic gas lights; on the outskirts torches and bonfires struck points in the darkness that showed where people lived.

The moon rising over Mexico made him think of feathered serpents, rain, corn, a flint knife plunged into a virgin's breast. A burning bed. Then he thought of candles, candle-lit processions, the Mexicans crawling into their churches on their knees, moving like a glimmering snake up the side of Christo Rey. The roaring smelter at its foot. Lent, light flickering under images of the Virgin. Sissy with an ashen cross on her brow. Mexico seemed a good place to to hide.

A police car was parked outside a diner, and a patrolman stood with one foot hiked up on the running board while calling out to another who leaned out of the diner to hear. Maybe they were talking about an ice-cold soda pop. Hunter checked his speed, held his breath, drove on with the hair prickling on his nape.

I am not a killer on the run. I am just a fellow going to court his girl, a bachelor....

No, he *was* a killer. He needed now to remind himself that he could do this, the coaching went both ways.

He was not going to court his girl.

And I'm not a bachelor, I'm a widower. And a father.

The reminder snapped a line of resistance, and images tumbled through his mind, a shoe box of snapshots. Pearl here, there. What time was it in California? Friday evening, about suppertime, he'd guess. Pearl and Mildred sitting at the oilcloth-covered table in the kitchen, maybe Pearl's favorite, meat loaf. She hated Ovaltine.

He felt sick. He'd called only this afternoon, but it now seemed so remote it might as well have been a week, a month, or a year. *I miss you Daddy. I miss you too, sweetheart. Give Gramma my love. No, I don't need to talk to her again.* (She would only tell him to come home. Well, he will, he *will!*)

If anyone ever harmed *his* daughter, he'd go nuts.

He drifted away, thinking about Pearl. Then, startled, he saw that the ghostly chauffeur who takes over when one ruminates had wheeled the Ford off Mesa and up Cincinnati Street and had brought it to heel behind a clanging trolley stopped at the end of the line in Kern Place. Now the Ford blocked the trolley from starting its return trip to town. At about this place just last night someone had hijacked a trolley and robbed the motorman, and now this one was glaring suspiciously out of the window at him.

Hunter cursed himself and swung the car around the trolley and made the turn onto Kansas. After a moment, he reached the grotesque gate to the exclusive subdivision at the base of the hills: constructed of pipe and wrought iron and festooned with illuminated globes, the contraption looked like two Christmas trees with the triangular gable mounted between them and over the street. This was the point of no return. He checked his watch, and, much to his astonishment, it was already 8:30. Sissy would be fretting. As he passed beneath the gate, white light drenched his arms and lap, then dried instantly with the darkness as the car moved on, and he thought of baptism, river water, coming up from a dive, going under again.

2

1917-
1920

THE BOY stared at a calendar on the wall. Thirty days hath September.

"Had bad luck all my life," his stepfather was saying.

"Aw, go on, now, Atlas," somebody goaded him. Three barber chairs were occupied. Six men waiting were smoking cigars and reading newspapers, and maybe they would've liked to speak to each another, but his stepfather had hogged the silence by talking in his booming voice. His face was red as the sand on their farm, and he had a stubble of beard, but he wasn't here for a shave or haircut: he was here to cheat a man whom they had observed from across the street enter the shop. That man now had a hot towel over his face. Maybe he was listening, maybe not.

"Well, hell, I ain't saying I'm the only one. I ain't feeling sorry for myself. And I ain't so dumb I don't know half the time bad luck's nothing but stupidity. You take for instance how I got stuck with that land in West Texas." He paused, as if to be prompted. No one spoke— maybe they'd heard this story—but his stepfather went on, anyway. "That was '87, I think. I'd just got married to my first woman and we'd had a baby boy. A man come up to Tennessee where we was and stood on a soapbox in the square talking about all that beautiful land, using a lot of flowery language just like a goddamned politician! He was reading all this crap out of a newspaper that come from there. 'Come have yourself a Garden of Eden!' it said."

His stepfather fumed in silence; one man winked to another. On the wall hung the head of an eight-point buck, eyes like marbles, its nose a prune.

"Garden of Eden my aching asshole! The winters was like Alaska and the summers were Hell's playground! If it rained any time the whole four years, I was either asleep or dead drunk, and when I woke up or sobered up that bastard of a sun had just sucked it back up again! There wadn't a tree in a hunnerd miles, and it was so flat it made flat look hilly!"

Somebody laughed, short, like a bark.

"Yessir," his stepfather went on, encouraged. "I plowed the ground and the goddamn wind just blew the topsoil away! The sorry-ass Comanches jumped the reservation every other day and come around looking for a handout or snatched up anything that wasn't bolted down, and them rich sonofabitching cowmen let their herds trample my crops! Then one day I come in after a four-day dust storm and found my old lady sitting on the floor making a noise like a hooty owl with her eyes big and blank as saucers. 'What in hell you doing?' I ast her. 'I'm a norther,' she says to me. She kept that up for two days straight. Then I packed up the wagon and we just up and left that shack and everything in it."

The boy caught a man sizing him up, and he wanted to say, I'm not that baby boy. I couldn't be. My real father was a genius, not a stupid farmer! He's talking thirty years ago, do I look thirty to you? Besides, it's all a bunch of lies, can't you tell? Turning away, the boy looked out the window. Town kids were going by, rolling hoops. Lucky.

"Yessir, thought we'd come here to the Promised Land. Might have known you can't have no Promised Land that's full of cheats and chiselers and a soil so thin you could read a book through it, even if you could read a book, which I can't because I never had the schooling that a lot of other people had, people like lawyers and other lying scum that learn how to cheat an honest farmer."

"You been out there on that piece a good while, Atlas," somebody put in.

"Yeah? Well, you couldn't raise an umbrella on it now! It's nine-tenths rock and one-tenth snake shit!" He groaned with disgust. "Like a dummy, I keep raising me one hell of a crop of rock. I keep thinking the price of a bushel a rock'll go up some day, and I'll be a rich man."

There was laughter. Even the boy smiled, despite himself.

"But it's all wore out. And it's about wore us out, ain't that right, boy?" Atlas clapped him on the back and expected him to speak, but the boy could only nod. He swallowed and looked away. Next would be the doorstep story.

"How many acres you got?"

"Two hunnerd," his stepfather said with bitter pride. It was as if the farm's smallness were still another way he'd suffered. "My livestock's dying of thirst. Don't know where I'll get the wherewithal to buy the groceries. But that's just about the story of my life. You hang around long enough you find that life's just a poxy old whore. I spent most of my sixty years with my hands on a plow and my eye on a mule's bung-hole, so what do I know, huh?"

Somebody clucked a tongue. His stepfather looked at the man under the hot towel.

"Water went sour on the place. Well coughed up some kind of black goo."

The boy held his breath, but no one spoke. "Welp," his stepfather declared, "best be running my errands."

Outside the barbershop, they stood on the wooden planking. The boy didn't know what was next. Back inside, the man who'd been under the towel was putting on his coat. The boy realized that his stepfather was waiting for him.

The man was tall, thin, and handsome, and his boots were always polished. When the boy and his stepfather occasionally saw him walking in his pastures next to their own, he was always wearing Sunday trousers with the cuffs tucked into the tops of the boots. The boy could imagine the man riding back to his house and going inside—he'd just lift out his cuffs and let them fall and he'd look right for being in his parlor. His house had a wide front porch and an upper story. His little girl had her own pony—she was only four or five maybe. When she rode it, she didn't notice anyone on foot. Sometimes she'd be sitting on the porch in a rocking chair when they went by in the wagon. If the man were present, his stepfather would wave, the man would wave back, and his stepfather would mutter, "That's right, say howdy, you conniving sonofabitch!" The boy's mother once objected to his stepfather's cursing the man, and his stepfather said, "Oh no, he ain't greedy for everybody else's land—he just wants all that butts up against his own!" The man had made offers for their farm, but his stepfather had turned them down. His mother wanted to move to someplace big like St. Louis where she'd grown up and lived until coming here.

When the man walked out of the barbershop, Atlas acted surprised to see him. They shook hands. His stepfather's hypocrisy galled the boy, and he walked over to the wagon a few yards away, filled a bag with oats and fed the horse hitched to the singletree. After a while, both men came over and climbed into the wagon. The man winked at the boy. "How you doin,' son?" Surprised, the boy blushed. "Where's your manners?" his stepfather said.

During the hour's ride, the man listened to his stepfather rant, nodding as if agreeing. When his stepfather was silent, the man would look off, and every time his stepfather started yammering again, he'd have to recapture the man's attention. The man was just being sociable and probably thought his stepfather was a smelly windbag. When they turned into the lane that led to their property, the boy saw everything through the man's eyes. The path was rocky and went by a field of withered corn bordered by a crumbling worm fence. Their skinny milk cow was rubbing her back against a pecan tree. Their house was a soddy dugout, a kind of log cabin whose lower half was buried, like a rodent's burrow.

"Go tell your mother we got company for supper, boy."

Sulking, the boy hoisted two sacks—one of flour, one of sugar—from the bed of the wagon and carried them on his shoulders around to the rear of the dugout. He resented being made a party to deceit. His mother already expected this "company," as the purpose of their trip—to judge by what the boy had overheard—had been to lure the man out here. His mother had told Atlas that the man always got his hair cut on Saturday afternoon.

Behind the dugout, smoke from a wash fire hung in the still air like a tattered question mark. A fire was blazing in a rock hearth and a black iron pot sat over it. Clothes were cooking in the kettle like soup. His mother was stirring them with a pole, but she was wearing her good dress; it had tiny blue flowers that matched her eyes and it tucked tightly into her tiny waist and made her bosom too noticeable, though the high collar trimmed in lace and the long sleeves covered her white skin.

He opened his mouth to pass on the message, but she nodded before he could speak and followed him to the dugout.

Inside, the boy let the sacks slip from his shoulders onto the floor in the kitchen. The men were standing at the table with their hats off. The man had coal-black hair like his daughter's and the boy's own, and the skin above his brow where his hat sat was a little paler than his cheeks. To the boy's knowledge, the man had never been inside here. It was dark as a cave. His stepfather said, "Opal, Mr. Kale here was kind enough to come have a look-see at our water problem, thinks he might have a solution."

"Why, that's nice of you," his mother murmured. "Won't you sit down? I do hope you can stay for supper."

"Certainly, if it's no trouble."

"No trouble dividing nothing by a higher number," his mother sang gaily.

But we're not having "nothing," the boy thought. His stepfather had trapped a rabbit and shot a squirrel. His mother had made a pie from hard little apples the boy had diced, and she started the biscuits as soon as the man sat at the table and placed his hat in his lap. Peeled potatoes floated in a pan of water. There'd be more to eat than they normally had on Christmas. What if the man hadn't come? How'd they know he would? She called it "nothing." Did she want the man to think they were poor? If so, why all the food?

His stepfather went to unhitch and water the horse. The boy sat off in a corner watching as the man rotated his head as if stretching his neck, but he was actually looking around. The dugout had a wooden floor that his mother had covered with carpets, and the furniture was better than the house, she always said. The dugout belonged to the place; the furniture had come from her family. She complained that dust fell from the rafters onto it. It'd be better off in storage, she said.

"You've got nice things, Opal."

His mother set a bowl on the table and gave the man a strange look, as if she were angry. She opened her mouth to speak then closed it when she spied the boy

27

sitting in the dimness. When she turned away, she said, "Thank you."

"You're welcome. You know, Opal, I've always liked the names of gems for women."

His mother turned at the stove and gave him a little twisted half-smile that chided him. Her cheek was pink.

"So you said."

The man chuckled. "An opal shines on the outside; it looks one color then another, but it's not clear. There's a mystery in the heart of it. A person has that name—you always wonder why they do things."

"Does that make you nervous?"

"Oh no. Just curious. Intrigued, you might say."

"Well, there's no mystery." She paused to give him a direct look. "Everybody does what they have to."

She stirred inside a pot—squirrel stew, the boy presumed—but she was looking at the man. Her eyes were twinkling. The boy was suddenly aware of how much younger she was than his stepfather. She was nervous, he could tell, but it was like being tickled.

What she did next astonished him. She carried a spoonful of stew to the man, holding a hand under it. "Try this."

He opened his mouth, and she fed it to him.

"Rabbit?"

"Yes."

"It's good, very good."

"Thank you."

Compared to this man, his stepfather was crude and loud. He dressed in a filthy shirt and trousers held up by rope suspenders. His mother nagged him for chewing tobacco and drinking whiskey from the bottle at the same time. Mr. Kale spoke nicely and walked about in polished boots, and he was admirable. With him, his mother seemed like a lady; their talk was quiet and polite, like a king and a queen in a storybook.

Even so, he wished his stepfather would come back. His mother's behavior began to upset him. He'd never seen it before. It was called flirting, and he could see it was part of the lie she and his stepfather were telling. That made her a liar, too.

But wasn't he just as bad? He knew the truth and couldn't (or wouldn't) tell it. Probably when the man looked at him, he thought: that boy's their son, I'll bet he's a damn liar, too.

◘ ◘ ◘

After supper, his mother said, "If you gentlemen will excuse me, I'll take a little rinse."

His mother carried a wash cloth, towel, and soap out the back door into the darkness. She didn't need a lantern.

The man looked puzzled. He and the boy's stepfather sat at the table, the man smoking a pipe, his stepfather cigarettes, so that the air was streaked with smoke like high thin clouds. Taking a rinse—his mother let them know she'd be in the makeshift shower in the yard so they wouldn't come out there. The shower was closed on three sides by barn siding, but the open fourth faced the house. An old towel tacked across the opening afforded privacy but not enough to suit her.

His stepfather chuckled. "You can set your watch by that woman's bath. She's trying to warsh this goddamn farm out of her skin. She's mostly Ladies Aid with a little touch of hellcat throwed in for good measure. She's city-bred, and there ain't a day goes by but what she don't remember it loud and clear. Been that way ever since she showed up here on my doorstep looking like something the cat drug in, with that bundle"—a nod to the boy, who cringed inwardly—"in her arms."

"People know you been good to them, Atlas. Folks appreciate a man who'd take in a stray woman and her child."

His stepfather rose. "Well, water over the bridge. Speaking of that, we might as well look at what I was telling you about."

Picking up a lighted lantern, his stepfather led the man out the front door, but the boy hung back, stung. His stepfather shouldn't talk that way about his mother to a stranger. His stepfather's loose tongue was like an unbuttoned trousers fly.

As if to make it up to his mother, the boy went out the back door and stood in the long rectangle of light laid down in the yard. The night was moonless, the stars hidden by an overcast. He couldn't see the shower stall, but the washpot sat big-bellied at the end of the rectangle, the coals glowing under it. The water sent up wisps of steam. She would dip a bucket into the pot, climb a ladder at the shower and pour the water into a perforated washtub stationed there, then go stand under the water. In the dark, she took her clothes off first because the water dripped out of the tub immediately. He worried about her climbing the ladder with the full bucket in hand and her bare feet slipping on the rungs.

"Mama?"

"Yes, dear, I'm here."

He heard a clank then the hiss of water being poured. "Are you all right?"

"Yes, of course."

"Do you want me to help?"

"No thank you."

He heard a drizzle like a cow pissing, then a tink and a clunk, and he could imagine her hurriedly stepping down the ladder backward in the dark; the idea of her nudity prevented any clear picture from forming, and the blackness in the yard matched the shroud in his mind.

In the shed beyond the corral, the lantern swayed, its light flickering in the cracks of the siding, and the boy picked his way to the door.

"Every morning I have to skim this junk off the well water." His stepfather knelt in a corner, prying off the lid of a lard can. The man slyly inventoried the room the way he had done the interior of their house. Hay was heaped in the center of the floor; on the walls weathered and broken tack hung from nails. An old saddle and rusty implements. The squalor shouted to the man.

"Here." His stepfather pointed into the can. The man bent, sniffed, dipped a finger down, inspected it in the light—it was the dark brown color of cockroaches—then dabbed his tongue with it.

"You say it comes up in the well?"

"Yep. A couple inches every day."

"I think it's oil."

His stepfather looked startled. "Oil? I'll be damned!"

The man looked about for something to wipe his finger on, then cleaned it on an empty feed sack lying on the floor.

"Yes, you could be rich, Atlas." The man smiled. "I don't suppose I'll ever get you to part with the place, now."

"I don't want no damned old oil," his stepfather said

unhappily. "You can't feed no livestock with it and you can't grow no crops with it. What I need is good water."

"If you have it here, why it might be next door, too, at my place, or over at that Indian's. Maybe we'll all be rich." The man turned, looked at the boy, and winked. He invited the boy to help make fun of his stepfather.

"Don't tell me any more bad news. You know what happened at Cement? Hell, ever place they hit it becomes a damned old swamp of black goo and ever kind of riff raff you can imagine comes tramping all over your pastures. Stuff runs in the creeks and rivers and burns, stinks to high heaven. Livestock drink it and die."

His stepfather set the can on the floor.

"There'll be people around, all right," said the man. "If word gets out on this, you'll have a dozen out here tomorrow wanting to buy your mineral rights. With the war on, that oil's a valuable commodity."

"Damnation! You reckon? I'll shoot the bastards! I don't want to sell no mineral rights. I don't want no drilling rig ranch here. They'll ruin my water. I'm a farmer, always have been, always will be."

The man tried to suppress a smile. "Well, you can't hold something like this back, Atlas. Be like standing in the Canadian and trying to bail it out."

"I reckon," his stepfather groaned.

The men stared in silence at the open lard can. The boy wondered what his stepfather would do now that showing the oil apparently had not enticed the man to make a higher offer for the farm.

"Maybe I ought to just sell the whole shebang and move on to where there's good land and water. The old lady's been agitating about it for a good spell now."

The man glanced at the boy as if to test the truth of the statement, then turned back to his stepfather.

"That so? Maybe selling's the thing, then."

"Hate like hell to leave this place. I've spent too many good years here. It's home to the boy and to his mother, despite everything."

Thus began the dickering. The man made an offer that his stepfather said was too low considering the value of the mineral rights, and the man said maybe there was oil, maybe not, and he wanted the place for the extra pasturage so convenient to his own land. But out of sentiment he was willing to up the offer a little. They went back and forth this way for a while. The boy expected to hear the man ask to see the water well. The oil in the can had come from a rig a hundred miles west. Dreading the request, the boy felt like a thief waiting anxiously for someone to discover that something he'd taken was missing.

But the man never asked. It meant he wanted the land oil or no oil, and badly. It couldn't mean he actually believed his stepfather's lie.

They went back to the dugout and sat at the table. His stepfather took a bottle of whiskey from the cabinet, and his mother served both men apple pie again. His stepfather said, "Opal, Mr. Kale here thinks that goo in our water is oil."

"Oil? My, that would be a nuisance."

Hearing her lie, the boy made a sour face in the darkness. He rose from his hunker beside the fireplace and climbed the ladder to his loft bed so he couldn't see them, but their sounds still drifted up as he lay staring at the ceiling planks. Their forks clinked and scraped on their plates.

"He's made us a fair offer."

"Oh?"

"The place might be worth more money now than

33

he's offering, but I sure as hell don't want to live on it no more. I was looking for a farm when I come here."

"Well, you know how I feel about this place."

The boy heard the false smile in her voice. His stepfather laughed. "Well, looks as if you bought yourself another piece of land, neighbor."

They got out paper and a pen; they toasted one another, then Kale gave his stepfather "good faith" money. Soon the boy's attention drifted away like an untended rowboat, but he was jolted awake later by hooves clattering on the stones outside. That would be Mr. Kale leaving, he thought drowsily. In a moment, he was aroused again. Voices murmured, lantern light splashed as if tossed from a basin onto the ceiling, and he heard the abrupt fart of a chair scooted back from the table. He looked down into the kitchen. The man was going out the back door. His mother was close behind him, a lantern in one hand, a quilt in the other.

"Mama?"

She stopped at the threshold, startled, and looked up.

"I'm going to get our guest settled in the shed," she said, answering his unasked question.

"Where's Atlas?"

Her eyes looked disapproving. "He went to town."

"Oh."

"Good night." She meant, do not bother us any more.

"Good night."

He lay awake. His stepfather would wake them when he came back. He would be staggering, and his mother would have to fix him something to eat. He'd call her "pretty thing" and try to grab her while she cooked. He'd sing loud, laugh, then before long he'd cry and moan, so drunk you couldn't understand him. His mother would have to undress him. If she caught the boy glowering at her, she'd say, At least he's not mean. But that bawling was sickening. When the boy grew up he would never drink whiskey. He would not be in any way like his stepfather.

Would he be like his father? Was he more like you? Yes, she had said. Much more. He had education, he was brilliant. He . . . invented things. An important family. But he, well, died. What of? She shrugged. Just died. A disease. This was puzzling, but he'd seen it happen to farm animals, too. When he asked about grandparents, a father and mother for this real father, she said, They never knew about us, but wouldn't say why. The father like her wouldn't be embarrassing. He might be like the man his stepfather was cheating. It was hypocritical to feed this man and pretend to be polite just to get more of his money. Then the man, thinking he was a respected guest, had been given a place to sleep—

The boy swung upright as if on a spring. Why should the man sleep in their shed? His house was just down the road. The boy blinked in the darkness. No answer came.

"Mama?" he wailed, like a child upset by a nightmare. He hoped that he'd been dozing and she had already come in from the shed unbeknownst to him. But she didn't answer, so she was still out there. Getting the man settled. It was taking too long, and he wanted her here with him.

⧈ ⧈ ⧈

Two days after buying the farm Kale appeared with a man who wore a monocle and spoke German-sounding English. A polished wooden box hung from his neck like an accordion; copper wires went from it to a tin skullcap which the man fixed carefully onto his hairless pate before he and Kale struck off on foot across the pastures.

Atlas watched the men from the door to the dugout. The boy was seated at the kitchen table. Having finished his arithmetic lesson, he was now looking at his mother's old schoolbook that showed a cross-sectioned diagram of an ant colony, the network of tunnels under a smooth bland surface. His mother was standing beside him, folding bits of torn sheeting around pieces of china.

His stepfather hee-hawed.

"What's so amusing?"

"They say old Kale's been buying up land right and left, thinking he's gonna be sitting pretty on an oil boom. I sold him a pig in poke, that's what."

His stepfather's gloating troubled the boy. He'd believed that his stepfather had only needed to sell this farm, but he now spoke as if beating Mr. Kale was the point, and he'd only be satisfied if Mr. Kale made a mistake that made him poorer than the Smythes. The boy thought of the girl not looking down when she rode her pony by him on the road. He saw her in rags, crying, her face dirty. In his mind's eye, he approached her, intent on insulting her, but she looked so pitiful he relented and won her heart by being nice.

His mother snorted. "You don't think he believes that snake doctor he's dragging around the countryside could find oil, do you?"

"Why else bring him out here?"

"You're so smart, you figure it out."

"He's wasting his time, I know that. Only oil here's what I brung."

"Maybe he doesn't care."

"Naw. That don't make no sense."

"Not to you it doesn't. You don't think he got to be the richest banker in this county by letting himself be hoodwinked by any simpleton with a salted mine, do you? He's a very tricky man." She paused, then added, "Believe me, Atlas."

"Well, he out-tricked hisself this time."

They had been arguing all morning. The money had been delivered in large bills yesterday morning by an officer from Kale's bank. Since then, his stepfather had kept the roll in his front pants pocket, where it formed an ugly lump against his loins, and he stroked it when he talked about fooling Kale. Last night he had taken it into town to show it off and came home drunk and happy. Along with the money had come a letter from Kale ordering them to vacate the premises within thirty days. His stepfather wanted to go looking for a better farm farther east; farther east was just dandy with his mother so long as it meant St. Louis. She was tired of looking at dirt. She said he could work in a blacksmith shop, or a foundry. He said he wasn't cut out to be nobody's wage slave. A better farm would have a better house, she'd see.

"You just better be glad what you wanted happened to fit with what he wants, whatever it is, and hope his plans keep working out. We'd better get moving, too, and you'd better stay clear of town with that money."

"You think I'm a simpleton, is that right?"

His mother turned her head down. She placed a cloth-covered cup into an apple crate on the table. "I just think he's not one, that's all. I doubt he believes there's oil here."

"Why would he pay as much as he did then, you tell me that!"

"Maybe he had his reasons. He's always wanted the place."

The boy thought, All you have to say is we'll move to St. Louis like we want and she'll tell you you're twice as smart as Mr. Kale.

"Yeah, well, he is a sentimental cuss, ain't he?"

"I never said he was. I said he probably had his reasons."

The ants were carrying large white things in their jaws in the underground tunnels. He'd seen real ants carry bits of chaff and such on the ground, but he'd never known this was where they were going with them.

"Well, I got mine, too!"

Atlas slapped the lump in his pocket and, to make certain his was the last word, stepped from the doorway into the yard.

"Are we going to get to go to St. Louis?" the boy asked the instant his stepfather was out of earshot.

"Yes."

"But he says—"

"I don't care. If not there, some other city. Any place there's civilization, I promise."

He was surprised to hear there might be an alternate destination. In the past month or so, all his "history" lessons had seemed to consist of her talking about growing up in St. Louis and the wonders of the St. Louis World Exposition of 1904, how she'd been a demonstrator for the new type-writing machines display. Aircraft, sewing machines, wireless—oh, he had no idea of the wonders you might see in such a place. People were civilized, had education, manners. They dressed well and knew what they were about, she said. The boy thought of a man like Mr. Kale when she said this.

"Did you meet him at the fair?"

"Who?"

"My real father."

She colored. "Yes, as a matter of fact."

"Did you demonstrate something he invented?"

She gave him a puzzled look. Then she said, "No, he asked me to a dance on a riverboat."

She said that in a city like St. Louis there were many parties and dances, and there'd be other children for him to meet, regular schools, restaurants, clean places, parades with bands. She was so excited when she talked about it that the boy wondered, then asked why they had left St. Louis in the first place—was it because Atlas wanted to come here?

"No, he was already here."

"Why did we come, then?"

"It's a long story. It doesn't matter now—we can go back."

"What if he won't let us?"

"Not everything is up to him."

Every night for a week, his stepfather went to town to celebrate. Each morning he'd report what the town gossips were rumoring. Everybody had heard about the foreign scientist that Kale was tramping about the countryside with in a search for promising oil-bearing formations.

"Pig in a poke!" Atlas would cackle. "And now I got him running around all over the county busy as a one-legged Chinaman in uh ass-kicking contest."

A week still later, a stranger drove up in an automobile, bouncing over the rocky wagon trail to the dugout. The man hopped out and began snooping about the shed and the corral.

"I'm the new owner," he said in a friendly way as he stuck out his hand. Atlas and the boy had intercepted the stranger on his path back to his auto. "You must be the cropper."

"I'm not no sharecropper. Place used to be mine before I sold it. How you figure you own it now?"

"Just bought it."

"Huh!" Recovering from his surprise, Atlas asked, "Mind my asking how much you paid?"

The man winked. "More than the last fellow, less than the next."

His mother came out to watch the man's auto bounce back down the trail.

"Who was that?"

"He says he owns the place." His stepfather's face was white. "I thought old Kale wanted it."

His mother smiled tightly, shook her head. "I told you not to worry about what he wants or doesn't want."

"Well, I'm gonna see about this."

When Atlas returned from town, crestfallen, he told them that rumors of Kale's widespread purchases had been false; he'd bought only one other place, for very little money, and resold it within hours as talk of an oil find swept the countryside. In addition, he'd unloaded on speculators several hardscrabble farms the bank had repossessed.

Knowing he'd been duped and that Kale was piling up an even greater fortune sent Atlas on a two-day binge. When he came home, he slept for a day while the boy and his mother packed their belongings. When he came awake, he bawled for an hour and wouldn't answer Opal's questions. Eventually he told them that because he couldn't stand being the butt of jokes, he'd gambled most of the wad on a horse race and lost. He'd meant to win the amount Kale had sold the farm for.

"What're we going to do, Mama?"

"Don't worry. I'll find a way."

Opal had to ask the new owner if they could stay and sharecrop. Soon three drilling rigs stood on the property, and trucks roared by the dugout carrying materials, raising clouds of dust and running over the chickens. The men worked all night, and their noises kept the Smythes awake.

The wells were dry holes. That Kale couldn't be hurt by them infuriated Atlas. Meanwhile, the activity drew oil prospectors by the scores. Next door to the south, on land owned by an Indian, a rig was erected, and a few weeks later a gusher exploded. The boy heard the noise and hiked down to the ferry landing where a crowd stood watching the black flower blossom over the treetops. "Stinking savage, stinking rich!" muttered one man. Another said sourly, "Well, there's one lucky sumbitch, all right."

"Goddamnit!" His stepfather slung a bucket against the shed wall when the boy told him about the gusher. "If that don't beat all the luck! What the hell use is that oil to a goddman redskin? Hell, I bet he can't even count! I'm the one who started talking about oil around here! If it wasn't for me, nobody around here'd know a goddamn thing about any goddamn oil!"

Atlas kicked the oat tins, slung opened feed sacks about, upended the sawhorses, then flung a shovel through the one glass pane remaining in the window.

The boy backed out of the shed and quietly made his

way down to the creek, where he sat pitching pebbles into the water. People said that when Indians got oil money they bought all kinds of foolish things. People took advantage of them because they couldn't read or write and didn't know the laws. He wondered what the Indian—his white name was David, but he'd told the boy his Indian name was Went On a Journey—would buy. It was hard to picture him doing something foolish. He could count; the boy had seen him make change for the passengers aboard the ferry he operated across the Canadian. He was big and strong and looked pretty fierce, but he joked with people, too. He worked hard; he lived alone in a cabin with furniture as good as theirs. The Indian had told him stories, had taken him hunting and let him shoot a .22 rifle.

So it seemed right that oil was found on the Indian's land. His stepfather had cheated, and the punishment was seeing Mr. Kale turn the swindle into a success. The boy was the son of the woman married to Atlas Smythe, so he was punished, too. The sins of the stepfathers were visited upon the sons. They would be poorer than ever, trapped in a downward spiral. The Indian had cheated no one; he did his work, kept to himself. They said he was "lucky" as if he hadn't deserved it, but to the boy this "good luck" seemed more like a reward for having character and "bad luck" was what happened when you lied and cheated.

Within a month, the crossroad village a few miles from the farm swelled like a bloated tick into a town of 30,000 restless, greedy boomers. Pastures on the outskirts were choked with groves of rigs, and the air stank of petroleum and smoke. Tent cities sprang up overnight. No one slept. Prices shot sky-high, and the family soon ran low on grocery money.

His stepfather bawled, whined, groaned, cursed. The boy and his mother sat day after day listening. Lady Luck the whore made everybody rich but him, when he was the one who told everybody about the oil! If anybody ought to be getting rich off an oil boom, it ought to be the man who started it!

Atlas hated the noise of the boom; he hated the scum who worked the rigs; he hated how much an honest man had to pay for an honest drink (an illegal drink, the boy thought); he hated how the dry-hole drillers had simply abandoned their rigs, tanks and pipe so that the land that Atlas had struggled upon for years, that earth so deep in his blood and his soul, had been ruined by Kale, who had sold it for a profit to someone who cared even less about it than he. Kale this, Kale that. His stepfather made it sound as if Mr. Kale had come and twisted his arm to sell for less than what the farm was worth.

He and his mother both sighed when Atlas would leave for town; perversely, he now seemed unable to stay away from it, due to the irresistible attraction of that which galls one the most. One night after he failed to return, a town boy rode out on a horse with a message from the sheriff: Atlas had been in a fight with an oilman and was in jail. He wanted Mrs. Smythe to come get him out.

While the boy was hitching the horse to their wagon, his mother came out and put a satchel under the seat. She let him drive and stayed silent until they reached Wetoka, where she directed him to the train depot. She had him carry the black satchel inside. She went to the ticket window, took an envelope from her coat pocket and pulled a twenty-dollar bill from it that looked to the boy as if it had just been scissored from greenish paper.

"Two tickets to Dallas," she said.

They lived in a boardinghouse in Oak Cliff. Opal took the trolley across the Trinity each morning to the Sears Roebuck warehouse on Lamar, where she sped down the aisles on roller skates, retrieving orders. He walked to his first real school, where he was up with the sixth graders in reading, behind in geography, ahead in arithmetic. He ran with a pack of boys in and out of stores on Jefferson, tumped outhouses on Halloween, fished in the river, learned marbles. He liked beating his mother home in the afternoons and having their room to himself or sitting on the porch and talking to the other boarders—Mr. Briscoe had worked for the railroad and could describe fatal accidents in great detail; Miss Arnold had a parrot that said, "Jesus wept." Mr. Peters gave him three empty cigar boxes. Where's your pappy, boy? He died, the boy said. But he was a genius, he invented things. What'd he invent? Mr. Peters said. The boy said, None of your business. He was certain it was true, but his grip on this truth was so tenuous that the facts seemed like a lie.

"What'd my father invent?"

"What'd he invent?" His mother shrugged. "Things."

"What kinds of things?"

"Just things. I can't tell you more than that. He was pretty tight-lipped about his business."

This vagueness disturbed the boy. It made him feel like a fugitive.

"Will Atlas ever come to visit?"

His mother was taking off her work dress. She'd cocked the door to the closet for privacy and stood in the mouth of it to shrug out of the garment.

"I hope not!"

Clothing rustled. He tried not to look; the vanity mirror would show something if he moved his eyes.

"Do you want him to?"

He thought about it. He could picture his stepfather still in jail, waiting. Okay, he was a fool, but he'd never been anything but friendly and had only once whipped him with a switch and that on the mother's insistence. Oddly, he missed that voice, the griping, the whining, joking. He wasn't a genius like Edison or Bell, but he was all the boy had had as an actual father, and he had become more important in his absence than he had been in his presence. His mother didn't want to hear him say yes, though.

"He wasn't so bad."

"I never said he was."

"You said he was a fool."

"People can be a lot of things all at the same time."

Flap, clothes on a line in a breeze. His eyes cut once to the mirror then back away quickly. Something white.

"Do you miss him?" she asked.

"Sometimes."

"You wouldn't want him to come here and make us go back to that farm, would you?"

"No."

"All right, then." After a moment, she added, "Besides, I think he went to the war."

War? Atlas Smythe, his stepfather, in uniform, with a rifle and helmet, on a ship, walking behind a tank, loading a big shell into an artillery piece; this flurry of mental images was so richly appealing he momentarily drowned in them, and when he surfaced into the room the mirror framed his mother's nude haunch and above it her eyes cutting at him. His face tingled. He jerked his head away, and she pulled the door closer to her like a sheet to her chin.

"You're getting too old. You need your own room."

She went downstairs in her going-out dress to help Mrs. Beasley with supper—she got a little off her rent that way. The war pictures played through his mind. Was his stepfather cavalry? Artillery? He could ask her. But how'd she know he was even there? Had she talked to him? If she knew he was in France, then there was no likelihood he'd be showing up here, was there? Then why raise the threat of it? When people said "Besides . . ." whatever followed was not a main reason for something.

She went out with Mr. Alexander. It was common for her to go out at night now. She told everybody the thing she liked most about living here was how people were nice and she didn't have to worry about her boy. In her absence, he was free to wander about and talk to the other adults. Something interesting was going on in each room. Downstairs in the parlor was a piano that Miss Arnold and Mrs. Beasley, the landlady, played. He learned "Chopsticks." Also there were magazines like *Liberty* and newspapers, pictures of battles in France. Chinese checkers. A bowl full of peppermints sat on a lamp table. For a while he worried that he took too many, but Mrs. Beasley just said, You like them green ones, don't you? and filled it up again. Mr. Briscoe taught him draw poker. Being here was like having a house full of uncles and aunts.

Mr. Alexander wore a suit and was bald; he had fat hands with a gold ring from the Masons. He was always patting the boy's mother on the rear as if he didn't realize that, as a lady, she wouldn't tolerate such behavior. The windows to their rooms overlooked Blaylock Street

46

and Oak Cliff Park, and when Mr. Alexander brought his mother back late during the night in his new Buick, the boy could look through the screen and see the car parked under the trees in the shadows. Murmurs, his mother's laughter. The glow from the man's cigar. When, eventually, they would emerge from the car, coming up the walk with his mother tugging at her skirt, the boy would sigh and surrender to sleep.

Mr. Alexander gave him a toy truck for Christmas that would've been okay for some kid, and the boy quickly traded it for a store-bought niggershooter and a bag of steelies to use with it. He shot two squirrels in the back yard, popped their eyes out. Thinking of his stepfather in France, he drew a bead on a calico cat sunning itself on a porch next door, but it was only half-awake so he let it live.

One night the door to Mr. Alexander's car slammed hard and his mother walked swiftly by herself to the house. His successor, Mr. Wilson, also wore a suit; he had little square spectacles and small wrists and a high voice. Once he took them to a church. Several times he took both his mother and the boy downtown to a restaurant and to the moving pictures, where once, to the boy's astonishment, he recognized the Indian from the ferry; here, he was dressed in an Indian costume and riding a horse while attacking a wagon train.

"He's a dope," his mother said of Mr. Wilson.

She was talking with Lila, her new friend from work. Lila lived down the street with her aunt. She would arrive evenings looking one way and leave with his mother looking another. The two women would put on lipstick, smoke cigarettes in the room, batting at the air to disperse the smoke out the window so that Mrs. Beasley wouldn't catch them. His mother wore Mr.

Alexander's jewelry when she and Lila went out to "private clubs."

Mr. Carcaccio wore cowboy boots that had a secret pouch on the side for hiding a knife.

When spring came, his mother talked Mrs. Beasley into putting his cot out onto the screened porch at the back of the house. Fine with him. Lila giggled and said stupid things and he didn't like the stink of their perfume.

The next winter they moved downstairs to a larger room that had a divider, but some nights he went back to the porch even when it was cold. One night in November the armistice was signed and everybody had a party in the parlor, a cake with little American flags stuck in it.

"So I reckon he'll be coming back now."

"Who? And don't say 'reckon' like a clodhopper."

"Atlas."

"Oh, honey, I don't know."

You don't know shit. "Maybe he's still sitting in that jail."

Now she gave him a look. She was fixing her hair. She'd had it cut short. "You're getting too big for your britches, buster."

Back on the porch during the spring. Back into the house during the winter. Mrs. Beasley retired to the country, and Miss Arnold moved her parrot to the parlor. Jesus wept. "Shut your hole," the boy whispered to it, close to the cage, just to see it squawk.

Jack Baxter had a trucking firm. He taught the boy to drive a truck around the yard south of town. He showed cards he'd gotten in France of women on their hands and knees like dogs. He told about shooting a German in the hand while the man was eating his dinner, and the man yelped and jumped back down into the trench. Jack, you shouldn't tell him such nonsense. And I heard about those 'postcards.' Aw hell, he's plenty old enough. Boy without a dad needs somebody to teach him things.

Lila got pregnant, moved to Houston. Mr. Briscoe died, a fellow with a moustache and a toothpick always in his mouth took the room. He called the boy's mother sister. Hey, sister. He's a pill. Miss Arnold gave the boy messages to deliver to his mother even though they all sat at the same dining table every night. Tell your mother not to smoke cigarettes in the parlor. Tell your mother to be quiet at night coming in. That bitch! What's she care? If she has anything to say, she can tell it to my face.

For his sixteenth birthday, Jack Baxter took him to a place in Deep Ellum where colored women did it for money. He drank "hootch," and Jack paid a big fat woman to "teach him what it's all about." She played with him. Oooo, you Mistah jissum! She showed him where to put it in. Mud. Mr. Jack, don't you bring that boy back here, he 'bout wore this girl out ha ha! Now he knew what went on between his mother and Jack. Mr. Alexander. Mr. Carcaccio. Mr. Wilson. Atlas and his real father.

One evening the following spring, he came home to find his mother sitting in the porch swing with a man whose face had an elusive familiarity like an old riddle whose solution has slipped your mind.

"Hello, dear. You remember our old neighbor?"

"Sir." The man's grip stung like a struck funny bone up his arm and down his spine. It all came back. Was Kale here to get even? Sent by his stepfather? Would he be punished, too?

"By God!" Kale grinned. "Here, I brought you a little something, son." He passed the boy a small rectangular package that turned out to contain a pearl-handled penknife. While he was inspecting it, Kale said to his mother, "I'd of hardly recognized him. He's a strapping lad, all right!"

His mother was beaming. "And so good-looking."

"Oh, he'll kill the ladies, I'm sure."

"Just like his father."

New information: his real father had been a handsome lady-killer? It jarred momentarily with his picture of the man dressed in a laboratory coat and working at an equation on a blackboard or standing and looking into steaming beakers, but he recorded it quietly behind his eyes. Then he sat motionless on the steps with his knees under his chin and his arms around his shins, curled into the shape of a giant ear. Kale got on a tear about the Indians with oil money. The Indian from the ferry had married a white woman, a white woman! and not trash, either, can you beat it? and had gone out to Hollywood where he was driving fancy cars now and acting in motion pictures. Stinking savage, stinking rich. Custom-tailored suits. You can't change genes, humans just breed down. Like dressing up a monkey. You see them driving their cars, they get a flat, they just walk away from the car. Buy cloisonné vases and cook out of them. Use a grand piano for a chicken roost. Indian with money was a bad joke. It ought to go to those smart and hard-working enough to get it.

His mother sought to soothe him. Oh, I'm sure there's not a one that's any match for you if you take it to mind to help them spend it. If you'll recall a certain John Deere salesman in the Drake Hotel and the fellow with the fresh mouth on the sternwheeler? Kale laughed. Walking gold mine, just takes the right miner.

Then: "Well, what about you, Opal? Have you been a good girl since last I saw you?"

"Well, sure!"

"Is that right, son?"

Kale was grinning. His mother's narrowed gaze spelled a warning. She should have been pleading for mercy.

"What you mean?"

"Has your Mama had fellows coming around?"

"Of course not!" laughed his mother. "I'm a married woman."

"Lots," the boy said.

"Lots?"

"That's not true!" wailed his mother in a mock-angry protest that he knew showed real pain. "Why, my own son makes me sound like a . . . well, like an I-don't-know-what!"

I do. And you're a liar, too.

They went on, ignored him. Kale wanted to know all about her life here. Poor but righteous, she said. That's us. Poor but righteous. His mother sat in the swing on one calf so that one foot dangled loose over the porch, and Kale was pushing them off, back and forth, with one toe.

The boy wanted to hear about Wetoka. He couldn't shake the idea that his stepfather was still behind bars. Or, if he'd gone to the war, was he back on the farm? Mr. Kale would know. He held back from asking, though; he expected his mother to bring Atlas up and relieve the boy of the duty of dragging into their present an unpleasantness from the past.

Soon, though, Miss Arnold turned on the porch light, and they got up. His mother was going to show Mr. Kale the town. Maybe it's too fast for me, Mr. Kale said. I doubt it, said his mother.

The boy sat in the vacated swing. He pictured the Indian riding in an open car, a big cigar, a custom-made suit, and a white woman in a fur coat beside him. California. An ocean and orange trees, palm trees, sunshine. An actor in westerns! It was amazing how different the Indian's life as a rich man had become in California. Thinking of that was like thinking of his stepfather wearing a helmet or of his father as a man who was handsome and broke women's hearts. People went different places or did different things and your picture of them changed. They went to California to be in the moving pictures. To get rich, famous. Go West, young man! Once they got out there it didn't matter where they'd come from; a person started all over. A person took a new name, whichever one he wanted. It didn't matter shit who his mother or father might have been.

At eleven, Miss Arnold turned out the porch light. It was a kind of game. Anybody gets in before eleven, they can see to come in, she said. We have bills to pay. Really, though, the rule was designed solely for his mother so that if she made noise walking onto the porch or getting the door unlocked, Miss Arnold could hit the switch and his mother and her companion for the night would be caught like somebody in a copper's spotlight or the flash from a camera.

He sat in the shadows waiting, a breeze rocking the swing. Kale's car pulled up after midnight. He was surprised that they didn't sit long in the car parked under the trees; then he thought—a hotel, maybe. He knew what went on, now. All they needed was a blanket and a shed with some hay.

She came down the walk alone while the car was pulling away. She was tiptoeing across the porch and yelped when she saw him.

"You scared me! You still up?"

He got out of the swing and stood near her in the darkness. He could see over her head. The cigar stink in her sweater was pungent as tomcat spray. Under the puddle of murky light, her face was indistinct, foreign.

"I want to know something."

"What?"

"What did you do to get the money for us to leave the farm and come here?"

His chin trembled. The darkness made it easier to ask, but her silence made him want to read her face. She raised her arms over her head, fiddling with her hair. Glint of metal in her mouth.

"I don't have to answer that, young man!"

"That's all right. I know, anyway!"

"Listen, Mister Smart Aleck, whatever I do is for you. Would you rather be back on that farm? I don't think so — you'd be doing the work of an ox by now, that's for sure. Just another beast of burden. The least you can do is show a little gratitude for the sacrifices I make."

"Do you take money from all of them?"

"I ought to slap your face! I'll have you to know that money was a loan."

"I'll bet I know how you paid it back."

Her hand went thump! against his cheek. Stung. He slumped against the railing.

"Oh, I'm sorry, sweetie! Here —"

"Get away!"

He pushed her back. Her mewling tore at his heart but he refused to look at her.

"It really hurts that you think so little of me! You've got a lot to learn about people, my friend. You think Bill Kale's such a fine fellow and a fine citizen, that it? You think I took advantage of his good nature? Well, you can think twice about that. I could tell you things—I could! Things that would curl your hair, that's what! And you taking such a high tone with me and not knowing anything at all about what things might cost me and I'm not talking about money! You have no idea at all of what it's like to be a woman alone in the world with a child and—"

The light burst on the porch like an explosion that didn't stop. His mother's make-up was smeared on her cheeks. A knuckle thrust through the lace and rapped like a thick beak on the glass door.

"Oh, go straight to Hell, you old bitch!"

They packed at 3:00 A.M. with everyone peeking out of their doors in their robes. Find us a house, yes, that's what's wrong, I know you've been feeling cramped. We should have moved a long, long time ago, that's all that's wrong, people breathing down your neck at every minute wanting to know your business! Don't you think that will help, sweetie?

He went along, sulking. He could picture a house. He might have a room all his own, yes. She'd have one, too. Hers would be empty at night. So would all the others. Unless she had visitors.

3

■ ■ ■ ■
■ ■ ■ ■
■ ■ ■ ■

1930   EL PASO'S new rich had built up
Kern Place the last ten years or so. The
isolated subdivision sat at the knee of a
rise with an Anglo name—Mount
Franklin—so its inhabitants escaped Rio
Grande flooding and the bilious smoke
from the smelter. Here, high up from
the border, they could hold Mexico and
its poor, dark-skinned peoples at arm's
length. Mexico meant cockfighting,

quickly withered. By watering the imported topsoil constantly, she was able to produce a thin patch of grass. She hadn't been able to bring a flower garden to glorious bloom, and the indigenous succulents were too foreign to be worthy of serious attention.

"I just do not understand why we had to move here," Hunter once overheard her complaining. She had spent thirty comfortable years in Oklahoma; why her husband had uprooted them "to go into this desert" was a mystery, though she agreed "this is a better place to bring up children." The way she spoke of the "desert" brought to Hunter's mind bearded men in colored robes trudging with shepherds' crooks to a distant place of exile.

Sissy met Hunter at the door wearing a chiffon party dress whose drop waist made her torso look tubular and breastless. Around her neck was a long strand of pearls. Her cloche hat sported two small feathered pins that looked like small cow horns in silhouette. The dress was red; so was her lipstick, and the color leapt to his eye against her crow-black hair and white skin.

"Do I look grown up now?"

She had one elbow chocked into her waist and the fingers of that hand languidly but affectedly dangled a lighted cigarette in an ivory holder that belonged to her father. She did indeed look startlingly older all at once, yet the inexpert awkwardness of her posture sent a pang of tenderness through his heart. He resisted it by looking over her shoulder into the foyer.

"Are you going to conduct an orchestra?"

She put the holder to her mouth and puffed.

"Trayz chick, no?"

He took the holder and cigarette from her. "You're too young to smoke. You look silly."

"Says who? You're not my father, you know. Besides, I'm eighteen."

"Not yet, you're not."

She stepped to him, ran her hand over his cheek. "Hey, smooth!" She laughed. "You look awfully skinny, though!"

They were standing under the porch light, so he moved past her and closed the door. She pressed her chest to his, cocked her head and half-closed her eyes. He could smell Scotch on her breath. It made him nervous for her to be close; she might smell or see something on him.

"Kiss me?" she whispered. "Oh, Will, I'm so excited!"

He bent up slightly to fit his lips to hers; she purred in her throat like a cat, and she tasted of tobacco and liquor. He broke off the kiss and held her tightly with her head over his shoulder.

"I'm normal?"

"Yeah."

She kissed her way around his brow and back to his mouth. "Only three and a half hours," she whispered, then giggled.

"I'm thirsty," Hunter said, careful to be gentle in pushing her away.

"You were supposed to bring me something."

"I'm sorry. I couldn't get it."

"All right. We'll drink Daddy's. Maybe he won't miss it. And if he does, it won't matter, will it?"

"No."

"Come on." She turned to lead him away, but when her hand went to take his, she discovered the makeshift bandage.

"Oh, Will! What happened?" She gently raised his hand and inspected it in the light.

"Car door."

"Oh, my God!" She held it as if it were a crippled bird and cooed over it. He had to laugh.

"It doesn't hurt much."

"Oh, you're just being brave. Come on, let me nurse it."

He followed her into the downstairs bathroom, feeling the pebble in his left shoe pinch his arch. She made him sit on the covered toilet, then arranged his hand on the basin. She unwrapped the handkerchief with more caution than was necessary—the wound hurt now only when he bumped it—and inspected the bite marks at the base of his thumb. She made a production out of her sympathy—oh, my poor Will's poor hand! etc.—and her too-bright eyes made it obvious she was tipsy. She dressed the wound with iodine, gauze and tape. Hunter licked his lips. The silver faucet was sweating. He tolerated Sissy's overly fastidious nursing job only because she enjoyed it so much.

He went into the kitchen, took a glass from the cupboard and filled it from the tap. He drank the tepid water in one long gulp. He set the glass next to a can of creamed corn on the counter.

"I thought you meant a drink." Sissy had gone to the sideboard to retrieve the Scotch. She sounded whiny, as if his ordinary thirst were a betrayal.

"Not yet. Later."

She held the bottle up by its neck. "I'll bring it with us."

"Okay, give me a shot now." He held out the empty water glass. She poured two fingers of Scotch into it, and he tossed it back, thinking a little would help. Too much would be very dangerous.

"That's the real thing."

"Nothing but the best for Daddy." She took a swig directly from the bottle.

"Hey, go easy."

"I know you'll take care of me."

When he saw her head swinging around to catch his gaze, he bent over the sink and rinsed the glass. "Let's go."

"Oh, Will, I'm not ready yet."

"You're all dressed. Haven't you packed?"

"Yes. But I got the undecideds."

He set the glass down on the counter.

"Golly, don't look so horrified! I didn't mean undecided about going, Will! I mean I couldn't decide what to wear."

"Oh. Well, you look swell."

"Are you sure?"

"Yes."

"I mean sure you want to do this with me?"

"Yeah, I'm sure."

"Come help me finish packing and we can go."

She led him upstairs and into what he presumed was her own bedroom, then realized that it must be her mother's. A four-poster bed of black walnut, a matching dressing table with three marble slabs and a huge oval mirror behind it on swivels. A silver-backed brush and comb set lay on one slab; on the other were crystal jars with silver lids. Sissy stood before the mirror, but she was too tall for it and had to reach out and tilt the top away from her to see her whole reflection. Hunter thought of the illustrations from *Alice in Wonderland*, the girl with the goose neck looking into the glass.

"I'm too ugly to go."

"Don't be ridiculous. You're very pretty."

"Maybe I should wear something else."

"I said you look swell, Sissy."

He eased down onto the bed. Her eyes caught his in the mirror. She looked a little panicky, then she scuttled beside him and sat. Now they were the same height. She draped her long thin arm around his neck and dropped her cheek to his shoulder. "You know what? I liked how you looked when I said I was undecided. It made me think you really want to go away with me. The reason I couldn't decide what to wear was I kept being afraid that you'd take one look at me and change your mind about going."

"No, silly."

She lifted his hand to her lips and kissed a knuckle. "But I really am a little undecided, too."

"It's only natural."

"I'm afraid that they won't be able to get along without me."

"Maybe if you're not around they'll just have to deal with each other."

"It kills me to think of Mother not having somebody to talk to."

"She can find somebody her age, Sissy."

"And Daddy, I know I'm something very special for him."

Hunter cleared his throat, then rose and slapped his thigh as definitive punctuation. "Yeah, well, you don't owe your life to him."

He went to her mother's dressing table, turned over the silver brush, and watched the girl in the mirror. She was frowning, her elbow on her knee, bony fingers draped across her cheek. One bare shin looked a yard long.

"Am I special to you, Will?"

"Sure."

Their eyes met in the mirror. Do you love me? she was about to ask. He was ready to lie but was also irritated that she would test him.

"But it's like I told you, Sissy, remember? Partners, buddies, friends for the road."

"But in California—"

"Oh, sure, I'm not going to desert you." He stepped to the girl and pulled her up by her hands; the way she uncrossed her legs and got to her feet made him think of ironing boards.

She hugged him close. "Doctor Hunter," she whispered hotly in his ear. "I'm ready."

He pulled away. "Where's your suitcase?"

"Downstairs."

He frowned, puzzled, and she said, "I wanted you to read my note."

She opened a drawer in the dressing table, pulled out a paper and handed it to him.

Dearest Mama, Please don't worry. I'm with someone who cares about me and who will watch out for me. This won't be like last time, so don't bother to look for me. Some day soon I'll let you know where I am, though. I love you madly, but I love Daddy too, and I can't choose.

He skimmed it quickly. It didn't matter what was said. When he looked up, she asked, "Are you sure this is the way we should do it?"

"Yeah. Why not?"

She shrugged. "I still think about standing up to him, you know, and telling him to his face we're going. That seems like the right thing to do."

"He might stop us. This isn't a case of being yellow

or anything, Sissy, believe me. But he has the law on his side."

"Not if we wait a few hours until I'm eighteen."

"Is that what you want? You want to take a chance and risk his finding some way to stop us just so you can spit in his face?"

"Oh, gee, I don't want to spit in his face, Will. I just want him to realize I'm grown up."

"He'll get the point."

Hunter's heart was pounding. The air in the room was heavy with something too sweet. He was eager to get away, but he was not the least afraid of her father. He was afraid of losing his nerve, his resolve.

"Do you think I should write something more?"

"No. What's to say?" He saw his own hand scrawling a note on a page: Here's an earring, you fuck. Next, an ear. "Did you leave one for him?"

"Yes, but then I tore it up. I wrote a bunch, but they all sounded too angry. I didn't want to sound like a child. I wanted to sound determined and mature, as if I knew my own mind and wouldn't be swayed by anything. I didn't want it to sound as if I was paying him back."

"Paying him back? For what?"

"For what he did to my friend last time. Or what Mr. Shingle did."

Hunter had a flash—the blood spurting from the neck wound. He shivered. "Mr. Shingle won't bother us."

She looked puzzled, but he merely waved her curiosity away with a gesture. "I mean we're safe, you're safe with me. I'm safe."

They went downstairs. Her packed valise was standing upright on the kitchen floor in a square of moonlight. Somehow he had missed it when they'd stood by the sink moments earlier. It was as if someone had placed it here while they were upstairs.

Hunter came out onto the porch, but Sissy lagged behind in the foyer.

"Leave the light off," he told her.

A tattered overcast blotted out the crescent moon; Hunter stood flexing his fist around the handle of her valise and rocking on his heels. Higher up the hill lights from the College of Mines glimmered against a scrim of barren black earth.

Sissy came out and pulled the door to behind her. She stood a moment with her hand on the knob.

"Gosh, it seems like I ought to say something."

"To the house?"

"Uh-huh."

"How about *'adios, muchachos.'* "

Sissy laughed, stepped to his side and wrapped his bicep in her long fingers.

"I hate good-byes. How about *hasta luego?*"

"Sure."

He heaved her suitcase into the back seat on top of his own, then he held the door open and ushered her in with a mock bow. By the time he'd gone around to the driver's side to get in, she'd opened the glove box and was poking about inside it. He shivered in panic — had he put the razor there? — then automatically patted his coat pocket to feel it.

"What do you need?"

"I'm just curious, that's all."

He reached over and shut the glove box door. "Hey, mind your own bees-wax, little girl." He tried to sound cheerful, good-natured, but he came off cross.

"Don't be such a grouch! Just thought maybe you

were hiding something." She bent to scan the floor-boards. She sniffed the air, tossed him a grin.

"Why would I be hiding something?"

"I don't know." Her grin blossomed in the dimness, and her eye teeth showed. "Maybe it's because you're a handsome devil and I don't know why you'd want to spend your time with a frivolous girl like me. Maybe you've got other girls. Maybe you're running from them. Maybe since I'm running away with you all of a sudden I'm wondering why."

"Because you're beautiful and smart and lively. And a good buddy."

She scooted over close to him and sighed. She laid her cheek against his shoulder, making it hard for him to steer the car efficiently, as his wounded hand was next to useless on a turn.

"Sometimes you seem mysterious to me, Will."

"It's the clean shave."

"No, I don't mean now. I just mean sometimes."

"Sometimes you women seem a mystery to me, too."

"No, I don't mean mysterious as in how people find the other sex to be strange. This is personal. You don't seem mysterious when I'm with you—" She patted his arm as if to prove his reality. "When I'm with you, sometimes you could be a brother or something, some-times a friend, sometimes a lover man." She burrowed her cheek into his arm. "But, you know, when I'm lying awake at night and I know you're not working and you're by yourself in your room, I've wondered what you're like or who you are when nobody else is around."

"That's crazy, Sissy. That makes no sense at all."

"I guess it does sound dotty."

"Truly."

"Maybe it's because you're older, I think. And you've been other places before you came here and you were with someone else maybe before you were with me—"

"I've told you you're the first, Sissy."

"Oh, I know. But that wouldn't be normal, you know, so I suspect you're lying to protect my feelings."

"You're certainly philosophical tonight."

The auto passed under the illuminated Kern Place gateway, and the pale light passed across her face; she looked earnest, vaguely troubled.

"This is a big step I'm taking here, Will. I'm just trying to think."

"Uh-oh! Call a doctor!"

She turned away. "I make very good grades," she said after a moment. "I may seem like a dumbbell and I act very childish at times, but Will—" She met his gaze with teary eyes. "I have a lot of good in me that hasn't come out yet. It needs encouragement."

"Yes, I know." He leaned over and quickly pecked her cheek. She smelled girly under her mother's perfume. Sissy was a nice kid. She'd done nothing to him, that was the horrible part of this. She'd be an innocent victim. Somebody just in the wrong place at the wrong time. A bystander just out for an evening's stroll when a truck runs up over the curb. Nothing she'd ever done to deserve it. Sweet kid, really. You couldn't think about this very much. Or if you do, you remember that Bobette was just such a person, too. Minding her own business when somebody greedy took her life like smashing a gnat. Eye for a fucking eye. So shall ye reap, the preachers say. It was a terrible world.

"What I meant about your being mysterious was that I think about the time you spent before you came here, and—"

"I told you I lived in California."

"I know. I'm not saying you didn't. I only mean I wasn't there with you. Why are you getting so upset? I'm just talking about a dumb idea."

"I'm not upset. But you say I'm mysterious as if I've been telling you lies."

"Forget it."

The sudden spat and its attendant estrangement felt comfortable. He could settle into it as if into the driver's seat for a long trip. But Sissy snaked her arm over his shoulder and across his nape and burrowed her mouth into his neck.

"Let's don't fight. Not tonight. I don't want to be childish tonight. I want to be all grown up."

"Grown-ups fight."

"Well, I sure know that!"

"I mean even people who care for each other."

"I'll have to take your word for it."

"Do."

"What if I asked you to provide an example from your own personal history?"

When he only shrugged, she withdrew her arm and slumped against the far door. "That's what I mean about your being mysterious."

"There's no mystery, kiddo. There's no past for us, just right now and how we'll be when when we get to where we're going, okay?"

He meant to reassure her, but his smile froze like the one you make for a cripple who's holding out a cup. She took whatever she could get and scooted back beside him. They were coming up on Mesa now, and the lights of downtown El Paso and Juarez were ahead, each city indistinguishable from the other except for the ribbon of river that divided them like a vein of black ore.

"Where are we going to spend the night?"

"I was thinking Las Cruces."

"Huh. I bet you didn't know that means 'the cross-roads' in Spanish?"

"No, I didn't." But it seemed appropriate. By the time they reached that town, Sissy's father would have come home to find the note, and Hunter could begin making his phone calls to the man.

"Are we going to stay in a hotel or a tourist court?"

"Hotel."

"Which one?"

"I don't know yet."

"Will they let us?"

"What do you mean?"

"Oh, you know. We're not married, in case you've forgotten."

"I'll just register us as man and wife, how's that?"

"I like that."

She fell silent a moment, working on something. "Only one bed, Will?"

"I guess. I don't care. You can have it if it's just one."

"I'll be eighteen."

"Holy cow, Sissy! I know that! You think I don't know that?"

"You don't have to yell. Maybe you've stayed in hotels a lot as somebody's spouse, but this is a first for me." Her lower lip quivered. "I meant it would be nice to know you're there beside me, say if I woke up scared."

"Sure I'll be there, kiddo, don't worry."

"And it wasn't only that, either." She bent closer. The horns on her hat were sharp against the light from the streetlamp. "We've never been in a bed. You remember last Saturday in your room?"

"Yeah, sure."

"I wanted to get into your bed then instead of being on top of it."

"Light me a cigarette, will you?"

Performing the chore momentarily distracted her, but as soon as she had stuck the burning butt into his mouth, she said, "You really did something nice to me. . . ." She paused, grinned. "Doctor Hunter. That's my new name for you."

He pictured the girl, eyes closed, head back, sitting up with her palms flat behind her on the bed. See if I'm normal. A horrific heat in his lap, the springy stiff thing, almost forgotten and rushing back with a rich familiarity like a scent from childhood encountered decades later.

"Doctor—"

"Let's don't talk about it, okay?" He rolled the cigarette between his fingers.

Sissy shrugged, cracked a sly grin. "Okay."

They reached the intersection where Cincinnati deadheaded into Mesa; to their left lay the town; to the right was the road to Las Cruces, Arizona, the coast. When he stopped to wait for the traffic on Mesa before turning west, Sissy said, "I'm hungry."

"We can stop soon as we get down the road a ways."

"I'd like to have a milkshake, wouldn't you?"

"Okay. Like I said—"

"The Five Points Oasis dairy bar makes really good ones."

"Okay." Presuming the place to be on their way out of town, he cocked the wheel and was about to pull into traffic when she grabbed his forearm.

"The other way." She pointed vaguely toward town.

"Let's keep going west, Sissy. You can get a milkshake about anywhere, you know."

"Yes, but they're special. Please, Will? It won't take long. And the thing is, you see, all the kids will be there. Maybe I won't get another chance to be here again, you know?"

"Aren't you worried about being seen with me?"

"Gosh, no!"

"Sissy, it just seems like an unnecessary risk. If you're hungry we can stop at a diner—"

"Please, Will? You know, it's not like we're going on a date—I may never be back here. I need to say good-bye."

The prospect of being detained while Sissy gabbed with her school friends at a hang-out rattled him. He also didn't like the idea of being seen with her—if her father did something so stupid as to call the police, it might make them easier to find. But her face—the wide mouth downcast like a sad clown's, her promi-ment dark eyes, the beakish nose—tugged at his heart. A horrible surprise awaited her down the road; it seemed unnecessarily cruel to deprive her of this small pleasure.

"Okay."

She squealed and kissed his neck. He turned the car left back toward town.

For a good half hour he followed her uncertain directions, first east, then north, then east again. No, she said. Down this way, I think—okay, just two more blocks. Oh, I guess I was thinking of. . . .

He'd presumed she'd been there many times, but he soon saw she was groping to find it; he was about to lose patience and head back to the highway when they came upon it where several streets converged.

"See!"

It was a tile-roofed hut with arched windows and a

parking lot that went all the way around it; many cars were parked head in toward the small building like cattle feeding from a trough. Other cars circled around behind, stopping and inching forward as the occupants yelled to one another.

"What you do is get your drink inside then come out, that's what all the kids do."

"Okay."

He parked behind a sedan and cut his lights, and Sissy jumped from his Ford to go inside to get her drink. He lit a cigarette, imagining her inside weaving in and around crowded tables, stopping to say good-bye to her friends. This would most likely take her a good while, he thought. Sissy among her friends. . . . When he'd called Pearl this afternoon, Mildred was giving her and some neighborhood kids a snack. They'd been playing in the yard. Mumbles had babies, she said. He'd wanted to crawl through the phone line and be there in that sunny kitchen. Be home soon, Sweetie. Yeah, well, you could just start up right now and ditch this kid and this town and this plan. Just drive off. Sure, she'd be hurt for a while, but she'd never know that she'd saved her father's life. Of course, he'd already killed Shingle.

He felt the spastic convulsions of the dying man under him and the greasy blood on his own fingers. He swooned with nausea; he grabbed at the door handle, laid his nape back against the seat, squeezed his eyes shut and waited for the wave to wash over him. It left him damp with his own sweat.

And before he could give the nagging voice inside another chance to argue, Sissy emerged from the hut and got back in the car carrying two large paper cups.

"Now you have to circle around a minute, okay?"

He shrugged, backed the Ford into a space in the circle parading about the building, and they joined the automotive paseo. Sissy sipped from her shake—his, set between his legs, made a cold fist in his balls—as they went by, and, although she kept uttering the names of people she recognized, she never waved to them nor did they seem to notice or recognize her. He felt they were on a treadmill. She said, "There's Melanie." She nodded toward a blonde seated in an open roadster with two young men.

"She the one you were supposed to be studying with when we were sneaking out?"

"Yeah."

"Don't you want to say good-bye?"

"I am."

"I mean do you want me to stop so you can say good-bye? We need to be getting down the road."

"Okay. We can go now."

"Yeah? But I didn't you want to. . . ." He left the thought unspoken. What occurred to him was: she had never been here before but knew it by reputation; she didn't actually know any of these kids except by sight and name; and she wanted to be seen with him to establish her own value and worth.

"How about your friend Melanie? Don't you want to go talk to her a minute?" he asked to test his hypothesis.

"She's not actually my friend. I just made that up."

"Really?"

"Yeah. And will you quit with the third degree? I said we can go now. Let's go, okay? I just wanted to get a shake like any normal kid, is that all right? It didn't kill anybody for us to do that, right?"

He got back on Mesa heading west.

"Will, I don't want to be a pest, but there is one more place."

When he looked exasperated, she said, "But it's very very special to me, and there won't be anyone there but us. Also, it's that way—"

She pointed ahead, through the windshield.

"It's on the way?"

"Yeah."

"What is it?"

"A surprise. You'll love it. I promise."

This time she did seem more in command of her navigational faculties; they went down Doniphan Drive but soon everything was unfamiliar to him, and he had to rely on her instructions. On a deserted dirt road west of the city, they weaved in and around foothills in the darkness—the final-quarter moon, still rising over Mexico, had been swallowed by the scud. They had driven onto what seemed to be a plateau. Lights of Juarez and El Paso glimmered on the plain. Below, in the distance, the zinc, lead and copper smelter churned and roared through the night, spewing sulphurous smoke Hunter could smell. Tiny points of light pricked the darkness from windows in the smelter's buildings.

At last, Sissy said, "Here. Stop here! This is perfect."

His lights made shivering mesquites look ghostly white and the stones were like eggs of prehistoric beasts. He cut the headlamps. Darkness swallowed the car; it was like being a mile under the ocean, he thought, the blackness penetrated only by a glimmer of phosphorescent creatures' eyes.

"Okay. What's here?"

Sissy giggled. "Us."

"Yeah, I can see that. But we can be us anywhere."

"It's my favorite place."

"Why?"

She sighed and moved close to him. He felt the warmth of her long thigh under the thin chiffon. The cloying milk taste made him long for a drink of cold water.

"You'll see."

"Sissy, this is stupid! Quit playing games!" He moved as if to start the engine, but she put her arms about his neck and kissed his mouth. She tasted sweet from the shake and Scotch and still brassy from the cigarette. She jostled him, and he grabbed for the cup between his legs. The shake was a slop of warm milk now.

"Please trust me?"

"Tell me why this place is special. Have you been out here with some other fellow?"

She smiled. "Nope, you dope. Daddy brought me out here on my sixteenth birthday."

A spasm jerked his gut. "Why?"

"To show me something."

"What?"

"You'll see," she said smugly. "In the meantime. . . ."

"In the meantime we're wasting time."

She went shhhhh between her teeth, disgusted. "What's wrong with you tonight? You're such a sour-puss."

She put her face close to his and ran her fingers around his ears. Her breast was pressed against his arm. She was twisted with her back to the dash now. He extracted the cup from between his thighs and tossed it out the window. She took advantage of his lifted arm to settle into him, shoved close by the wheel.

"My doctor," she murmured. "Check my temperature. I think I'm getting warm."

bullfighting, and bloody politics—Hunter had heard that El Pasoans had watched from the roof of the First National Bank while battles raged across the river during the Madero Revolution. Mexico meant the Old-World mumbo-jumbo of the papacy and heart-eating rituals of pagan Indians; it also meant quick divorce, paid-for sex, gambling casinos and nightclubs along the street called the "Calle Diablo" in Juarez.

The richer you were, the higher you built. Sissy's father had erected a two-story house on the northern rim of the subdivision on a one-acre tract surrounded by vacant sand lots choked with mesquite and cactus and stones as big as bread loaves. Made of red brick, with a gallery-porch off both the first and second floors, the house, like some others nearby, was stubbornly midwestern in design and would have fit perfectly along a leafy Ohio avenue. Here, though, surrounded by rock and arroyo, where the tallest green object in the foothills was a bush, it looked misplaced, as if it had been plucked from that Ohio setting by a tornado and deposited neatly but inappropriately onto the lot. During the rare but torrential rains, the dry arroyos behind the house sluiced a raging run-off of red gravy that slid across the lot and ripped off the top-soil trucked in especially to grow the fine-bladed grass Sissy's mother wanted in her yard. To hold off the water and to shut out horned toads, lizards, and rattlesnakes, Sissy's mother had a six-foot fence of red brick built around the house. Like the stockade about a cavalry fort, the fence declared that inside lies civilization, and nothing outside shall enter uninvited. And like most newcomers, Sissy's mother had fought the desert, but even after three years she'd neither surrendered nor adapted. She'd planted a dozen trees, but they had

Heat from her torso burned against his chest. He passed his hands over her shoulders, her long back, the filmy chiffon thin as oil on her flesh as his fingers glided over her hips. She reached up, removed her hat, tossed it aside, shook out her hair. It smelled of cologne. He swallowed. Lying on her side and facing him, she shifted her legs and her stockings whistled. He bent to kiss her, and she met his mouth with hers open, her tongue flicking against his teeth. He gave in, touched her tongue with his, went hard instantly. She arched her torso, pushing her breasts toward him, inviting. His palm passed across her chest, found the hardened knot under the dress and camisole, and she groaned into his mouth.

"Golly!" she gasped, breaking the kiss. "What time is it?"

He laughed. Waves of energy were pulsing through his limbs, flooding his cranial cavity. Desire, it was like a drug. They'd been on their way. Now were stopped. They should be moving on. But his arms were full of warmth, silky flesh. It was so dark no one could see, not even the dead.

"What's it matter?"

"Because I bet I'm eighteen in New York already. Or maybe Bermuda, what do you think?"

"What's it matter?"

She hugged him, spoke to his left ear. "Because when I'm eighteen no matter what we do you won't get in trouble."

He wished she would stop snaking her hot breath into his ear canal and squirming in the seat, moving her hips against his thigh. They kissed again. His heart thundered against his breastbone and his stiff cock swelled like a painful tumor. He kept his hands gliding across her back to hide their shaking, but her skin against his palms blotted out his intention. He splayed his hands across her back and pressed her close to him. No one would know if he had her, would they? And if her father learned it, so much the better.

"No, wait," she said, "Look. Here's what we came for."

She twisted about and faced the windshield. He looked. The desert about them seemed black as obsidian; only a few stars glittered against the sky's flinty hardness. A ridge ahead was faintly silhouetted against the sky. He caught a movement, vague, not clearly discernible, heard a rumble.

"Oooo," cooed Sissy, just as he saw it: a glowing orange river tumbling down the hillside in waves, each moving like swift lava over the one before. The air held a faint metallic stench. A clank came from the crest of the hill, then a new outpouring rushed out in a pop that sent sparks rocketing into the sky over the river of red-orange-yellow sliding down. For an instant, shocked, he thought volcano but knew that made no sense.

"What—"

"Slag," she said. "They dump it out."

They watched in silence as several more carloads were poured down the mountainside, Hunter feeling mesmerized, tugged down into himself where he didn't want to go. The deck exploding in splinters under his feet, hurling him upward, then he was coming to in the water of San Pedro Channel, something bumping the nape of his neck, and he turned to see Bobette's disembodied arm wearing his grey cardigan floating by him. Ugly flames were nesting in the stern of the boat like angry gargoyles. He tried to shake off these pictures.

The slag heap pulsed while cooling like some beast breathing its last. It glowed in the darkness. If you were out in space, he thought, it would look like a big eye, and the earth would look desperate and angry, enraged in helplessness, imprisoned by its own round circumference. The air was heavy now with fumes that made his eyes water. He thought of the grime-faced smelter workers on the slag carts, the carts going down to the molten core, loading up, the men being marched with a whip, Volga boatmen. Below the surface of the earth an engine rumbled constantly, unstoppable, oblivious.

"Will, do you believe in Heaven and Hell?"

He snorted, compelled to mock her. "What a question."

"No, really! I want to know."

"How come you're so full of philosophy tonight?"

"Gee, you'd think it was obvious! Here I am eloping on my eighteenth birthday. I'm not a kid any more and I have to start thinking about such things. And my future, what I'm going to do."

"I wish you wouldn't talk about crap like that!" he thundered suddenly, astonishing them both.

"What's the matter with you?"

"Nothing, I'm sorry, I really am." He took her hand.

She stared him down, he looked away. The river of slag had dulled, covered by a translucent skin. Looking at it made him thirsty.

"I want to know if you believe in Heaven or Hell."

"Why do you care?"

She didn't answer for a time, then she said, "Because Mother said things like that don't seem so important at first but later on they can be."

Elope? Things that don't matter at first? Maybe he should remind her again that he'd promised nothing, but why bother? Tomorrow everything would be inside out and upside down for her, anyway. In this moment together here in the utter darkness they could be whoever they wanted to be to one another; he could be a young man who had never known a young woman, just as she was a young woman knowing a man for the first time; there didn't have to be a past or a future so long as they just sat here, girl and boy, breathing each other's sweet breath, breast to breast. Then there would have been no Bobette in his life, and, better luck for her! no man such as he in hers. Just him and this nice kid, eloping.

"She's right. Tell me, what do you believe?"

"I don't know what to believe. When I had instruction it all seemed to make sense, but I really don't know. They both seem so . . . far away."

"You mean because one's way above and the other's way below?"

"Yeah, that too, I guess. I meant a long time off. You never told me what you believe."

"I believe what you believe."

"You're just saying that to get me off the subject."

"Well, maybe this is a personal matter, Sissy."

"You should be willing to share something important with me, if I'm at all important to you." She faced him squarely, snagged his gaze, and held it. "I'd share anything I have, anything I feel or think with you, Will. I'm all yours now, body and soul, do you know that?"

Her look was too pleading. He felt panicky. "My leg's cramping." He squirmed clear of her, straightened his legs, and pressed his soles against the floorboard. His knee popped. He frowned at his toes.

"Will?" she whispered. "Did you hear what I—"

"You wanted to know about Heaven and Hell, right?"

After a moment, she said, "Yes."

"Maybe I do believe in Heaven and Hell, sort of. It's an idea people carry in their heads of the best and worst that can happen. You look at the newspaper and see somebody tied somebody else up in a bed and set fire to it, or maybe threw some kid up against a wall and broke his neck. Those people are living in Hell, both the ones that do the stuff and the ones to whom it's done. You know the Bible story about Job? Think about some modern-day man like that, say who has a loving family that means everything in the world to him and some scum bastard comes along and kills them. You could call him the Devil. And the man has to find the Devil and take his revenge and that's all he can think about night and day, how he lost his family because of that man. Even if he gets even, he'll still spend the rest of his life missing them, he'll never be whole again, he'll never know any kind of Heaven again."

He was clenching his jaw; Sissy looked on, drawn back slightly in alarm. He let out a breath. "You, you've been living in Heaven, Sissy—your parents love you, you've never wanted for anything, your every wish is granted, you're healthy, you have friends—"

"I have you!"

He nodded slowly and blinked. "You have me."

"But none of it's forever?"

"Right. I don't believe in the forever part." He gazed very seriously into her eyes as if to send a message. But she gave him only sympathy in return: his "philosophy" apparently made her feel sorry for his having to take on the burdens of the world; her brow knit, she leaned forward and smoothed his cheek with her palm. Once again they kissed. Her hand fell casually, palm up, into his lap, and he swelled to an ache. Why not? Last chance, why pass it up? It might hurt her father worse than anything else. Blood of her maidenhead, here on the seat.

But his desire was tainted with hatred and guilt. He wanted to be monklike, clean, purged of unhealthy complications; he didn't want to sully his intent or his act by taking this kind of advantage, like a soldier grabbing the spoils of war. And he didn't want to be distracted or swayed from his purpose. Already he was full of torment over her, hating her or what she stood for, hating her because she was alive to bring pleasure to her father, knowing even as he did that he hated her out of necessity and not from anything she might say or do, and the truth was that he wanted her, even liked her, felt guilty about what he must do to her. It was just too damn bad she was in the wrong life at the wrong time. This was as good an example as he could imagine of Hell.

4

1920-
1930

THE WOMAN in the room across the
hall painted in a wild style he'd never
seen before, and he wondered if she
were truly sane. She called her paintings
still lifes. If you stood back from them,
they did look like normal pictures—a
room, a table, and on it a vase of flowers—but when you bent close you could
make out faces in the blossoms, a mouth
gasping for air, another wrenched in a

silent howl, still another with a lolling purple tongue. They gave him the willies. She asked to do his portrait. He made excuses. Then, though, she smiled oddly when they passed in the hall, and in the next still life she put on display in the parlor an outlandish floral tropical horn with a red and yellow gullet was swallowing him to the neck.

This artist popped up in a dream as his mother, and she made him sit for a portrait but wouldn't show it until she was finished, then she faced it at him like a barber showing you your new self in his mirror. The portrait looked at first like a desert landscape, then the horrible realization sank in even before he saw the evidence—she had punished him by breaking his body into pieces which she'd only half-buried in the forms of the lizard, the snake, the rock. I tried my best, she said, but I couldn't make you fit.

He woke up glad to be in California. He stretched his legs, his arms, his neck, straining to reassert his connections. His muscles were thick as hawsers from working the loading docks in the freight yards.

On his way to the bathroom, he met the artist coming out. On her kimono were a cherry tree in bloom and a snow-capped peak. She smiled.

"Hello, Mr. Wyse."

"Hello." He couldn't meet her gaze; her human reality was soaked in the hue of the night's dream.

"I hope I left it clean enough."

"I'm sure."

She'd leave her hairs, though. A compulsory intimacy. Even a single tiny curled spring could inflame like a splinter under his imagination, but he bet she knew that. She was maybe five years older, good-looking, but those paintings scared him. He didn't see why, since he was in a land of milk and honey, he should have to tolerate anything that would scare him. Anybody like her who lived in a boardinghouse was here today, gone tomorrow. Trash, probably. What was the point of coming here if you were just going to duck right back into that same burrow?

Days off he'd walk to the beach below Ocean Avenue in Santa Monica. He strolled a mile or so out of his way to go down Carlisle and to pass where the Indian from the ferry lived with his white wife. He'd looked up the address in the telephone book. It was something, that place. Soaring palms lined the street, a sweep of green lawn dotted here and there with Mexican gardeners, behind it a two-story white stucco with balconies and a red tile roof shaded by huge eucalyptus trees. It lightened his step to take it in. To think the Indian used to work day in day out poling a ferry over the Canadian and lived alone in a shack. As he looked at the arched windows he could almost picture the Indian moving about inside. The house meant the Indian had a new life, and that gave him hope for change; yet the house also meant the nearness of a friend from the past, and that made him less lonely.

Copperfield's wife had yellow hair and nearly ran him down as she came speeding out of the driveway in a red roadster one morning; he didn't see her up close, but she looked young and beautiful. Maybe if he walked by enough times the Indian himself would be coming down the drive or might be practicing his putts on that carpet of lawn, and he'd reintroduce himself. Not that he wanted anything, really—it would be nice to shake the hand of a man who had come so far, come from a place he knew, through luck that was deserved. Since the Indian's life had turned itself inside out here, maybe the magic could rub off.

He was coming back up Wilshire one Saturday afternoon not too far from the Indian's place when a swirling candystripe ahead caught his eye, and he thought he'd stop in for a shine and to eavesdrop—he might get a tip on a nag at Santa Anita or maybe a prospect for a job that suited his I.Q.—and he'd no sooner set foot inside a cloud of tobacco smoke and bay rum than he spied the Indian in a barber chair under a teepee of white sheet with his head sticking out. He was leaned back peering at the ceiling while the barber, who didn't look happy, was about to slather his cheeks with soap. And here—this was a surprise!—the Indian had grown his hair long and now wore it in two braids that were dangling down from the headrest. Bits of red ribbon cinched off the black ends. When the Indian had run the ferry he'd worn overalls and his hair was always cut close. Now, in a place as modern as Los Angeles, he went around looking like an old-fashioned savage.

Wilbur got a shine and sat hiding behind a paper listening to fellows talk about strikes—new oil strikes, old railroad strikes, yesterday's baseball strikes. Nobody had word one to say to his childhood friend. When the barber had shaved him and whisked off the apron like a magician, the Indian stood towering over everybody in the place. It made you blink, the things that turned out to be so different—had he been expecting Copperfield to wear a loin cloth under that sheet? The Kiowa had on khaki slacks, a pale blue cotton dress shirt, and a navy blazer. The way rich white fellows dressed casual.

Copperfield walked out of the shop leaving a huge tip, which, to judge by how his barber was the first to insult him the instant the door had chased his heels, was only large enough to buy him entrance, not acceptance. Can you beat it? He gimme a dollar tip on a two-bit shave again! Then the moron's chorus: yeah, what do you expect, junk they spend money on, they can't hardly count, why my brother-in-law lives in Tulsa and he—

Wilbur angrily rattled the newspaper, then slapped it to his lap and broadcast a glare around the room like a yellow spotlight. They looked. They had never seen him before. He was in a strange land, among strangers who were insulting his friend.

"He gave you a tip that big because he counted on you not giving an Indian a shave unless he did. He was counting on your greed being larger than your bigotry. He was counting on you just doing your job and keeping your trap shut because you thought he was going to tip you a buck, so he had you dancing like a monkey on a leash for it. Looks to me like he made that dollar spread pretty far. Looks to me like he bought your dignity with it, and I know I sure as hell wouldn't let mine go for that little!"

The next Saturday afternoon he strolled by the shop and saw that Copperfield was getting a shine. He waited outside, and when the Indian came forth, he stuck out his hand and said, "Say, there, Mr. Copperfield, do you remember me? I used to lived up the river from your place in Wetoka County—"

Copperfield squinted at him, then said, "Sure, I see it now. You're grown."

"You used to let me shoot your rifle."

The Indian laughed. "You were a pretty good shot." He shook Wilbur's hand. Wilbur grinned. It'd been a long time since he'd spoken to someone who could remember something about him.

"You told me some good stories, too."

"I'm glad you remember them. There's not many out here want to hear them."

Copperfield had three cigars sticking out of his shirt pocket, and he offered one to Wilbur. Wilbur took it but in turn insisted on buying Copperfield coffee. Copperfield insisted on treating Wilbur to lunch. An hour later, seated on an outdoor terrace in the small cafe run by a Lebanese family where Copperfield ate breakfast most mornings, they had finished lunch and were drinking coffee and smoking the cigars like old chums. Wilbur described life in his boardinghouse; Copperfield talked of playing an Indian in westerns. Wilbur listened attentively but behind his smile he was calculating furiously—how to keep a hold? How to latch on? Copperfield could buy gardeners, cooks, houseboys, maids, mechanics. What could Wilbur do for him that could not be bought? What service could he perform that could keep him close to this good luck charm? What did Copperfield need?

He needed somebody who could hear the moron's chorus behind his back. He needed someone he could trust, not someone whose opinions and dignity were on the block for a buck.

He told Copperfield he was looking for a position in business. What kind of position in what kind of business? Well, hard to say exactly. He wanted to work for somebody he respected who would trust him to be kind of personal assistant maybe, like a secretary, you know, arrange things, write letters, think about all the details, keep books—

Copperfield was grinning. "You're thinking maybe I'm such a man?"

"To tell the truth, yes. Maybe you need somebody to watch your back, too. I get the feeling that a man in your situation excites a lot of people's interest and envy."

86

Copperfield, it turned out, had recently been considering new ventures. Oil strikes could turn into a glut. He'd been thinking of getting into California real estate; the wave of people coming west—"All these white men coming out here to take a tiny little piece of land and build these little white houses: I'm thinking of selling them the land and building the houses for them. I need somebody who's willing to study these things with me."

"You could hire a lawyer or some fellows who specialized in this kind of thing, you know."

"Sure. Which ones should I trust?" Copperfield winked at Wilbur. "That's your job, you tell me that."

Luck had struck. He'd come upon Copperfield at just the right moment. It was a good omen. So he went to work for Copperfield learning and helping him to learn what they needed to know to do what Copperfield thought needed to be done. The next several months they pored over newspapers in the mornings during their breakfast at the cafe, drove in the Indian's Packard to see plats of vacant land, and when Copperfield was busy making a picture, Wilbur rooted about in county records running down deeds and titles. He talked to lumbermen, subcontractors for plumbing, painting, electricity, carpentry.

The good luck formed a chain of circumstance. Landing this position meant having to work not with his brawn but his brain; it forced him to learn in a way that his mother or school had never done. He took an apartment in Santa Monica and wore a suit and tie now. And with each new scrap of knowledge came strength and more confidence in a future, and it was possible to think of himself as having outgrown his past.

Having to learn sent him to the Los Angeles County Library. One day behind the counter there was a young woman who had so many freckles he couldn't take his eyes off her face. They were like the little chips of mica seen in streams, what they call fool's gold. Her long hair was reddish-blonde and almost matched her cheeks when she blushed.

Which was frequently, during the first ten minutes he talked to her. He didn't know why he had such a strong urge to linger at the counter. She seemed like a mere schoolgirl in her yellow dress with a lace choker, not at all his picture of a librarian; he wasn't interested in schoolgirls—he was disdainful of children because he considered himself an adult.

He had no reason to hang about after she had logged his books on accounting and keeping ledgers. However, he grew aware of a peculiar effect he alone had on her: she smiled and said something "nice" when talking to other patrons, but she blushed and averted her gaze when she silently handed him his books. He was curious and fascinated by this effect; it was if he were playing a strange musical instrument with more accomplishment and ease than his unfamiliarity would normally allow. It was, naturally, quiet in the library, and so he leaned forward to whisper, "Do you have any more?"

"What?" She spoke much louder than he thought a bonafide librarian should.

He held up a book. "Books."

She grinned, then bent forward to whisper. "Thousands!" she hissed.

"On accounting, I meant," he said stiffly.

Chastened, she went to the card catalogue and returned a moment later with a card. *The Sum Total of Accounting*, it read. She had included numbers and the author's name. She had what he would call a very girly hand, a neat cursive with loops all properly proportioned and in place.

"Do you know the Dewey decimal system?"

"What?"

"It's how books are shelved. How you find them."

He looked away. "Well, not in this library, I know the one in my own."

She snorted. "I'll show you."

She led him into the stacks, and he studied her girlish figure from behind. She irritated him. Dewey decimal system. She'd only meant the numbers on the books. Of course he used the numbers! He had had quite enough messy exchanges with a female for one day, even though he dimly recognized that she was doing something for him or with him, and not to him. But he hadn't any clue as to what it was; this terra incognita was new and therefore troubling, so he vowed to stay business-like.

She found his book, he made no remark, and he stood at attention while she recorded it at the counter. She used a yellow lead pencil; her hands were long and slim and covered with those bronze freckles. Her nails were bitten off. She wrote something wrong on the card and had to erase it. Her head cocked to one side while she wrote again. She had high cheekbones and full lips that were a deep red but not with lipstick, more like mulberry stains. Her eyes were beer-colored. A minute line of perspiration was visible at her hairline.

She handed him the book. He realized he would have to walk away now.

"Are you really a librarian?" He grinned as if he doubted it.

"Only a helper part time."

"You go to school?"

She nodded.

He put the books down and made a show of straightening his cuffs, but once he had done that, instead of lifting the books, he set his elbows on the counter.

"I thought so." He grinned again. "What do you study?"

"Geography and history, reading and writing, algebra, French, Latin."

"What grade are you in?"

"I'm not in a grade, it's college. I go to the Normal at the end of the Vermont Street line."

"Oh. They let kids go to college around here?"

She laughed. "Only college kids."

"I didn't go. But I'm learning on my own." He indicated the books which she'd handed him only minutes before.

She bent over to place a book under the counter, and a scent like bath powder wafted up. He decided he was talking to her only to teach her that you didn't have to attend school to become educated.

"This fellow I work for, he's rich but he never went to school."

"Then he must be ignorant," she said quietly but without malice—it meant poor man!

"Well, he studies on his own too and he has tutors, that's what I meant. He's as smart as anybody you see around here."

"I didn't say he wasn't smart. I said he must be ignorant. Not smart and ignorant aren't the same. You can be brilliant and ignorant both."

It wasn't wise to banter with this girl. Twice now she'd made a fool out of him. He gathered the books under his arm.

"Well, see ya."

"See you, Wilbur."

He came back to the counter, grinning again.

"Now how did you know my name?"

"It was on the card."

He slammed his palm against his forehead: of course, you moron! But then, she didn't have to use his name, did she?

"You memorize it?"

To his gratification, she blushed a flaming ruddy color that almost glowed. "I have to work now." She strode away from the counter. He was afraid he had made her mad.

He went outside but turned to look through the glass doors. She was straining up to shelve a book; the long yellow skirt rose over her calf, and her breasts almost vanished as she straightened her arms, gave a little uunff! and shoved the book home, bouncing on the balls of her feet.

He thought about her during the night. It had been fun to fluster her and see her discomfort flag madly across her face. Did she have a boyfriend who teased her? He imagined a thug on the street, catcalling to make her blush. If he caught some guy. . . .

Whoa!

He returned the next day, but before he could even reach the counter, she called out, "Well, hello!" People all over the library turned their heads. She looked him squarely in the eye and grinned impishly. "Here's old Abe Lincoln himself, his pore old eyes just burned out from studying by the light of that fireplace!"

If she'd smacked him in the face with a custard pie he wouldn't have been more surprised.

"Well, what are you so red for?" she asked with mock innocence.

"I'm not red!"

"Oh. Sorry!" She pressed her hand to her mouth in a transparent effort to hide a snicker.

"That's just...windburn. I got it from fishing."

He put the books on the counter.

"You read them already?"

He nodded once, dramatically. She whistled, then gave him a sassy, mischievous wink.

"So what now? An overnight symposium in paleontology and trigonometry with maybe a little philosophy thrown in for relaxation?"

He flushed, speechless, shifting his weight, unable to look at her. He didn't know whether to be a good sport and work up a rejoinder or let her know he felt hurt. "I try to improve myself. I've been on my own since I was sixteen." He sounded like an injured child, and he wished he'd kept his mouth shut.

"Poor little orphan boy, huh?" she cracked as if she would never for one instant believe it.

He nodded, his face woefully earnest. Her grin faded, the color came back to her cheeks, and she turned away.

"I'm sorry," she murmured.

Now he wasn't glad to have made her blush, though he was happier to be the object of her sympathy than of her sarcasm.

"I get along. It's all right. I'm okay," he said to ease her discomfort. "Nobody to push me around—"

"Like a wife or a girlfriend, huh!"

"—or to tell me what to wear or do. I wouldn't have it any other way."

He leaned on one elbow at the counter like a loafer. She moved opposite him, hands playing with a yellow pencil entwined in her fingers. Very fine copper-colored hair veiled the freckles on her forearms. She pressed her ribs against the counter, which made her breasts look bigger.

"My brother's in the Navy," she said confidentially. "My dad died, and I live with my mom."

"Sorry to hear it."

"Yeah, me too," she said drily.

He'd meant sorry your dad's dead but didn't seek to correct her misconstruction, though their having that in common reassured him. She gave him a friendly look, without challenge. He wondered if he could tell her things without her using that wicked laugh, and he wanted to hear about her school. He wondered what she could teach him. He liked this girl. It seemed safe enough; after all, she was a child without a father, and it wouldn't hurt him to play her big brother. He'd always wanted a sister.

"What're you thinking about?"

He looked away. "Nothing."

"You're handsome. You're bashful, too."

"No, I'm not!" Her quick judgments made him feel she could read his mind.

"Which?"

He was flustered. "I'm not bashful at all!"

"Does that mean you think you're handsome?"

She'd reverted to bantering. He was willing to concede that she was superior in this area, so long as she would quit using this wit on him!

"No!"

She clucked her tongue. "I can tell right now that you want to ask me if you can come to my house on Sunday and see me, and you just can't get it out of your mouth. You want me to say it for you?"

"If I want to come to your house, I'll ask for myself."

There was an uneasy silence. He was afraid he'd have to leave.

"Well?"

"Well's a hole in the ground," he said. "Too deep for your shallow mind."

She laughed, as if in pity. "All right, then. We'll have to pretend you asked, how about that?"

"That all depends on what you answered when I asked," he heard himself say.

They both laughed.

"I said yes, of course."

He put the girl—Bobette—out of his mind; or, rather, he fixed the girl in his mind so that he didn't have to treat the invitation as an obligation: he might show up, he might not. She was too forward. A girl that forward, well, you didn't who'd been there before you. Might even be p.g. and looking for a sucker to pin it on. They didn't call it fool's gold for nothing. So he didn't have to go. You didn't owe somebody who tried to trap you.

But, so long as you knew that, you were safe. You could wear your watchfulness like a suit of armor.

Bobette and her mother had a frame house near Echo Lake that her mother had purchased with her father's life insurance. Worked his heart out, said the mother, but, behind her back, the daughter winked, mimed a bottle with fist and thumb and went glug glug glug. The mother was short and dark-headed, pleasant enough but cool in a way that said "prove it." She and the daughter demonstrated their homemaking skills and invited him to sit in dad's easy chair. Seems he arrived a tad early. The chair fit him nicely and he could picture the father sitting there enjoying the show, so to speak. Though even a cement-headed dunce could tell they were trolling for a sucker, he could see how some fellows might be tempted to bite. They weren't boardinghouse trash, for one thing. Carpets, drapes and lamps, framed pictures of men the mother called Big and Little Harold, and end tables with knick-knacks, each item placed in a way that suggested care and a fondness for things. The lace doilies were clean, starched, and, most significantly, not tattered. The house smelled of pies and roast and ginger and a lot of feminine scents mixed together, and he kept inhaling the aroma as the women yammered on and bustled about to complete Sunday dinner, still in their church clothes.

At the table, while her mother said grace, his gaze roamed the platters and bowls decorated with lacey blue etchings of country scenes and filled with steaming potatoes, gravy, green beans, and under the china a white tablecloth trimmed with embroidered flowers. On the sideboard were mincemeat, chess, and apple pies. Their plates shone and matched the bowls, their napkins were rolled into silver rings beside the plates. They had the kind of house he thought his mother had always wanted or had occupied in St. Louis before she'd fallen.

After they ate, they remained at the table while he talked about himself. Bobette laughed no matter what he said, and he felt like a chocolate malted she'd been waiting all day to consume. To impress them, he told them about the oilmen in Dallas he'd worked closely with. He wanted the women to know just how good a catch they were going to lose. He also had the feeling that the instant he stopped talking about himself, the mother would interview him, and he would rather dole out answers to unasked questions in his own sweet time than to field the mother's chosen queries. He gave amusing thumbnail sketches of other boarders in his former house—the landlady who dipped snuff and who was never seen spitting, but if an unsuspecting visitor lifted the cover of a candy dish in the parlor he discovered that she had, the automobile salesman who kept cockroaches in matchboxes to see how long they could live without eating. In his story about the artist—"she's a looker but pretty darned crazy"—the woman bought him dinner at a fancy restaurant before taking him across the hall into her own room to unveil the painting.

"She thinks you're just a bragger."

He blinked back his shock. "What do you think?"

"I told her you were an orphan."

"What's that got to do with anything?"

"You've never been loved enough to trust that somebody might accept you as you are."

He clenched his jaw. He was smarting from her mother's judgement, and the insulting speculation about his personality seemed a gratuitous intrusion on his privacy. "I'm not an orphan."

"Why'd you lie?"

He shifted his feet as he stood inside the doorway to the little storeroom on the library's third floor. Her bracing him this boldly was so outrageous he could hardly think straight.

"Why'd I lie about being an orphan?"

"Yes."

"Aw, you know how it is. You're on a train, and a fellow sits down next to you who you don't know from

Adam's off-ox, and next thing he's pumping you full of hooey about himself and you know it isn't true, and you just nod and let him go on because it's harmless if he wants to pretend to be someone or something he's not. You're not going to see him again."

She was smiling. "And you can pump him full of hooey, too."

"Yeah."

"And so were you—"

"I wanted you to feel sorry for me."

"I did, it worked. You bamboozled me. But then why'd you brag?"

"Which time?"

Bobette smiled. "My mother would say about the rich men you've worked for, but I'm saying about the 'looker' who painted your portrait, of course."

"Maybe I was lying about that, too. She did paint my portrait, but it wasn't like I made it sound."

"But why make it sound like more than it was?"

"Well...."

He was sweating. The storeroom was hardly larger than a closet. Two long tables were against one wall and held stacked cartons of books; along the other wall was an old horsehair sofa. The room's one tall window overlooked the street; it had no shade or curtain but the milky glaze of neglect on its surface diffused the strong sun so that the room was bright but the light didn't hurt his eyes. Bobette was using a carton next to the sofa as a table, and it presently held a square of waxed paper and two triangles of a white bread and bologna sandwich which she had continued to eat though he was standing with his hat in his hand just inside the open door. Was he sure he didn't want half? On a little shelf above the sofa were *Little Women* and *Great*

Expectations, because, as she'd explained, normally she stayed up here reading for the whole of her lunch hour. His unannounced visit had disrupted her routine. The room smelled dusty, like old books and paper, even though after he had knocked on the door and she'd opened it, she'd left it ajar so that "no one will get the wrong idea," she said, grinning, "especially you."

He had been up here what seemed the whole day, though he knew it was only a matter of minutes. He'd come to the library expressly to see her and had been directed to her hideaway. He wanted the girl to realize that, though he might be ignorant, his manners were so impeccable that he would make a special trip just to deliver this message: would she please tell her mother for him how much he enjoyed the dinner on Sunday? Her reply had been that her mother thought he was a bragger.

He sighed. "Well, I suppose I wanted you to think that other girls were after me. I thought it might make you more interested."

She wadded up the bread crusts in the waxed paper, then she stuck a hand into her lunch sack and extracted another item. Unfolded the paper. Mincemeat pie, left-over from Sunday, he guessed. His stomach growled. She lifted the point of the wedge to her mouth, putting a free hand under to catch crumbs. It struck him that she wasn't uncomfortable to be watched by a man while she ate.

"Well, it actually made me less interested," she said finally. She dabbed at her fingertips with the tip of her tongue to snag flakes of crust. "Telling me lies like that just seems pathetic. If you'd had better things to do than be with us, you'd have been doing them."

"Everybody likes a home-cooked meal."

"I see. I suppose your artist is too creative to cook."

He started to protest that the artist lived in a board-inghouse where nobody cooked but the landlady, but he saw that how people took their meals wasn't the point. To think he'd come to express his thanks!

"Well, I can see why you need your mother's help in getting a fellow to come around, that's for damn sure."

"I actually don't give a damn if I get a fellow or not. Bringing one home gives my mother somebody to fuss over. If you came back a second or third time she'd show you the broken porch rail, and there's a wardrobe she wants moved out of my dad's old room—do you want the rest of this pie? It's too sweet—I guess she could hire somebody to do that stuff quick enough, but she'd rather barter her wares for it. If you have some-thing that needs mending, bring it by. Any further transactions can be negotiated between you two with-out my help. I picked you out because you looked capa-ble."

Where was he in that speech? Being cast aside or invited in? She was a puzzle, and for the first time he found himself more interested in learning about her than afraid of what she might learn about him. This moment—this event—which had suddenly been con-jured unexpectedly into his day was so wholly unprece-dented and strange that it made his head spin. The sen-sation of having his thoughts rush out of his mouth without being censored was terrifying, yet exhilarating. So far no damage had been done, but that seemed like luck.

"How come you don't care if you get a fellow? Do you already have one?"

"No, not now." She looked out of the window. "I was engaged last year."

"What happened?"

"It's personal."

"Oh, well! Excuse me! And how about when you say I've never been loved enough to believe that people will accept me!"

"I didn't know if that was true. It wasn't anything you told me, you know. I was only guessing."

"It's rude to make guesses like that to people's faces. What if I say I'm guessing your fellow jilted you and that's why you sound so bitter and angry."

She snickered. "You'd be wrong. Maybe he got sick of my being bitter and angry. Or maybe I jilted him because I'm a bitter and angry woman by nature."

"Is that it?"

She sighed. "No. No." She looked up, frowning in earnestness, but no longer challenging him. "I did break the engagement. We parted friends. No, not friends, but with a handshake, and I think we were genuinely wishing the best for the other's happiness. No, I'm not angry or bitter about him."

"What about, then?"

She smiled. "Nothing, really. I mean I'm not that way to people who really know me."

"Why act that way with me?"

She lifted her shoulders to shrug, and when they fell, they were rounded. "Talking to you is exhausting."

"It's no picnic for me, either," he said. "I've had more fun with my eczema."

They laughed.

"Here's what it is," she said after a pause. "I've been working it out." She looked into the air near the ceiling and seemed to be talking as much to herself as to him. "I got tired of lies. My mother lied so much for my father she got to where she couldn't tell any more what was really true. Oh your father, he's so sensitive, she'd say when he'd get fired. She'd make excuses to his bosses and to me and to herself. Truth is, he was just a drunk. When I was a kid I'd have to make excuses about why he didn't come visit my school or come to my piano recital. If I sat next to you on the train I'd have told you he was Sergeant York if you asked about him."

She gave him a frank and direct gaze as if to judge whether he deserved to hear this. He'd been standing with his hat in his hand leaning with one shoulder against the wall, but now he eased down onto the sofa so that their eyes were on the same plane.

"I hadn't realized how naturally I'd picked up my mother's habit until Paul and I got engaged. My dad was already dead by then, and so I felt really relieved of the burden of keeping people from knowing he was a drunk. I just let my mother pump Paul full of hooey, as you say, and kept my mouth shut."

She rose, picked up the remaining chunk of piecrust and carried it to the window, where she shoved the casement up, broke the crust into crumbs and spread them on the sill. She looked out the window and into a tree as if for birds. When she spoke, it was to the pane. "Then Paul told me something that worried me. He said he'd asked me to marry him because he was certain I was 'unsoiled.' He was talking as if he were grateful to me for being a virgin, congratulating me about it. You see?"

Dread seeped into his blood. He cleared his throat. "You aren't? I mean, you weren't?" he was astonished to hear himself ask. This was not his business!

"No." She said it lightly but firmly, as if unconcerned about his judgement. Her candor was ferocious, he thought. A weapon. "I never told him I was a virgin; he just presumed it. But from then on I had to live with the choice of lying about it or not. It all seemed too familiar, you know, worrying about hiding and being found out. That's why I broke off the engagement."

"Why didn't you just tell him the truth?"

"I didn't think he could take it."

"You could have given him the chance."

"Yes." Now she blushed for the first time. "I guess I really didn't care enough. Maybe I wanted to stay a virgin in somebody's eyes."

"What reason did you give him?"

"I said I was unworthy of his love."

He chuckled. "Boy, talk about your hooey...."

"It was true, Wilbur. I was a liar."

She looked at her wrist watch, but then made no move to leave. She yawned and stretched. When she saw him watching her, she said, "I usually take a cat-nap."

"I guess I stole it from you today."

The rhythm of the moment seemed to call for him to take his leave. But he felt vaguely helpless. He'd never learned so much about someone in so short a time, and he felt so enormously full of information about her he was itching to cart it all away on the run and sort it out slowly at home. But it also seemed an opportunity had come, and he was afraid that if he left it would vanish too. Full as he was, there was more to be learned. Why was she willing for him to know these things about her? Maybe to her they two were like those fellows on a train: they were as free to tell the truth as they were to lie to one another. Safe in either case—they wouldn't occupy each other's future. Maybe she had no plans for him.

"So are you angry and bitter because you think this fellow couldn't take the truth about you?"

"I told you I wasn't angry or bitter. I was just acting horsey with you."

"Why?"

She sighed, looked away. It gratified him to see that at last he'd asked a question she found uncomfortable to answer.

"After I broke off my engagement, I decided that whenever a fellow came along who was the least bit interesting I'd put everything on the table and if he didn't like it he could walk away and we wouldn't waste time on play-acting. I guess I was just protecting myself from having to be nicer than I felt like being later on."

"A test by fire."

"If you like."

"So I'm an experiment?"

"I guess you could say that."

"That must mean you find me the least bit interesting."

She grinned. "You were up until you said that."

"I take it back, then."

"I'm a little glad."

They spent another hour talking. Later, he was amazed to think back on what he'd told her about his mother. He'd not called her a "whore" outright, but he'd said she lived mostly by taking money from men. He said his father had been an inventor like Edison or Alexander Graham Bell, and before Bobette could ask what he had invented, he added that his father worked on secret projects. Saying this out loud made it sound false, and he wondered, for the first time, if it were true.

He told Bobette about Atlas Smythe, of leaving the farm, living in Dallas, running away to come here to

103

make something of himself. He didn't want to be trash like his mother. He'd kept looking at Bobette's face to observe her reaction, saw her wince once or twice, just as he'd winced to hear her confess that she wasn't a virgin. It sure was a novelty to spill your guts like that on first meeting somebody, but maybe it wasn't good to let them know everything—or to learn everything—if you were going to include them in your life. If things turned sour, then they would be holding information that could damage you. Of course, it worked both ways. This kid did have guts—how did she know he's not going to scrawl her telephone number on the wall in the pisser at the Armory now? She'd done the dirty deed at least once in her life already.

Who with?

He fixed the porch rail and scooted the heavy wardrobe out of what had been the drunk's bedroom and put it in Bobette's. It was quid pro quo, as the lawyers say. He showed up Sundays to work and Mildred fed him either before or after. She wasn't so aloof to him any more. It still burned in him that she'd called him a bragger. Like most widows, she missed having a man to advise her, and with Little Harold out to sea, who could she turn to? Did Wilbur know anything about home insurance? About car noises? Roofing? Buying stocks? Each time he'd answer with, I'm not one to brag, but. One Sunday while he was putting up a shelf in her kitchen, he said, half thinking aloud and being so accustomed to speaking his mind around Bobette. "I understand I didn't make much of an impression on you the first time I came for Sunday dinner, Mildred."

"Oh," she said. "How's that?"

He tried to make a joke of it, as if it were something far behind them now and could be treated lightly. "I heard you called me a bragger."

"Why I said no such thing! Who says I said that? Why, I wouldn't no more say such a thing about you, Wilbur! I'm really hurt! Who says I said that? Bobette? Bobette, you come in here right now! How can you say I said this boy was a bragger! I said no such thing!"

Mildred started crying, stamping her feet. "My own daughter made me out to be so ungrateful! I said no such thing!"

"All right, Mother! You didn't say it."

"I most certainly think so I didn't say it! And you ought to be ashamed for saying such a thing! Whatever possessed you to say such a thing! I'd think you'd try to behave yourself just once and not be running some nice young fellow like this off with that ugly way you talk. I just wish your father or Little Harold were here!"

Bobette shrugged, gave Wilbur a look of long suffering. Unlike her daughter, Mildred went to pieces if you uttered anything remotely real to her. If he'd have accused Bobette of it, she'd have said, "Yeah, I did it, so what?" The mother seemed more fragile than the daughter. You had to watch what you said. She took things the wrong way and pouted. She'd say, "You think those biscuits are light enough? I think they're hard, my baking powder's too old." You were supposed to say, "Oh, no, they're light as clouds, Mildred!" Bobette would say, "Well, Mother, they're a little like hockey pucks, it's true, I'll get baking powder next time I go to the store." Mildred would retreat quietly to her room with a wet washcloth draped across her forehead; she would be having a sick headache. You were supposed to feel sorry for her and guilty for having called her biscuits hockey pucks.

All her relatives were wonderful folk, as were her friends. Little Harold had been a model child. She lived in a world where no one stole, lied, cheated, murdered, or betrayed anyone else. She spun a cocoon of her own wishes and lived inside it. She seemed so innocent in regard to what the world really was that Wilbur felt protective of her. Sometimes he wondered how Bobette had managed to grow up, with her father drunk and her mother so helpless.

"Oh, she's not helpless. How do you think she raised two kids when her husband was drunk all the time? She thinks that if she can make you believe she needs you then you won't run off like Harold did. You'll stick around and marry me. I get tired of her childish tricks."

He nodded. He didn't ask if Bobette was dropping a hint. Later, he wondered. People could be honest even when they were being devious, and the contrary was also true. Marry her? What did Bobette want? What did he want? What was she to him? He to her? He'd become addicted to talking to her, point number one. She seemed vitally important to him now because she knew everything there was to know about him. If he should misplace himself she was where he'd be found. And so far as he had been an experiment for her to discover the value of frankness, he'd been a success: he was still coming around. It wasn't likely he'd stop. A day without talking to her was a day away from talking to her. He didn't notice much but her when he was with her. Her freckles were tea leaves in the bottom of a reader's cup. Her face was always a congratulatory telegram. He liked to hold her hand when they sat on the front porch. One of these days, he'd kiss her. He kept watching her lips as she talked as if expecting them to tell him when to do it.

He was drying while she washed the Sunday dinner dishes. Mildred was on the phone to her sister across town. Bobette's hair was pinned up, showing her freckled nape. A few long strands had fallen loose. An invisible hand square between his shoulder blades pushed him gently forward until his lips brushed her neck. She shivered all over, like a horse twitching flies.

"Ooo, Wilbur. Do that again!"

He was so nervous he could have leapt out of his skin. His erection embarrassed him. He leaned forward and pecked her neck very gently, cleared his throat, and returned to drying the dishes. Her hands circled slowly in the murky dishwater as if she were trying to find shards of broken glass.

"That did it."

"What."

"Made up my mind about you." She twisted her head and grinned at him. "You're the one."

"I'm the one what?"

"The one who's going to wind up being my husband."

"Don't I have any say so?"

"Sure. So what do you say?"

"This is all backwards. I'm supposed to ask."

"I never asked anything. I made a prediction."

Later, on the porch, Mildred having long since gone to bed, he held her hand in the shadows of the porch while out in the moon-washed yard a cat sat twitching its tail and studied a moth floundering on the grass.

"I always wanted to honeymoon at Coronado."

"That sounds nice."

"I guess I should ask if it's important to you if your wife is a virgin."

To answer this was also to answer the more important question. "I don't know if it is or not."

"I want to tell you what happened so you won't imagine the worst."

She was thirteen, her father had been sent to the "hospital" for the first time for a "lung" condition, it was summer, her mother had gone for the day to visit him, Bobette was supposed to babysit with some neighbor's children.

"—and this encyclopedia salesman came to the door. He said he was a college student. He was nice and polite. I was lonely, and I was feeling pretty blue, too, and maybe I was mad at my dad and feeling guilty because I hadn't gone to visit him. Everything seemed kind of, well, hopeless. The empty house, the heat—oh, I don't know, Wilbur, it doesn't make much sense. I didn't want him to leave is what it amounted to. He asked for a drink of water. He told me I was pretty."

He waited in her silence then realized no more was coming. "A door-to-door salesman? I thought that only happened in dirty jokes, Bobette." He felt stung, inexplicably cheated. "You didn't even know him?"

"I'd never seen him before."

His ears burned to imagine the story the guy told back at his office. A pushover. He felt tainted by what had happened. If her being a character in a travelling saleman's joke was not the worst, what was? The story she told wholly baffled him; it suggested that some facets of her character might always be enigmatic no matter how candid she was.

"Did he ever come back?"

"Oh, yeah. But I never let him in again."

"That's good."

"I told you I was thirteen." Her voice was quiet but icy. "He was an adult, I was a child. It was his fault, not mine."

He thought about that for a few minutes. She looked hurt, rocking on the step as she hugged her knees to her chest, her chin resting on them. Like a child. Like that child must have looked. Needing something. What could he give her but his best?

They spent their wedding night in a resort hotel at Coronado, with her tugging him up the stairs before dark and into their room, where she pressed her willowy body to his and kissed him passionately.

"I'm so excited! Let's get in bed! What should we do first?" she burbled.

He laughed uncertainly. "I guess take our clothes off."

"You go first."

"I think the woman is supposed to go first."

She guffawed. "Who says?"

"I dunno."

"Okay, we'll do it together. Only you do mine and I'll do yours!"

They stood beside the bed and unbuttoned each other's clothing, from the top down. She smelled so good he had to nuzzle and kiss her, then they were clinching and kissing while trying to finish their undressing; he tripped on his trouser cuff and they fell on the bed.

Later as he lay under the covers, she got up and pranced about the room, nude. This was like a dream to him. Her tall form showed boyish hips with a reddish-gold triangle between her legs, and her large breasts were round and firm. Her long hair fell over her shoulders.

She stood at the end of the bed and held out her arms.

"Da-da!" she said, imitating a fanfare. "Here's Wilbur's woman and his wife!"

He laughed; suddenly recovering her modesty, she scurried to her side of the bed, slipped under the covers, and pressed her warm flesh against his flank.

"Let's do some more! Something else."

"Something else?" He nibbled at her lower lip. He could smell her sweet breath. "Such as what?"

"Whatever you have in your storehouse of manly lore. If I'm going to have to be married to somebody who visited bordellos at age sixteen, the least I can do is take advantage of what he learned there."

"To tell you the truth, maybe I don't know as much about this as you think I do."

He presumed she would be disappointed, but she wriggled against him like a puppy.

"Good!"

"Good? Do you want me to be a virgin?"

"Well, let's put it this way—it's going to be fun for us to work to find out what things there are that we haven't yet learned about."

Marriage could be a glorious erotic adventure? He'd never imagined it. Complete trust combined with inexpressible pleasure? Inconceivable. Yet here they were. For years he had been satisfied to be alone and had not imagined such intimacy; once married to Bobette, he could not dream of having to live without it. One person on this planet knew him; with and through her he was connected to all humankind. Wasn't it ironic that he'd run away to California to escape the past and being known only to find that being truly known is the only gold that's true? Ironic that he'd come to "make something of himself," had even taken a new name like some movie hopeful, only to discover that the man he and Bobette had made was only the man he'd always been?

He'd stepped through a door into another world: The fixtures about him—streets, autos and crowds—were identifiably the same, yet they glowed with an new, rosy aura of benign intent.

He surrendered, let himself adore Bobette; he could sit for hours watching her comb her hair, and he would sometimes brush it out for her, feeling the cool, silky texture of it pass across his palms and through his fingers like water. They were completely at ease with each other and would spend an afternoon at home simply fingering and nuzzling and inspecting and lapping at each other's parts, without urgency, as if practicing for a wonderful ceremony an eternity away.

Too, she unlocked an almost ludicrous generosity in him, and he would catch himself reaching into his pocket when he encountered kids on the street, feeling as if his good luck was so far out of proportion to what he deserved that he had to find ways to bleed off portions of it.

They quarrelled only about Mildred. Bobette wanted to leave her mother's house to start their own family, but Wilbur wanted to have a house big enough to include their future children and her mother. Being too greedy for happiness might offend the gods, so giving up privacy seemed a necessary sacrifice to appease them. Now that he could recognize the condition, he could empathize with her mother's loneliness. To leave her house would be to steal Bobette from her, he said. Bobette's answer was, "She's not a baby, Wilbur! We'd only move to Santa Monica!"

Lack of funds made the debate moot, but soon they both had raises large enough to afford a mortgage for a house of their own. Against his better judgement, they left Mildred's house, and several months later, Pearl was born.

◰ ◰ ◰

"You'll see a smiling face, a fireplace, a cozy room, a little nest where blah blah blah and ro-ses bloom. Just Molly and me, and baby makes three...."

The song was a thread stitching tight his days. Happy in his blue heaven.

"Look, Daddy! Dolly's riding Mommy's mountain!"

Pearl had put her doll on Bobette's belly; Bobette, laughing, shook it off. They were lying on a blanket in their back yard. Leftover chocolate cake stood in vanilla ice cream puddles on plates in the grass. The night was inky black, moonless, and glimmering stars hopscotched one another like tiny white fires blazing a path to the outer rim of space.

"Put your ear here."

Pearl grabbed Bobette around the waist and pressed her cheek to her mother's abdomen.

"I don't hear anything. Is it only air in there like a balloon?"

They laughed. "Of course not. I told you, it's your brother or sister."

"Which?"

"We don't know."

"Why not?"

"People don't know those things until it's time."

"When will it be time?"

"In a few months."

"I'm tired of waiting!"

"We get that way, too."

"How old will it be?"

"It won't be any old when it's born, sweetie," Wilbur said. "You start getting old when you get born."

"Then I'll always be older."

"That's right."

Soon she'd fallen asleep between them. She'd been up since six, itching to rush through breakfast so she'd know whether she got her dollhouse or not.

Bobette was chuckling.

"What's so funny?" he whispered across the child's body.

"How old will it be!"

He smiled into the dark sky. To think that two of them might be twice as delightful. He and Bobette had been trying now for a long time and had finally struck a spark. Not that failing hadn't been a heap of fun. Six years old, this kid was. She'd been conceived at Coronado, in the hotel. Before that, there'd been their meeting at the library, his living in that boardinghouse, Bobette at home, her dad's dying, his being in the hospital—when you traced a line back, the present was up from it.

"I'm a lucky guy."

"Yes, you are. I'm lucky, too."

"You know who I feel sorry for?"

"Who?"

"That salesman."

"What salesman?"

"The one who kept coming back but couldn't get in your door again."

◙   ◙   ◙

The launch cleared the pier off the Catalina Yacht Club; while Copperfield piloted from the stern, Bobette sat in the middle gripping each gunnel white-knuckled, struggling to keep her body from swaying as the craft dipped and lurched. Despite the sour morning—Santa Ana winds had whipped the harbor water into grey chop and soiled the sky with a skein of dust—it had been a good weekend, Wilbur was thinking. Getting to come along on the Copperfields' excursion to scout locations for a movie had been a happy accident.

Contrary to her worst expectations, Bobette had not gotten seasick on the way over and joked that her belly gave her a lower center of gravity. Even though Copperfield and his wife were quarrelling and others of the party were grumpy or discontented, he and Bobette had managed to keep everybody else's problems at arm's length; they had enjoyed a much-needed respite from their own troubles, and Pearl seemed happy to tag along with adults.

He was glad now that Bobette had argued him out of inviting Mildred along. She would have been a pain in the neck. She was getting more squirrelly by the day. Now it was seances where she talked to Big Harold, but about all Harold had to say to her from the Beyond was to tell her to invest her life savings in some mining outfit that Wilbur was ninety percent sure was bogus but he didn't have proof yet, and if the truth were known he was a little weary of watching her back for her, especially when, as Bobette pointed out, not only was she ungrateful for their efforts, she was positively hostile. She would hear no criticism of Madame Werzowsky. Werzowsky! Wilbur's guess was that the woman's real name was Betty Breland from Lincoln, Nebraska, having come out west to be a movie star but, like Copperfield's white wife, she'd gotten too old too fast from bad company, bad habits and her own bad character, and had fallen back on acting the part of a European aristocratic gypsy with a bath towel wrapped around her head and an accent so thick you knew it was a phony the second she answered the phone. Los Angeles was full of people who were sailing along through life on some other sucker's money. Running a gimmick was an indigenous crop, like wheat in Kansas.

The latest wrinkle in "Madame Werzowsky's" game had been to convince Mildred she had special powers as a graphologist. He didn't know yet what this angle meant. He and Bobette had visited Mildred in Echo Park Monday night only to find the place stinking to high heaven from incense and flickering candles, while Mildred was seated at a card table in a flowered caftan and spectacles nobody had ever seen before. She was poring over scraps of paper on which he and Bobette had written inconsequential notes—a grocery list and instructions on how to check the oil in Mildred's Ford. The instructions were meant for her son, Little Harold, who, having returned home from the Navy, insisted upon doing things for his mother for which he had no knowledge, aptitude, energy or perseverance. To Little Harold the expression of intent stood for the deed.

Mildred said, upon reading Wilbur's instructions, "Wilbur, you have an impulsive personality. You are often guided by your emotions. I can tell by how you slant your letters." He laughed. Bobette said, "Mother, I doubt if you can tell anything from somebody's hand-writing except whether they used a pen or a pencil. Is this your spiritual advisor's doing?"

"Well, I don't know what you mean by 'doing,' but Madame Werzowsky has been kind enough to help me nurture my God-given talents, which is more than some."

There ensued a brief argument whose course Wilbur knew so well he hardly had to listen. The gist was, Mother, don't let yourself be taken in. Daughter, don't be so cynical—why, you would never meet a more wonderful person who was so willing to help even a stranger.

"How much have you given her?" asked Bobette.

"Whatever I've given her I've gotten back many times over in other ways."

Most of the trouble between them and Mildred went back to Mildred's feeling abandoned when he and Bobette bought their own home, though what she said was, "Why, I can understand perfectly why two young people just starting a family wouldn't want an unhappy old woman underfoot all the time. I've been looking forward for years to having my house to myself."

She'd never forgiven them for taking her at her word. Bobette sought to solve the problem by coaxing Aunty Nan to move from El Segundo up to Echo Park. The sisters talked on the phone daily, anyway. To keep them both from feeling like sympathy cases—neither would openly admit to being lonely—the move was proposed as a business arrangement: two could live more cheaply than one, which allowed each to say, in her own way, that she didn't need the money herself, but of course she would be willing to give up a little privacy to help the other. Thus Wilbur was trapped into moving Aunty Nan himself to avoid her having to pay for it. He spent three days driving a hired truck back and forth from the seaside village to near downtown, and he and a hired fellow both nearly wound up with hernias from getting Aunty Nan's solid walnut furniture and six decades of memorabilia packed into Mildred's house. "My goodness!" sang Mildred gaily. "You sure came well stocked!" Aunty Nan told Mildred she had had to put two rooms of perfectly good furniture into storage where she was sure the mildrew would ruin it.

The phone calls to the Wyse house began immediately. If Bobette was not available, Wilbur's ear would do. Mind you I'm not complaining, but Aunty Nan.... Or I'd be the last person to ever say anything against my own sister, but Mildred (Or Nan)...hogs the icebox. Won't pull the shades all the way down in the living room in the evening. Was supposed to be the one taking out the garbage. Parks the car with the rear end hanging over the sidewalk. Keeps taking my sewing scissors and won't put them back in my basket. Move again?! Oh, gosh, no! Never—I couldn't survive it. All in all, this is for the best, I do know that. After all, two old women with nobody else and she can't afford to live alone.

He and Bobette agreed to include the two in Sunday dinners. The baton had passed to them, now officially a family. Tablecloths, good silver, suit and tie, cooking half the day on Saturday, taking up their entire weekends, and the old women calling to say the other has too bad a headache to drive over there and I don't like that traffic. So he had to go pick them up, to boot, and take them back. Next time they didn't even offer an excuse—it became something "nice" he did for them which they praised him for. Treating us like royalty, I'll say! What it was, though, was this—Mildred was extracting her payment from him for taking Bobette and for forcing her to put up with her own sister, while Aunty Nan no doubt felt that since her niece and nephew had made her move from that nice house near the beach where you got that strong ocean breeze in the evenings the least they could do was to give her a lift in their auto so she wouldn't have to get sick from being so nervous in the traffic which they didn't have down in El Segundo.

This went on for two years. When Bobette complained about them he had to be careful not to chime in too quickly or else he'd find himself suddenly out on a limb alone while she burst into tears and defended them. But he could not defend them, either, while she criticized them, because she took it as a personal affront; it would light a fire under her that might take half the week to put out. They were her relatives; that gave her exclusive rights to claiming them as a burden and airing out any grievances she had, even though they cost him as much time, energy and frustration, and he knew damn good and well that he'd be the one straining under all those dark, heavy tables when the end inevitably came, and he always felt like the world's greatest husband when he helped her with the Sunday dishes while the two women sat in their parlor interrogating Pearl and waiting for him to spend the rest of his afternoon driving on the streets between their houses, though Bobette would get to collapse the moment the door was shut and they were on their way. One Sunday night he was winding the clock and noticed that the alarm had been changed to 3:30, puzzled over it a moment then realized that Bobette had set it so that she'd be up from her nap before he got back from taking Mildred and Aunty Nan home and had neglected to reset it so he wouldn't know she'd taken one. It was a fine state of affairs when they had to hide something like that from one another. He laughed, pointed out her oversight. She said, "I sometimes wish you knew where your mother was so she could come to dinner and make us miserable, too. Then we'd be even."

What she said worked on him. It was funny how being grown up you understand how adults can make mistakes. His mother—whatever her faults, she couldn't have been any worse as a mother than Mildred. Though she'd obviously been deserted by the man who was his biological father, she hadn't done the same to Wilbur. She loved him. She took care of him. She'd tied herself to a man like Smythe just to keep body and soul together, and when she couldn't stand it any more she'd gone to work. Maybe all those men were just prospects for marriage. So she took presents from them. So what?

Could what she did be any worse than what he'd done to her by running away and breaking off all contact? If Pearl were seventeen and had done that, wouldn't he be worrying every night of his life about where she was and if she was well? Whatever she might have done with those men, it was to herself. What he'd done had probably hurt her badly, and still did. And here he'd now given her a grandchild. He was cheating both his mother of a granddaughter (and a son!) and his daughter of a grandmother.

He contacted an agency that located "missing" persons. If he were reunited with his mother he might learn about his real father: she might feel free to tell an adult son things best hidden from a child. Possibly, his real father was alive and well in St. Louis or elsewhere.

During the next Sunday dinner he told Mildred and Aunty Nan that he was now searching for his mother, because he wanted her and Pearl to know one another. "Why, I think that's just wonderful!" said Aunty Nan. "I do too," put in Mildred. "I suppose it would be wonderful for this child to have a grandmother living right here in her own house with her."

Wilbur didn't rise to this bait, but Bobette took it. "Mother, we don't even know if this woman is living, let alone where she might want to set up housekeeping." To his dismay, she didn't add that they had no plans to have his mother live with them. Mildred said, "Well, I know you don't have a lot of extra room, but then, you've got more than I do." Wilbur said, "I would never think to impose upon you, Mildred." Both old women gave him a look. Aunty Nan said, "I had worlds of space in my house in El Segundo."

A few Sundays later, Mildred reported that she'd gotten a letter from Little Harold. He was getting out of the Navy. Bobette, sounding alarmed, said, "When? What's he going to do? I thought he was going to make a career of it."

Mildred said, "I imagine he's had a belly full of people telling him what to do. You know it's hard for an especially smart person to be constantly doing the bidding of people who are beneath him."

Bobette said, "What? Did he get thrown out?"

"I certainly wouldn't think so, not after all the years of faithful service he's given to his country!"

"But, Mother, do you know what his plans are? Maybe Wilbur could help him find something. You know, he and Mr. Copperfield work with a lot of contractors and people who might hire a veteran."

Wilbur couldn't account for the odd desperation in Bobette's voice, but her mother cut her off cold. "I'm sure he'd appreciate your efforts, Bobette, but you know he can't just take anything just to be doing something. It'd have to be up to his mentality. I suspect he'll want to rest a while before he goes to work."

"Rest? What in the world has he been doing besides lifting a beer bottle that's so strenuous he can't work like everybody else in the world?"

Through all this discussion about Little Harold Aunty Nan had sat without saying word one. She somehow managed, nevertheless, to radiate such billows of self-pity that Wilbur finally caught on: on returning from his hitch in the Navy, Little Harold would "rest" in his mother's house, thereby displacing Aunty Nan. This might have been the first Mildred's sister had heard of it.

A day later, not to his surprise, Aunty Nan said in his ear, "You know her place is not near big enough for two of us let alone Little Harold, too."

So Wilbur took Aunty Nan house-hunting three weekends in a row, and she at last settled on one that was literally within sight of her former dwelling in El Segundo, only not nearly so nice, she said. He and Bobette worked frantically to get her moved before the next weekend because Little Harold was due in on a Saturday from New York on the Santa Fe. Of course Mildred expected Wilbur and Bobette to drive her to the Pasadena station to meet him. Meanwhile, in El Segundo, Aunty Nan, standing about in a sea of unopened cartons, said, "Much as I'd like to meet my nephew at the station, I guess I'd better stick to my unpacking now that I'm here alone and nobody to help me with it."

Bobette had also worked nights all week long helping to turn the drunk's old study into a place for Little Harold, as the second bedroom still contained furniture and cartons that Mildred had agreed to store for Aunty Nan because the new house in El Segundo was so much smaller than her old one. They had scrubbed and swept. Mildred had insisted on buying a new bedspread. She wanted to make new curtains. "Mother, you're wasting your time—he's not going to care!"

"Bobette, I care, even if you don't!"

Mildred's machine broke down and she had to hem the curtains on Bobette's, but Bobette's was too complicated for her to use, and so Bobette wound up finishing the curtains.

They drove Mildred to Pasadena on the appointed day and waited for the train. Little Harold wasn't on it. "Why, that just worries me sick!" said Mildred. "I just know something happened to that boy!"

"Everything about this deal is very typical so far," said Bobette.

Mildred called a few days later to say she'd gotten a telegram from Little Harold. He'd be coming the following Saturday.

"Did he apologize for standing us up?" asked Bobette.

"I'm sure he had a lot on his mind," said Mildred. "What with his new bride and all."

"His new bride!?"

Mildred didn't have any details, only that Little Harold was married. Big Harold's old study was not going to do at all; it was too small for both Little Harold and his wife. They were going to have to find some place to put Aunty Nan's furniture—

"Mother, why can't Harold and his wife get their own place?"

"Well, I'm certainly not the kind of person who won't offer her home to her own family!"

Wilbur carted the rest of Aunty Nan's furniture down to El Segundo, where it was stored with the original leftovers from the first move, articles which, so far as Wilbur could tell, had not mildewed—but only because the wet weather hadn't set in, said Aunty Nan. They would. He'd see.

They primped and scoured the second room. Mildred fretted because she didn't know anything about Little Harold's new bride's taste and worried that she might think the drapes were tacky. Bobette said, "Wait and let her decorate it herself, Mother."

"What? And have her think I didn't care enough to make it attractive?"

Little Harold was a baby-faced, hulking tub of lard with curly red hair and an anchor tatoo that looked ludicrous on his pink fat bicep. One look told Wilbur that this was a kid whom other kids had picked on with relish and some reason. Little Harold's bride was named Pei-Ling, but she hadn't accompanied Little Harold on his journey west. He showed them a snapshot of her. You never could tell with Orientals, but, even so, this girl looked twelve, at most. Perched on a barstool in a slitted dress. Little Harold told his mother she'd love Pei-Ling. The bride didn't speak much English—a couple of words, maybe—but somehow they had managed to understand each other. "Language a love, Ma!" he chortled.

"I'm disappointed she couldn't come with you," said Mildred. "We all—" she turned to include Wilbur, Bobette, and Pearl, in case they had second thoughts—"wanted to welcome her to the family." Little Harold explained that Pei-Ling had stayed behind in Hong Kong because he didn't have the money for her passage. That was the first thing he was going to do, of course, when he found work: save up to bring his bride home to America.

"My god!" shrieked Bobette when they were driving away from having dropped off Little Harold and Mildred. "A barfly! You think she'll mind those curtains? My god! No English! Help me! My brother is a cretin! Do you think it's legal to marry a child prostitute?"

"Now, hold on," Wilbur said, trying to remind Bobette that their daughter was in the back seat listening. "You don't know anything about her, right?"

"She married my brother—that sure doesn't inspire much faith in her intelligence."

Fortunately, Little Harold could drive an automobile, so he chauffeured his mother to Sunday dinner at the Wyses'. Aunty Nan still had to be picked up in El Segundo, however. Little Harold ate two helpings of anything that was put before him without ever praising it or thanking his little sister—of whom he was terrified—and immediately upon eating would stand in the back yard to smoke Egyptian cigarettes and exchange childish insults with Pearl and the children next door. You have snot and boogers hanging from your nose! Oh yeah? You pick your nose and eat it!

"Mother," said Bobette, "Little Harold doesn't have to come for dinner if he doesn't want to."

"Who says he doesn't want to? If he's not welcome, though, I'm sure he'd as soon stay home."

Little Harold was not looking for work, yet. He was resting. It's because of his nervous condition.

Nervous condition? Yes, being around those big guns on those ships, it has given him a nervous condition. "Mother, are you going to support him for the rest of his life? And what about this child bride of his? I thought he was going to work to get her passage—"

"Bobette, I'm not about to put the boy out on the street because he suffers from a medical condition. And we're working on getting his wife over—"

"You're going to pay for that, too?"

"Maybe I am, maybe I'm not. Maybe I don't mind

helping my family. He'll pay every penny of it back, believe me."

Eventually the girl arrived on the train. Her only baggage was a cardboard box tied with a rope, and she was wearing a man's greatcoat whose origin couldn't be determined since no translator was present. She was tiny and looked like an urchin. She smiled readily but vacantly when spoken to, but it seemed more like a plea for mercy. Little Harold installed her in their room in Mildred's house, where the drapes made no apparent impression on her. She could say "like" and "not like," however. Her universe in Echo Park was quickly ordered into categories corresponding with her command of English. They soon learned what she'd eat and what she wouldn't and what music she preferred on the radio. She was rather distressingly fond of strong drink and all forms of tobacco.

"She's like a pet," groaned Bobette. "All she and Little Harold do is sit around that room looking at movie magazines and eating candy bars. I can't believe that my mother is willing to tolerate this. She's become their maid and cook, and she even gives Little Harold an allowance!"

Wilbur said, "Let's just hope the girl doesn't get pregnant."

"Not to worry. I doubt if she's had her first period yet."

This went on for a year. Naturally, Pei-Ling also had to come to Sunday dinners. Unlike her husband, she was very particular about what she ate. Once it was discovered she would eat plain white rice, Bobette included it on the menu. The girl said "good," "rice," and "I like" in separate little utterances. She gravitated toward Pearl and, when her husband vanished out the back door to smoke, she would let Pearl lead her into the child's bedroom where they would play with Pearl's dolls. She would sing to a doll in a high thin voice whose profoundly foreign character made it audible all over the house despite its softness.

"You know what she did today?" Bobette asked Wilbur about a month prior to the present weekend outing at Catalina. "She came into my bedroom and stood looking at my belly, then she put her hand on it and started crying. It about broke my heart. I hugged her and she bawled. I don't know what she expected coming here, but I wish the child could talk to me. I said where is your home? Your family? You know, she hasn't even had a letter from Hong Kong since she came. She said, you fambly. It about broke my heart I'm telling you. So far away from anything or anybody she knows, and people can't even talk to her. Maybe we should take her to Chinatown and let her make friends. You think she'd like to be an au pair? She and Pearl really hit it off. What do you think about moving her in over here? We might be able to get her in a school, she's just wasting her life over there with Little Harold—"

"For God's sake, Bobette, you can't just move a man's wife around like a chess piece just because you feel sorry for her!"

"Yeah, well, he moved her all the way to the far side of this planet, Wilbur! Besides, I'd be very surprised if they were really married. She probably doesn't have any idea what her status truly is. God only knows how she got into the country. She may be an alien. She might be caught and whisked off before we even have a chance to help her."

Resolving the case of the displaced Oriental child bride was temporarily shunted aside, though, by the ongoing crisis of Mildred's new hobbies of graphology and seancing with Madame Werzowsky. Surprisingly, it had been Little Harold who alerted them to Mildred's new interests, no doubt because once the ghost of Big Harold began advising Mildred on her finances from The Beyond, Little Harold feared she might be taken for everything she had.

So they'd gone over last Monday night. Ostensibly they were present to hear Mildred interpret their characters based on their handwriting specimens (Bobette's the grocery list, Wilbur's the instructions about changing the Ford's oil). But they tried to steer the subject to Madame Werzowsky's influence on Mildred. While they argued with Mildred in the dim living room amidst the incense and flickering candles, Little Harold and Pei-Ling were back in their room eating an entire chess pie and drinking whiskey from water glasses. The girl was smoking a cheroot while she looked at the pictures in *The Ladies Home Companion.*

"Mother," said Bobette, "This is just a bunch of foolishness! These won't tell you anything!" Bobette snatched up the scraps of paper and flung them down onto the card table. "We just scribbled these things!"

"Well, it's true that you could probably give me better samples, but you know Madame says sometimes it works best when the person is simply being unconsciously him or herself. You take this note Wilbur wrote to Little Harold, for instance: I could tell you that Wilbur's probably better off leaving well enough alone in regard to looking up his kin." She gave Bobette a significant look. "And I can tell from looking at the way you form the humps on your Ms and Ns that you're the kind of person who isn't grateful for what others do for you."

"That's it!" declared Bobette. "May I drop dead before I put on another Sunday dinner!"

🖂 🖂 🖂

Copperfield tied the launch to the buoy where his yacht was anchored, and Wilbur climbed the rope ladder first so that he could stand on deck and help Pearl and Bobette up. Then Copperfield heaved up their overnighters and Wilbur caught them and took them below. When he got back to the galley, Bobette was tugging Pearl's sweater over her head. The child was shivering.

"She got wet from the spray."

Bobette took her own cardigan from around her shoulders and gave it to Pearl.

"Sweetie, go get Daddy's gray sweater for Mommy to wear, will you?"

When Pearl had disappeared down the hall to retrieve his sweater from where he'd stowed the bags, he hugged Bobette and rubbed the goose bumps off her arms. The weather would be hot later on, but he'd known to start the day on a sailboat with a windbreaker. Bobette almost always dressed for what the weather would be later, not for what it was.

"There's something between us."

She squeezed him, bending forward to lay her cheek on his shoulder. "Last night I was wishing there wasn't."

"One thing about being pregnant—it never lasts forever."

"Tell that to the woman who is."

They rocked back and forth with the sway of the boat. He thought of Mildred and Little Harold and Pei-Ling.

"So are you missing anything yet?"

She laughed. "You've been thinking about it, too?"

"Yeah." He raised his arm to peer at his watch. "Right about now they're going to be awake enough to wonder what they're all going to do for Sunday dinner."

"I feel guilty, but not much. It's for no good reason so I'm not paying attention to it."

"Sometimes I wish it was just the two of us."

He didn't know how she'd take that, but she only squeezed him for an answer.

"I wonder where everybody else is," she said after a moment. They'd grown aware that Copperfield was walking methodically about the deck overhead. Wilbur had presumed that they would wait for the rest of the party to arrive, but the thrum of the idling diesel under his feet suggested Copperfield was about to lift anchor and sail for home. "Did he say anything to you?"

"While he was settling up the bill, he told me that he and Laura had a big row last night."

"Oh, well, what else is new."

"Daddy, I can't find your sweater." Pearl came and stood on his foot and tried to wedge herself between them. "I'm hungry, Mama."

"I'll get the sweater."

"I'm going to make some tea."

He went down the dark, narrow passageway feeling his own footfalls shake the decking. Overhead he heard a scraping sound, then a clunk and a ratchet's clacking. He ought to go help Copperfield, he thought, but he wasn't much of a sailor and might only get in the way. Still, he could offer. Laura Copperfield was nimble as a goat on deck, and when she and Copperfield worked together to sail the boat you'd never know they had a rotten marriage. It was like a kind of strange dance, the only thing they did together that seemed harmonious. Sure, they'd had a row last night. It was hardly front-page news. In all the years he'd known them he couldn't recall a time they weren't fighting, unless it would be when Copperfield was out in Utah or some place shooting a western and she'd be hitting the speakeasies and running with the movie crowd. The woman was poison. A gold digger. Why Copperfield let her take advantage of him was a mystery. Looking at such a marriage made you appreciate what you had, Little Harold or no. It made him sick to see a good honest fellow like Copperfield with a collar on his neck and the other end of the leash in the hands of a witch like that. He wouldn't be surprised if last night's row wasn't tied to how cozy Laura obviously was with that would-be "director" who was supposedly going to cast her in a Biblical movie about Ruth that they'd written together and were now expecting Copperfield to finance; never mind that they were making the beast with two backs in his own house whenever his head was turned. Laura Copperfield as Ruth! What a joke! To Copperfield's credit, he'd cast a skeptical eye on the deal, and that was a relief—Wilbur had often wondered lately whether it wasn't his reponsibility to tell his employer of his suspicions about his wife's infidelity. To judge by the uproar last night, Copperfield had learned anyway.

When he stepped into the room, the boat lurched forward as the engine surged. They were under way; they'd sail with the motor until they cleared the harbor, he knew. He found his sweater hanging in the mahogany closet of the stateroom where he'd left it when they'd debarked for the hotel on Friday afternoon. Then, while Pearl had gone off exploring with the other adults, he and Bobette had retired to their room and had two whole uninterrupted hours alone to nuzzle and talk. He'd forgotten what that was like. In fact, until this morning, he'd managed to put Big and Little Harold and Pei-Ling and Mildred and Aunty Nan out of his mind.

Now he and Bobette were on their way back home. No doubt the second they returned the phone would ring and Mildred would be hinting at how they'd managed just fine thank you! to get Sunday dinner for themselves despite her daughter. She would probably claim Little Harold took them all to a very nice restaurant where they had a wonderful meal.

He sighed. This new baby would not make anybody's life less complicated.

He carried the sweater back to the galley where he stood behind Bobette and helped her slip it on. The sleeves were way too long and covered her hands to her knuckles. Water in a pot was simmering while it sloshed from side to side as the boat struck the swells.

"Want some?"

He nodded. She set out three mugs, dropped tea bags into them. The galley was, like the rest of the boat's interior, trimmed in shining red mahogany and leather upholstery that together exhuded a rich aroma. The ladder to the deck jutted into a vertical rectangle that framed a roiling grey sky and Copperfield's bright yellow slicker as he stood at the wheel in the stern. The third mug. It was like her to think of Copperfield, too. It was an admirable trait to be always thinking of others, he supposed.

She handed him one steaming mug.

"Thanks."

"I'm going to take some to David. He looks all lonely out there."

Then came the moment which he has now fixed forever in his memory: he sips from the mug. He doesn't want her to go topside. Pearl is nowhere to be seen. He wants to hog Bobette if only for a second because this new baby will be here before they know it, and because although Bobette has vowed never to put on another Sunday dinner, it won't hold, and if it's not Sunday dinner, it'll be something else.

The minute this ship hits the far shore they'll be back in the cage of family.

She steps onto the ladder, puts one hand to the rail to steady herself, holds the other carrying the mug away from her body, gyroscoping it to keep the tea from spilling.

"You know what I wish? I wish one of these days you'd pay attention to just me." He wants it to be a joke, but he sounds whiny instead; he wants to flatter her by letting her know how important she is to him, but she hears a reproach, she hears one more person wanting a little more from her.

"Buck up, laddie, things aren't so tough," she says evenly, but she won't meet his eye, and he can tell she means get off my back. He watches from below as she mounts the ladder a step at a time like a cripple. Behind her, in the sky, the sun breaks through the tattered overcast, and suddenly a billow of yellow sunlight bursts over the boat and glows in a nimbus around her rising form.

◧   ◧   ◧

Ifs descended upon him like a plague of locusts. If Bobette hadn't been standing over the engine. If he had kept her from going topside. If he had been there

132

instead. If they stayed at home and held their usual Sunday dinner. If he'd never gone to work for Copperfield. If he'd not run away from Dallas. If his mother had not run away from Atlas. If his mother had not run away from St.Louis. Then Bobette might be alive. And Copperfield, too.

Why do accidents happen? Bobette and Copperfield had been standing over the engine. Why there and not elsewhere? Why them and not someone else? He and Pearl had clung to floating wreckage until another boat arrived. Why couldn't Bobette have been with them?

Why a cabbage.

As the weeks after the funeral crawled by, Wilbur groped in the dark to make his loss rational. He had three choices: there was a God, and He was diabolically clever at seducing his creatures into falling into a pit; the cosmos was godless, and there was only a random arrangement of events without purpose or guidance; or there was some mechanical Fate operating according to enigmatic laws. Though the first gave him the satisfaction of having an adversary, he leaned toward the last: he had seen Bobette's mutilated body scattered about the aft deck of the boat like so much butchered meat, and no God he could conceive would have been so cruel as to force him to witness that. Something without compassion, however, something required by contractual arrangement to punish him might, though.

Had he been too greedy for happiness? His love for Bobette had had a holy aura to him that repelled any thought that his luck might turn bad. Or that he and she had to pay. He'd reveled in his good fortune. With Pearl the bounty multiplied. He'd felt blessed, though the word had no specific religious connotation. Being blessed meant he'd been awarded something extraordinary by fate or luck or chance without having applied for it or otherwise wanted it or even known that it was available. And it had come not because of looks, family connections, intelligence, talent, or strength, but by whimsy, it seemed. Like how it will rain on Santa Monica but not downtown.

Was a blessing only a set-up?

Was adversity the way you paid for a blessing?

Or was bad luck as arbitrary as good?

He became a functioning corpse; he walked, he talked and heard, he worked, but he lived as if miles of space extended between the outside of his skin to where the center of his being had withdrawn—from an oak to an acorn in the space of only weeks. He was inconsolable for a time. A well-meaning friend said to be thankful he had Pearl to remember Bobette by, but that sword cut two ways. He was bewildered and distressed by ugly thoughts—why not Pearl instead? or if it weren't for this child, you could go away and forget this part of your life!—and sought to escape them by avoiding her. He let Mildred comfort her, feeling guilty that he couldn't help his own child, knowing that Pearl had lost a father, too—he could read her pain plain as a photograph on her face. Mildred said, "She thinks she's done something wrong." But he felt helpless to explain or to act otherwise; he was tormented by the guilt of hurting his own daughter and was angry at her for showing the pain that made him feel guilty. He thrashed about in a straitjacket.

Then he was bedeviled by dreams and snippets of memory. Copperfield comes to the hatchway of the boat and says, You want to be alone for a while? and he nods eagerly. He looks about. Where's Bobette? Bobette? he calls out. Copperfield, on deck, yells back,

Thought you wanted to be alone. Later, he and Bobette are talking in the galley, and her eyes get big. Oh, my God! What did you forget? Did he forget something? Oh, my God! she says. She's panicky. Wilbur, you forgot something!

He remembered telling her he wanted to be alone with just her, and her answering, Buck up, laddie. Things aren't so tough. In the last exchange they had on earth he made her feel a little more burdened. He hated that. He would have liked to have made her feel that much safer, happier.

He got into the habit of leaving a light on in the room where he slept in their bed. The burning light discouraged sleep. It helped diminish his fear of what might creep into his head and illuminate itself like a horror picture show while he lay unconscious and vulnerable. Soon, though, his eyes would droop, his mouth drop open. He would glide through the gate into the other world. In this dream, he is sleeping in their bed just as he is in reality; in the dream, he is overwhelmed by a horrible nightmare that Bobette has died or has been killed, but he is awakened from that nightmare by Bobette herself, who is shaking his arm. He comes to consciousness there beside her, sees that she's alive; he embraces her with joy and shouts into her face, 'You're alive! Alive!' And she says, laughing, 'Of course, silly! You were just having a nightmare, wake up!' So inside the dream he comes fully awake and, relieved to find that that her dying is only a nightmare, he hugs her fiercely. He then wakes up in their bed alone sobbing for joy and clutching her pillow.

The inquest concluded the explosion was an accident. Fuel leaking out of a line from the tank to the engine had gathered in the compartment and had been ignited by a spark. The insurance investigator's report mentioned that the line "had loosened from its connection."

Normal wear and tear, he thought. Vibrations? Maybe the last time the engine was serviced, the mechanic had not tightened the nut. Negligence? If the mechanic was negligent, then he was at fault. Sue the fucker's ass off! Get a charge of manslaughter brought against him! In court: Because of you two innocent people have died.

No. Calm down. No proof.

But, thus, the idea of a human agent, a cause that wasn't Fate or Luck or chance, crept into his thoughts. Not something made it happen; someone. Then it would say "had been loosened." What a difference one word made.

He couldn't sleep. One night lying awake he traced the line of Fate that had led to the awful moment and arrived back at the time in front of the barbershop when he stuck out his hand and introduced himself. You tell me who to trust.

A terrible sensation smothered him like a blanket.

The next day he drove over to Copperfield's place. Laura, his widow, greeted him at the door in a flowing white satin robe such as choir singers wore. It was trimmed in gold, and she had a large gold cross hanging between her breasts. He blinked in surprise, then quickly recovered. He recalled how, at Copperfield's funeral, she'd been with Copperfield's old missionary teacher, Sister Alice Roberts, and her Foursquare Gospel crowd. He'd never have dreamed, though, that she'd be a convert. On the other hand, what made more sense than a reformed sinner? Still, he was wary.

She leaned forward, cupped his elbows, and pressed her cheek to his.

"Brother Wyse! I have prayed for you. I feel such kinship with you in our mutual loss."

He nodded and let himself be led into Copperfield's study. The woman had bulldozed it, and now workmen were busily scraping and painting. Copperfield's desk and red wing chairs were gone, as well as the mounted arrow and spearhead collection. The woman perched herself upon the edge of a new brocade sofa and waved him into the matching love seat. She folded her hands in her lap and gave him a look of pity and concern. In the years he had known her he'd never seen an expression even remotely resembling this one on her face, and his puzzlement must have shown.

"I know this must be a shock to you, to be here in David's house again, and to be seeing me thus attired." She plucked at the robe so that it lifted, coyly, an inch or so over her ankles, and dropped it. She smiled wryly. He found the irony reassuring. She'd stepped momentarily out of this new character and, paradoxically, made her performance a shade more credible.

"Yeah, but I do know that when terrible things happen to them people change, Mrs. Copperfield."

She smiled as if to thank him. "Is there something I can help you with?"

He shifted his feet. There'd been no offer of coffee. She'd also not shooed the workmen away or showed him to a room where it was quiet. It wasn't exactly the bum's rush, but it wasn't rolling out the red carpet, either. She wanted him to get to the point.

"I was wondering about a couple of things, Mrs. Copperfield. You know the insurance investigator's report?"

He watched her face; her expression didn't change,

but she moved her head slightly backwards as if to fine tune her focus on him.

"Why, yes, certainly."

"You know how it mentions the fuel line being loose? I got to worrying about how it got that way, you know? I got to thinking about how maybe someone did that. It worries me because, you know, Mr. Copperfield put a lot of faith in my ability and he relied on me to take care of things. I was supposed to tell him who to trust."

Laura Copperfield looked stricken. "You don't suppose—? Oh, Wilbur, that would be horrible! No, you're just overwrought and jumping to conclusions! Why would anyone want to kill David and that wonderful wife of yours? We all need the comfort of thinking that things have clearcut causes, but, Wilbur, when you learn to put your faith in Jesus Christ, it will give you peace of mind, believe me! Put aside these suspicions—they're unworthy of you."

Her face was screwed up as if she were about to weep in pity for him. It was disgusting. When the Holy Ghost struck, it seemed to blow out your common sense like a fuse. She was speaking in ready-made phrases.

"Well, Mrs. Copperfield, you know after being married to him for over ten years that a lot of people are bigots and don't much care for Indians in the first place, and if they're rich, that's two strikes against them, and if they're rich and married to a white woman then they're out, you see? I just thought maybe you had an idea of how some particular person might benefit if Mr. Copperfield were...deceased. I just thought maybe you'd keep your eyes and ears open for me. I'm feeling pretty low about it, to tell you the truth, because he trusted me to watch his back for him. I don't want to think I let him down. If it turned out somebody did this on purpose, I'd want to know who and I'd want to be right there seeing to it that justice was done." His throat caught, and his eyes stung. No—not in front of her, of all people! He sat perfectly still for a moment, clenching his jaw, then blinked and swallowed.

"That person was responsible for my wife's death."

They sat in silence, the woman looking intently at him, her brows slightly arched. He couldn't read what she was thinking or even guess for certain what she felt.

"You have no reason to feel guilty, Wilbur." Her eyes brimmed suddenly and her chin trembled. "It was an accident. Let it rest. Don't think about it any more. Bobette is in Heaven; she knows peace now. She's happy. Be happy yourself in her joyful reunion with our Lord."

He sat in his idling car a moment before pulling out of the drive. Stymied. He couldn't say for certain why he'd come—maybe he just needed to talk, maybe he'd been looking for someone to talk him out of a nutty idea or reassure him by confirming his doubts. She'd done neither, really. He couldn't buy her reassurance that it had been an accident because she seemed so caught up in the jargon of McPherson's followers. Bobette peaceful in Heaven—God knows it'd be nice to believe! Either Laura Copperfield had completely bought the Foursquare Gospel line and had transported herself halfway to Heaven already, or it was all a phony act.

Of course, another possibility was that she felt guilty about something and needed to feel her sins were washed away—the way she treated Copperfield when he was alive might be gnawing on her. Maybe Wilbur and she were kin when it came to wishing you had acted differently.

Funny, when he was talking about somebody doing something to the fuel line he meant it might have been an accident or on purpose, and she leapt to the conclusion he meant somebody meant to do it. She said put it out of your mind. But it was obviously in her mind, too. Why not admit it?

He went to the downtown office of the Copperfield Foundation where he and Copperfield's other assistants had operated the man's businesses. He hadn't been here in well over a week, nor had he kept in touch with Iola Conroy, Copperfield's executive secretary, a Kiowa whom Copperfield had known since childhood. The office was in an uproar. People were packing their belongings in cartons.

"What's going on?"

"The grieving widow," cracked Iola. "She's gotten an injunction against further spending. All David's assets are frozen in probate. Looks like we're all getting the sack."

He told Iola about his interview with Laura Copperfield and about his doubts concerning the accident.

"She didn't throw you out?"

"No, why should she?"

Iola shrugged. She was ferociously angry, he could tell. "Because you were accusing her."

"I was?"

"You weren't?"

Hair on the back of his neck rose. "No. Should I have?"

"Can you think of a more likely suspect?"

When he didn't answer, Iola said, "I imagine she's got her hands full now, anyway, fighting off this new will."

"What new will?"

A petition had been filed at the Los Angeles County Courthouse three days ago that made a claim against Copperfield's estate. A new will was filed with it. The primary beneficiary was a banker in El Paso. That's all Iola knew. The petition claimed that the banker had been granted power of attorney by Copperfield.

The more Wilbur thought about it, the more furious he grew that Laura Copperfield had hidden this from him. He called her immediately.

"What can you tell me about this new will?" he asked bluntly.

"New will?" she sang.

"Yes, the new will filed in—"

"Ignore it!" she snapped. "Whatever Bill Kale has up his sleeve—"

"Kale? Kale?" Wilbur's hand shook. "The one from Oklahoma?"

"How do you know him?" Laura asked, alarmed, but Wilbur hung up. He was trembling: the "coincidence" of his own connection to the man evoked a violent fear in him. It was as if all these years his life had been on the end of a very long leash. Someone on the other end had given it a yank.

◙   ◙   ◙

The train to El Paso went East across the Mojave from Los Angeles. By day, the hot wind blowing through the open windows baked the passengers' skins. Outside, the landscape shimmered endlessly into a vague horizon where dim humps of mountains lurked against the sky. Stickers and barbs clung to the sand or rooted in rocky pockets to defy the climate. Things here survived despite adversity by mimicking the harshness of the habitat, enduring poison and thirst, blistering heat and nights clear as the sky over a pole and every bit as cold.

You could learn a lesson from it. He sweat but kept his suitcoat buttoned, pushing his body against the heat for the pleasure of resistance. Cultivating discomfort had become a habit, honing his spirit while he searched for the fire to lay his metal in. He put pebbles in his shoes and ate only those things he had no taste for and never when he felt too hungry. He'd given up cigars because he liked to smoke them; when he'd become used to doing without them, he took them up again to make himself sick, dropped them when nausea grew into craving. He allowed himself no more than four hours of sleep a night, though his body would crave two more, and when he got drowsy, he pinched his arms and stomach or jabbed himself hard with a pencil. He exercised until he was ready to drop.

He'd be ready. This time he'd be alert, nobody would sneak past. No, it wasn't punishment. It was training. Protecting himself. He welcomed the challenge of pain; he wanted to be so familiar with it that it wouldn't deter or weaken him. When the time came to settle the score, he wouldn't be turned aside by his own body—it would be an instrument of his will until it was lifeless.

He got off the train in El Paso and checked into a hotel on San Jacinto Plaza under the name of Will Hunter. In the room, he looked out the window into Mexico, thinking that if he were not driven to unravel any mysteries here, then he might go to a such a place. Your anger and pain would shrink against the backdrop of such a rough, enormous landscape. He was tired; he couldn't distinguish weariness of travelling from something more permanent and deep-seated. Pinching himself awake, he removed a sheaf of papers from his valise and sat at the desk.

But before looking into the folder, he picked up the phone and called Mildred's house. Little Harold answered, and Wilbur gave him the hotel's telephone number. Was Pearl still up? No, she'd gone to bed an hour ago.

"What are you doing in El Paso, Wilbur? You're a man of mystery!" joked Little Harold.

"Just business. Looking into something."

"Well, don't worry about Pearl. Pei-Ling loves that kid, you know, and we'll take good care of her."

He didn't want to think about Pearl in that household, but, then, it was unfair always to think the worst of them.

What was he doing here?

He opened the folder and leafed through the papers in it. A private investigator he'd hired in Tulsa to dig around in Wetoka had come up with a little bit of fact and a lot of rumors. Kale's bank had gone bust a while back and Kale had moved to El Paso, but he still had his ranch and several other parcels of land (including, Wilbur discovered, Atlas Smythe's old place), and everyone said he'd been too smart to get hurt by the crash last October. The Feds in Oklahoma City hinted that Kale and others with whom he was associated were currently under suspicion and investigation for the deaths of several Indians in a three-county area of Oklahoma. All victims were oil-rich, all had died when dynamite blew up their homes, and all had had dealings with the bank in Wetoka. The investigator guessed that no evidence had been uncovered sufficient to support an indictment at this time. Nobody around here has gotten much riled up about it, though.

People there knew, though. They had to. The obviousness of the conspiracy was distressing. Creeks and

Osages and other Indians were being murdered for their oil money in a systematic fashion, and people chose to look the other way. Maybe they didn't have any real proof; maybe they didn't want to root around for it; the "law enforcement agency" in Wetoka consisted of a county sheriff and one hand-picked deputy, a run-down three-cell jail, and a Model A the sheriff appeared to use at will for his personal business, which included looking after large tracts of his own land. Given these circumstances, public apathy could be explained.

But he knew people looked the other way because the victims were only "savages" who, not so many years ago, were wielding axes on white scalps and were now getting what they deserved. And never mind that the Creeks and other members of the Five Civilized Tribes had been uprooted from their homes in the South and marched at gunpoint to Oklahoma and had never practiced scalping!

People looked the other way because they hated the idea of a rich Indian; it was a crime against nature; it was a bad heavenly joke. Destitute farmers and unemployed laborers with the bust of 1929 ripe upon them seethed inwardly to see a man in a feather headdress behind the wheel of a fancy automobile. If they were being murdered for their money, good riddance.

People looked the other way because they preferred to think that each death was a separate, unrelated instance of conspicuous and foolish extravagance having lured a single, greedy transient—"oil trash"—into a criminal act. They could reassure themselves the guilty man was already seven counties away, on the run. No one wanted to believe there was a conspiracy in their own town of a banker and a lawyer and a sheriff to kill Indians for their money.

Bobette had nothing to do with any of it. Except that she had married a man who worked for a target of the murdering bunch.

He closed the report. He didn't need to know more to be convinced of Kale's guilt. He had arrived at it through an agony of self-reproach and tantalyzing guesses. Chance was out now; to blame Fate was to let everybody off the hook. He'd blamed himself enough for not being watchful, and of course Copperfield was at blame too for marrying that woman, and she was guilty, too, for being a tramp. And he supposed she and Kale were co-conspirators.

But it came down as always to the man behind the wheel, didn't it! Naw, hell no, he ain't greedy for land—he just wants all that butts up against his own. Kale the gentleman was also Kale the confidence artist; he'd broken Wilbur's stepfather, made a fool and whore of Wilbur's mother, killed Wilbur's friend. He had killed Bobette. Kale was a dark magnet that sent out invisible rays to grab you before you even felt them. For whatever reason, William Kale was behind every malign event in Wilbur's life. Maybe it was coincidence; maybe there was a design. It didn't much matter—it was time for it to stop.

Seated at the desk in the El Paso hotel room, he read through the insurance report trying to think, once again, of how such an accident might be rigged. Then he rose from the desk, lifted the valise and put it on the bed. He opened it and drew out a bar pin, a hank of red hair in a large heart locket, and a camisole top that smelled of Bobette when he pressed it to his face.

Then he removed a hinged triptych album from the bottom of the suitcase, unfolded it and set it on the desk. A studio portrait of Bobette, another of Pearl, and a third of the three of them together. Formal poses. The one of Bobette had a radiance about it, like a halo. Going up those stairs, the sun backlighting her. Buck up, laddie.

He put away the bar pin, took another last look at the hair in the locket before snapping it shut, folded up the camisole with trembling hands, and shut the valise. He shoved it under the bed so that he would have space on the floor to perform his nightly 250 situps and pushups.

When he had finished his exercise, he felt calmer, and he lay on the bed with his heart thundering in his eardrums and his skin tingling as the air of the desert night dried his sweat. The bare bulb hanging from a wire swayed gently to and fro, and after a long struggle he surrendered to the darkness in his skull.

5

JANUARY-
MARCH
1930

ON KALE'S desk sat a souvenir paper-
weight from the St. Louis World's Exposition of 1904.

Beside it were two framed photographs, one a studio portrait of an
odd-looking young woman with
owlish eyes. Kale's wife? "Hunter"
ground his teeth—still alive. Several
more photographs hung on the wall,
same female subject.

Kale glanced up from Hunter's letters of introduction, caught him gawking, frowned.

"You're not a family man, Mr. Hunter?"

"Not yet, sir."

"You want to sow some wild oats first, I suppose."

Kale was eyeing him closely. A loaded question.

"Well, no sir. It's just I haven't met the right girl yet. California girls were a little fast for me, to tell the truth."

"I see. You mind if I ask your national origins, Hunter?"

The question seemed strangely irrelevant. Should he try to mirror his interviewer? What sort of name was Kale? "My father was Scotch-Irish, my mother German."

"Good stock."

"I think so."

Kale examined his paper briefly then excused himself and left the room. Wilbur worried that his ruses would be detected, that Kale had gone to telephone the phony name on his letter of introduction to verify the recommendation. Wilbur had concocted an employment history that matched his qualifications and skills but which withheld the significant facts that his former employer had been an oil-rich Kiowa who'd been murdered, leaving an estate tangled in probate because Kale had moved to freeze the assets until the courts could determine the validity of a false will.

He surveyed the desk. Several loose papers, covered with numbers not words. The other framed photograph showed Kale standing with a group of men in hunting attire. They were hoisting rifles triumphantly into the air.

Kale returned and sat behind the desk. He wrote on a pad for a moment, and Wilbur broke the silence.

"Excuse me, sir, but I couldn't help but notice the photographs on your desk. Would this be your wife?"

Unexpectedly, Kale flashed him a look of alarm. "No. That's my daughter. She's still in school, Mr. Hunter. She's not nearly so mature as the portraits might lead you to presume."

Wilbur checked his surprise. He recalled Kale's daughter from those Oklahoma days as a haughty child astride a blaze-faced pony. But, of course, she'd be a dozen years older now, and Kale's wife would be Kale's age. Looking about, he saw no other photographs.

"As you know, Mr. Hunter, several banks here have gone under in the last few months, and a lot of their employees have come to us looking for positions. Some are conversant with the accounting procedures we use."

When he paused and stared, Wilbur accepted the opportunity to defend himself. "I can understand that, certainly. But I'm a very quick study, Mr. Kale." He leaned forward, lowered his voice. "Mostly, though, from working with your truly superior men, I've learned a lot about being discreet and about carrying out orders and wishes in a way that's efficient and quiet."

Kale studied Wilbur a moment. "Have we met before?"

Wilbur rubbed his sparse beard. He should've waited another week to show up here! "Well, not that I know of, sir. This is my first week in Texas."

"You ever live in Oklahoma?"

"Never been near the place, sir."

"Huh." Kale's eyes dropped to Hunter's paper. "We'll let you know soon."

Certain he'd be passed over for the job, Wilbur spent two days struggling to invent another means of becoming intimate enough with Kale to secure usable evidence of his guilt. Then he was called in for a second interview with Kale and two other officers, who explained the various secretarial and clerical duties of the post, and the salary, then offered it to him. Apparently his claim to discretion had been effective.

On Monday when he reported to work, he sat calmly across from Kale taking notes on several matters Kale wanted done, but found himself preoccupied. In his braces, tie loosened, Kale sat talking, breathing, smoking a cigarette, his suit coat hung on the hall tree behind the door. It was January, but the office was overheated; sweat beaded on Kale's forehead. It was one thing to read about a cold-blooded murderer in a newspaper or in an investigator's report and another to sit in the same room with him and think: I knew this man when I was a kid and I thought he was sharp. He was a boyfriend of my mother's. Now he's actually killed people. He's responsible for my wife's death. Why did he do it? Even if I knew why—say, he's a gambler deep in debt and has to hide it and needed a lot of money—how could he have brought himself to do it, have it done? What's in him that isn't in other people?

He wanted to crawl inside Kale's skin to understand; it would help put his mind to rest about why Bobette had died. Sometimes he would furtively observe Kale working at his desk. Everything appeared normal on the exterior: Kale was of medium height, going a little tubby around the waist but no more so than most men in their mid-forties, his coarse black hair not thinning but frosted at the temples like an Indian's hair, that's ironic!, with a dark but sparse beard that hardly needed shaving by the end of the day. Wilbur supposed women thought him handsome—his nose was thin and sharp; his lips had a surly, girlish shape; his eyes were such a dark brown that the iris bled into the pupil and was indistinguishable from it. He sported a thin little moustache like a flag of vanity, and you could tell he thought he was some John Gilbert or Rudolph Valentino. It was disgusting to watch secretaries flirt with him. When he spoke to them he'd lower one brow and twist one corner of his mouth into a smile as if to let them know that even if he was talking about ordering note pads he was thinking about tickling their pussies. Wilbur hated that, and he hated the way the secretaries smiled back. He hated the way Kale put his cigarette in an ivory holder to smoke it and clamped the holder between his teeth so it jutted out and up from his mouth at a cocky angle; he hated how Kale splashed bay rum lavishly when he shaved so that it stank up the office and you could tell where he'd been five minutes after he'd gone; he hated Kale's habit of cleaning his teeth with a penknife when Wilbur was giving him information; he hated how Kale talked to his wife over the telephone as if she were an idiot who constantly tried his patience; he hated how Kale never took the blame for a mistake and required anyone who worked with him to attribute a botched communication to their own faulty hearing; he hated how Kale curried favor with the editor of the *El Paso Times* and had instructed Wilbur to "volunteer" a letter to the editor suggesting that his boss would be an excellent subject for a story; he hated the sound of Kale's voice—it had the overly practiced enunciation of an orator, as if he were polishing its lustre and listening

with admiration even as he spoke. He talked too loudly and used more words than needed; he interrupted
you without apology or ignored what you said when he
didn't feel like listening.

Wilbur hated hearing Kale speak with mocking con-
tempt of Indians and their wealth. The subject obsessed
him. Once it grew almost unendurable. Kale was rant-
ing to another bank officer while Wilbur was working
with a letter opener to screen the day's mail, and for a
moment he almost plunged the opener into Kale's
back. Holding himself back, he closed his eyes instead
and imagined the knife puncturing Kale's flesh. Would
it resist the knife like a watermelon? Would there be a
satisfying sound, a humpf! and a groan from his victim?
The movie in his mind cut abruptly to a chase on the
street, he was cornered and caught. The headlines:
Banker stabbed, Lives! And even if he died, it wasn't
enough. Justice required a trial—then he could be
hanged, as they said in the Old West. Then he'd know
he was paying for something.

Hatred lodged in Wilbur's gut like a wad of raw
dough. After a month of working with Kale, Wilbur was
consumed by these fantasies of rage. Watching him
from nearby while Kale was occupied with someone or
something else, Wilbur would imagine twisting a
corkscrew into the man's ear, shoving a hot poker up
his asshole, pushing needles under his fingernails;
pushing pencils through his eyes into his brain—

His violent thoughts sometimes revolted him, and
more than once he'd dashed for the lavatory to puke his
breakfast. Trying to contain this rage sometimes made
him tremble. It was astonishing to think that Kale never
really noticed it; or, if he noticed anything peculiar
about this assistant "Hunter," he apparently had not

connected it to himself. That made Wilbur wonder about himself, that he was so capable of keeping his rage hidden. Having these two selves—the public and cooperative self, and the raging demon beneath that screamed to be let go—brought Wilbur uncomfortably and unexpectedly close to an understanding of Kale. But he refused to compare himself and Kale. No, Kale's shadow-self was not motivated by anything so clean or essentially human as revenge or rage.

Wilbur kept tabs on who came and went in Kale's office and to whom he spoke on the telephone. When he had the opportunity, he dug into Kale's files for incriminating correspondence, but soon decided that Kale had either left any in Wetoka or kept it at home.

He made himself responsible for passing out the mail to the bank's officers and departments, and on the first Monday of his fifth week of employment, Kale received a personal letter with no return address but postmarked Los Angeles. On a hunch, Wilbur took the letter home and carefully steamed it open in the bathroom, his hands shaking. The note inside didn't say much, but it said enough: Bill, I don't want our lawyers to argue about how to carve up this pie. They make too much noise. I'll grant you've got a lot coming. Call. There was no signature, but Wilbur knew Laura Copperfield's handwriting like his own. He'd always taken her to be a gold-digger and a tramp, but never until now had he believed with certainty she would help Kale kill her own husband.

He resealed the envelope and slipped it back into Kale's mail. When he handed the letter to his employer along with several others, he watched Kale flip through the envelopes. When Kale reached the letter from Laura Copperfield, he dealt it to the bottom of the deck, and when he'd gone through the stack, kept it and another and handed the others to Wilbur. He was so eager to read it that he sent Wilbur on a pointless errand.

At four o'clock Kale called him into his office.

"You're a bachelor fellow, right, Hunter?" he asked merrily.

Wilbur nodded.

"My women are out of town visiting relatives, and all of sudden I'm a bachelor fellow, too." He smiled. "I thought maybe a couple of hard-working bachelor fellows like ourselves deserved a night on the town down in old Juarez. We can celebrate."

Wilbur, startled, fumbled for an answer, and Kale added, "My treat, of course."

"Thank you. Yes, that would be good."

Kale said he would pick Wilbur up at seven at his hotel then left the office early himself. Normally, on his way home, Wilbur stopped off at a cafe near the hotel to eat supper. His usual evening routine was to read in his room or go to the movies across the plaza from the hotel; on Tuesday nights he called and talked to Pearl. Now and then he'd sit with old Sanchez in the lobby. Frustrated that he could do little in the evenings to investigate, he'd driven by the Kale home several times and debated dropping in on him but hadn't out of a fear of arousing suspicion.

Kale had given him a chance to learn more now. He left the bank and drove straight to the hotel, bathed, changed into a fresh shirt, then sat at the window sipping whiskey from a shot glass and watching the dusty yellow light of evening fall on the mountains to the south. He'd been on edge for hours, eager and excited about the chance to get Kale alone and watch for a slip, encourage his confidence. The whiskey hit his empty stomach and made his head swim, so he diluted it with two glasses of water that sloshed in his gut when he moved. Then he felt less eager, a little queasy. Why had Kale chosen him? Didn't he have any cohorts here? Had Kale made a call to Laura Copperfield, and had she alerted him that Copperfield's former assistant was known to have gone back to these parts for unknown reasons? Had Kale guessed his true identity? Was this excursion to Juarez a trap?

He wasn't afraid to confront Kale; if anything, he welcomed a fight. He sat at the desk chain-smoking, his mind racing in circles. Now that he had proof of guilt in the note, his pulse was pounding. He should write a letter explaining what he's doing here in El Paso and what his suspicions were in case Kale had something planned for him in Juarez. Describe the note from the widow. Belatedly, he realized Kale could destroy the note. Wilbur should've kept it, even if Laura might have then called to ask Kale if he'd gotten it.

Should he take a weapon tonight?

Kale probably had thugs on his payroll. He couldn't fight many of them off.

What would Pearl do without a father? The one tug he felt for staying alive—and it was a strong pull, all right—lay here, in his duty as a father and his love for the girl. And when he allowed himself to play out his present course of action in a way that put him into a trapped corner, he could feel his resolve to pursue all this drain from him and leave him faint. There was no law that said Wilbur could kill Kale and not pay for it with his own life, even if Kale had killed Copperfield and Bobette. Besides, it wasn't killing Kale that he wanted: it was making him hurt. And hurt. And it wasn't his own death he feared: it was leaving Pearl, causing her more pain.

Oh, this whole thing is crazy! Let the G-men take care of it! You're no copper.

But his attempt to discuss the case at the U.S. Attorney's office in El Paso three days ago had left him discouraged. He'd been parked in the outer office a half hour after the appointment time, and when he finally was allowed to see an assistant, he was afraid to tell all he knew: Kale had lived in this town for over two years. There was no telling how far his tentacles reached.

However, he dutifully described the accident, the insurance investigator's conclusion, his Tulsa private eye's report, his suspicions.

"You say the situation is being looked into there in Oklahoma by the Justice Department?" asked the assistant.

"Well, yes, that's my understanding."

"What about the California authorities?"

"I suppose someone would need evidence that the accident wasn't an accident to reopen the case."

"Have you tried the District Attorney in Los Angeles?"

"Yes."

"And?"

Wilbur shrugged. "They would wait to see what what was turned up in Oklahoma."

"I see." The assistant's face closed like the cover of a book.

Wilbur left the office feeling that he had failed to interest anyone here in furthering the investigation but had succeeded in revealing to strangers that he was personally interested in Kale's criminal activities. He'd gone in for help but had come out in danger.

The note from Laura was new evidence, true. But it hadn't said anything, really, had it? And he didn't have it.

☐ ☐ ☐

When Kale's Chrysler rolled to a halt in front of the hotel, Wilbur had been standing at the curb for several minutes watching a flock of glossy black grackles amass like huge flies in the branches of a diseased elm in the plaza; when they spoke in a raucous clack, their opened beaks disclosed pointed red tongues, and their dissonant squawks seemed a commentary. Wilbur's straight razor lay folded in his right coat pocket, and he kept pressing his elbow against it to reassure himself.

On the way to Juarez, Kale shot the breeze about office politics. He was chatty, full of chuckles, and stank of toilet water. The ivory holder jutted out of his jaw like a skinny hardon. What put Kale in such good humor—the prospect of slipping a knife into Wilbur? Was it learning that Laura had caved in and now the door to Copperfield's safe had been blown open? Wilbur struggled to keep up his end of the conversation and hoped that whatever reticence he showed would be read as shyness and respect.

"So where to?" Kale asked as they crept across the bridge in a stream of traffic. It was Friday evening and the first night of Mardi Gras; Juarez would be jumping with Anglos from the sister city to the north. Below, in the ruddy eddies of the Rio Grande, urchins stood holding long poles on which paper cones were affixed to catch pennies tossed at them by tourists.

Wilbur shrugged. "Don't get down here much myself."

"What? Young bachelor like you?" Kale winked. "I'm surprised." His grin mocked Wilbur's innocence. "It turns out I do know a place or two myself."

"I thought you were a family man."

"Oh, yes. But a little recreation never harmed anyone. Moderation in all things, you know."

They were on the Avenida 16th of Septembre, passing a sign: "Mexican Curio Shop: While You Are Sober Write Some Cards." The bourbon Wilbur had downed in his room on an empty stomach hadn't made him drunk, but had turned his stomach fluttery.

"I think I'd like to eat first."

"Sure." Kale laughed. "First? Before what?"

Wilbur shrugged. "Before whatever."

"What'd you have in mind?"

They stopped behind a campesino leading a burro that had decided to rest in the street, and Kale tooted the horn. The horn rattled the campesino but didn't intimidate the burro. Overhead was a billboard: *** DIVORCE ***

"I didn't. Like I said, I don't get down here much."

"You find some nice girl in the office?"

Kale edged the car's bumper to the burro's flank, honked again, and it shunted, hooves aclatter, to the curb, its load of pottery cookware rattling dully as it shifted in the net.

"Not yet." He remembered telling Kale Calfornia girls were too fast.

"How about Celia Montgomery?"

Wilbur drew a momentary blank then fit the name to a buxom brunette who always emerged from the ladies' toilet redolent of tobacco smoke. Kale had pronounced her name with that special urgency reserved for women who arouse one; Kale seemed interested in her out of proportion to any feature that Wilbur could see, but if he played the choir-boy too earnestly Kale might back away.

"She's a looker."

"I'll say. You had her out?"

"Naw. I asked her, though."

Kale said, looking ahead, "Pretty titties."

"Yeah."

"I'd bet that field's been plowed before, too."

"Could be."

Kale drove on for a moment without comment, as if languidly contemplating the prospect of having been the "farmer" who plowed Celia Montgomery's "field," but Wilbur felt uneasy, having no idea what the drift of their conversation signified.

"What do you say to a show?"

"A show?"

"Floor show."

"Fine. Let me get some chow, a couple of drinks, I'll be up for anything."

"A fellow I know gave me the name of a club here that's supposed to have a special show—some gal, she does, uh, tricks." Kale laughed uneasily.

"That the one with the zucchini?" Wilbur guessed. Bordertown legends—Tijuana supposedly had such shows.

Kale laughed. "Coke-cola bottle first, then a donkey. You ever seen anything like that?"

"Nah. Just heard about it."

"That might be something to see."

Wilbur thought watching a woman take a donkey on a nightclub stage would be the saddest experience he could have as a spectator.

"Might be," he said.

Fortunately, Kale's tastes in food were strictly ortho-dox, and he led Wilbur to the Central Cafe at Lerdo and 16th de Septembre for steaks. It was a large, barny place filled with Anglos. Wilbur counted Kale's three Manhattans, managed to nurse his one bourbon and water but finally surrendered to Kale's urging a second to keep from seeming a wet blanket. While they ate, Kale continued to assess each girl in their office for her "sex potential." Wilbur confirmed his credibility with Kale by mildly agreeing on each account. He was sur-prised by the turn of events; he had had no idea that this night with Kale might consist of two "bachelors" trading stories of sexual conquest, though in truth Kale revealed only smutty conjectures about the reputations of the girls and, wittingly or no, his own randiness.

When Kale said, "Janet Johnson," Wilbur nodded. He had taken the blonde with the delicate features out one night for coffee and listened to her complain about having to live with her mother and grandmother. He'd had no desire for her, and before the evening was over he realized he'd asked her out because, like Bobette, her living in a manless household encouraged his brotherly instincts.

"Yeah? Nice girl, Hunter?"

"Yeah, too bad." Wilbur chuckled.

They'd now gone down the roster, and Kale seemed deflated; whether he was disappointed in Wilbur or dis-appointed in Janet Johnson's virtue wasn't clear. To keep him up and talking, Wilbur invented a waitress and spun a lie about sneaking her up to his room.

"Hell's bells, son! No wonder you don't get over here very much!" Kale said. "In your room, huh? She stay all night?"

"Yeah."

Kale laughed, slapped the table with his palm. "I thought you've come to work looking a little peaked sometimes. What kind of girl is she?"

"Not so nice, I'd guess you could say."

"No, no, no. I mean is she...." He bent forward, lowered his voice, "a white girl?"

"Uh, yeah."

"Thought maybe she was colored. Or maybe a Jew girl. Lebanese, we got some around here. You ever had a colored girl?"

"No."

"I had a colored mistress. She about bucked me off. How about a Mexican?"

"No."

"You've got something to look forward to, then."

"Maybe so." Wilbur couldn't tell if Kale was referring to an immediate or an indefinite future. But he was stricken in the pit of his stomach by a memory of this man sitting in the swing on the porch of the boarding house in Dallas, sitting with his mother. And another of the night in Wetoka when he looked down from his sleeping loft to see this man and his mother going out the back door of the dugout, her with a blanket.

"Some fellows say Indian women are a special treat, but I couldn't stand the stink. Make a man puke."

Kale's mood had taken a sudden side step that alerted Wilbur to something dark. Watching Kale, he said, "I don't know myself, but you know, some say the wilder the better."

Kale snorted with derision. "Some fellows fuck sheep, too. Far as I'm concerned we'd all be a whole lot better off it they'd sew up all the squaws and deball the bucks. Sheridan wanted to wipe out the whole mess of them. Too bad Grant didn't let him. Now we have to

161

live with all these savages walking around our towns and leering at our women. They might be all dressed up like white men and some preacher might've taught them a verse or two of the Bible, but a parrot can preach, you know, and you can put a gorilla in a custom-tailored suit. What I hate is knowing my own girl has reached the age where she'll be going about in the world without my protection and everywhere she turns there'll be some...."

Kale shook his head and cut into his bleeding steak. Wilbur thought with a start: That's why Kale moved his family from Wetoka to here?

"You've had some trouble?"

"Well, yes and no. Nothing I couldn't get taken care of. I saw them looking, saying things, making gestures. You take a kid like Sissy, innocent and well-intentioned, she doesn't know things. She's friendly, too friendly for her own good. Well, this young buck took it wrong." Kale's grin told Wilbur everything; the grin said, I'm glad the buck gave me a chance to do what I'd been itching to do. "I'd gut the first dirty savage who laid a finger on that girl. No, I'd cut off his pecker first." He frowned. "My grandmother. As a girl...."

Was raped by an Indian? Wilbur wondered when Kale didn't continue. It might have been some trouble less dire, but leaving it unstated invited the worst conclusion.

"In any case, I imagine it's easier to raise a son than a daughter."

Kale looked directly at him, then he winked. He gave Wilbur a peculiarly gleeful grin. It invited Wilbur to give him a cue.

"How's that?"

"Well, a daughter you try to keep from learning

about the world; a son it's your job to teach him about it." He looked at Wilbur then waved his hand toward the room, though the gesture seemed to include all of the seamy city's illicit pleasures. Kale's notion of a father-son outing would be a trip to Juarez? Was this Kale's motive for bringing him here—a kind of fatherly instruction in vice?

"You know anything about the study of genetics?"

"Not much."

"You know what happens if you put a couple of pure-bred dogs into a pen with a bunch of mutts?"

"I'd say sooner or later you wind up with all mutts."

"Exactly. And if you're trying to make a first-class orchard, you have to be careful where the bees get their pollen, am I right?"

"I'd have to take your word for it."

"Well, do. That's my philosophy. Mutts are fine but you don't pen them up with your pure-breds. Anybody with livestock can tell you that the first thing you have to learn is to breed carefully and breed for quality."

They ate in silence for a moment. Two shoeshine boys came to the table, Kale nodded to them, and each went to work silently under the table, propping first one of the men's shoes then the other up on the lids of their shoeshine boxes. Wilbur felt the boy's brush across his shoe as he ate.

"What's your philosophy of life, Hunter?"

"Oh, to get ahead, I suppose."

"That's not a philosophy, son. That's merely a plan, call it a desire. What're you going to get ahead of, what are you going to get ahead for, what means are you going to use?"

"I guess I haven't thought about it much."

"Are you a religious man, Hunter?"

"As much as the next fellow, I'd say."

"You haven't seen behind the veil, then?"

"Behind the veil?"

Kale smiled. "Of illusions."

"I don't believe everything I've been told, if that's what you mean."

"Somewhat."

The shoeshine boys surfaced and Kale paid them both. Immediately, a third child in a dirty t-shirt and bare feet appeared with a tray of packets of gum and cigarettes held by a string about his neck. Wilbur bought a pack of Fatimas.

"Chew wanna see pitchurs?" the boy asked.

"What?"

The boy leaned close, looked about furtively (though it was a practiced gesture), lifted a door under the cigarettes and extracted something flat wrapped in cellophane.

"French postcard," said Kale.

The boy sat the packet on the table and kept looking about. Kale, too, was taking quick glances around the room. Wilbur thought, a lot of people he knows probably come here.

"No?" the boy asked when neither Kale nor Wilbur made a move toward the card. He was about to retrieve it and move on when Kale said, "Take a look." He winked at Wilbur.

Wilbur slipped the cellophane sheath off the card. As he looked at it, Kale bent forward and cocked his head to see it from across the table. A woman on her back, knees up and hams exposed, a man with his root in his hand, grinning and winking at the camera. Wilbur glanced up quickly and caught a gleam in Kale's eye.

164

"How much?" Wilbur asked the boy.

"One dollar."

Wilbur paid the buck.

"You wanna fock my seester?" the boy asked Wilbur.

"She's a virgin, right?" said Kale.

"Chu bet, meester."

Kale coiled his index finger tightly against his thumb. "Leetle poosy, es correcto?"

"Si, señor. Leetle poosy."

"How much for your virgin seester with the leetle poosy?"

"Ten dollar."

The shine boys carrying their boxes whistled to the cigarette boy from the entrance. They'd made the rounds among the customers here and were about to migrate elsewhere. The boy waved them on.

"He thinks I'm a hot prospect," said Kale. "Too high," he said to the boy.

"Seven dollar for you, señor."

"How old is your leetle virgin seester with the leetle poosy?" Kale chortled.

The boy scanned Kale's face as if the girl's age were written there. "Thirteen, señor."

"Too young, muchacho."

"Fourteen next week, señor."

Kale laughed and the boy laughed with him.

"Tell you what," said Kale. "You keep your leetle virgin seester with the leetle poosy, but I'll give you a dollar just for thinking so quick."

Kale got out his wallet and gave the child a dollar bill. The boy reached under the flap in his tray and pulled out another postcard and put it on the table, then he strolled off toward the front door. Wilbur thought that the boy had either completely misunderstood Kale or understood him far better than Kale understood himself. The boy was about Pearl's age, maybe a little older. The boy's sister would be older still, but only some. To think about these children was to look into the darkness. Maybe the girl wasn't a sister, and maybe she was sixteen, not thirteen, certainly not a virgin, oh yes, Mr. Kale, let's look behind the veil. Even if the girl in question were twenty-six, did it make a difference in how this child had to live? And Kale protected his precious Sissy from "savages!"

Both cards sat on the table. Wilbur pushed them toward Kale.

"No, no." Kale protested. It was as if they were fumbling for the check.

"Please. Least I can do." If Kale didn't take them, Wilbur would be stuck with them; he could toss them into a shit can, but he'd never be able to forget where they came from and who sold them.

"Well, I do know a fellow who appreciates this kind of humor, and I owe him a favor."

Kale covered the cards with his palm and slipped them into his coat pocket.

Kale drove them to the area just west of the main drag where they went past several blocks of noisy, neon-lit bars with doorways like wide-open mouths. Women stood about in knots or leaned out of windows baiting men who strolled in groups down the cobblestone pavement. The traffic was heavy and pedestrians weaved in and out of the auto caravan. Everybody seemed drunk and in high spirits. This quarter might have been the site of an important sporting event that had just ended or was about to begin.

"Pussy paradise."

Kale parked the car and tossed a coin to an urchin to

watch it, then they struck off down the crowded side-walks bumping shoulders with cowboys, soldiers from Fort Bliss, and clumps of well-dressed Anglos in suits. Wilbur followed Kale under a blue adobe arch and into a small dirt courtyard where several older women were seated on wrought-iron chairs fanning themselves; beyond were lighted archways that allowed a view into the nightclub. Inside, the air was thick with smoke and noisy with talk and laughter. The place was jammed with men. Kale slipped a bill to a waitress, and she took them to a small table against the wall and near a low stage. Wilbur nursed a watered-down drink while a vaudeville comedian and an aging fan dancer warmed up the crowd. Then the men shouted, whistled, and tramped their feet, and the star came out to an orches-tral fanfare. She strip-teased down to pasties and a g-string, then the comedian emerged from the wings grinning and carrying a Coca-cola bottle on a velvet pil-low, and the men exploded into cheers and clapping.

"I gotta piss!" Wilbur shouted in Kale's ear.

The plumbing had broken in the men's restroom and a half inch of water stood on the floor tiles. The adobe walls were painted an aquamarine blue that soaked up the light from the single hanging bulb. A tin trough was mounted along the wall, and three solitary men were standing at it in silence. Wilbur sloshed to the trough and took his place on the left. The other men all leaned to the right. The strench of urine burned his nostrils. Outside the door, the crowd noise shot up suddenly.

"Must be missing something good," one man said.

"When you gotta go, you gotta go," said another.

When the others left, Wilbur stood about for a moment. No sink, no mirror, no crapper—only the trough, a light, a stench, water creeping into his soles. He didn't want to stay, but he didn't want to return to the table. He slipped out of the restroom, passed along the bar as the donkey was being led onto the stage to a thunderous ovation, and walked out into the courtyard. He stood, stretching, then lit a cigarette. The courtyard was dim, and the sky was a coal-and-diamonds display, the stars sharp cold points and the new moon a black disc rimmed in silver and set against a black sky. Aztec moon, he thought, swallowed by the night.

"Round the world?"

One of the three old whores seated in the shadows about a wrought-iron table had addressed him but with no apparent expectation of success.

"No graciás." He smiled at her. They were drinking something out of tall glasses. Before them on the table was a plate holding a stack of corn tortillas.

"You no like the show?"

Wilbur shrugged then walked away to an empty table and sat. The whores returned to chatting among themselves like housewives over coffee. He leaned back and peered into the blackness overhead, heard a whir of wings—an owl? Nighthawk? Then it all blurred and his cheeks were cool where the breeze touched the wetness. A year ago, one night in their backyard, lying on a blanket, holding hands, Pearl between them, humming herself to sleep. I'm lucky, he said. Bobette said, I'm lucky too.

If he'd known what lay ahead, he would've secured a poison, fed it to them and swallowed it himself.

He rose and went back inside, where the comedian was coming onstage to close out the first floor show.

"Where you been? You miss it?"

"Naw, I was watching back by the bar."

"How about that?"

"That's something, all right."

Kale got up, hitched his trousers. "Damn!" He was grinning from one side of his mouth. "You see that?"

"Yeah."

"Damn! She took that thing!"

They followed the crowd out of the club, through the courtyard, and into the street. The men were boisterous, laughing, and yelling to one another. "Jeez, that was disgusting!" somebody said. "Yeah, wadn't it, though?" another answered him merrily, and they both exploded into laughter. Hyenas!

"Fellow told me about a place. What do you think?"

"Fine with me."

"He says it's clean."

"Okay."

Kale gave him a searching look. "We'll have some fun."

"Sure."

Apparently satisfied, Kale lengthened his stride and turned down a side street; within a block, they reached another open archway, and Kale passed under it and onto a tiled patio brightly illuminated by lights strung across the space. A trio of musicians was playing a lively, bouncing tune, and the patio was packed with couples dancing. They took a table, and within seconds two women in peasant blouses and full red skirts had come to the table. They wore heavy lipstick, rouge on their cheeks, and their Spanish combs were pitchforked into their hair. One seemed to recognize Kale; she called him "Meester Jones" and sat on Kale's lap. The other tried to sit on Wilbur's, but he pulled a chair closer and ushered her into it. Kale kissed the other woman and ran his hand up her skirt.

"Oh, Señor Jones!"

"Damn!" Kale laughed. "Let me feel that thing."

"Buy me a drink?" The woman beside Wilbur was wall-eyed, and her left front tooth was gold. Wilbur shrugged. The "drinks" arrived on the instant, as if by magic. Kale paid $10. Wilbur's tasted faintly of champagne. The whores' would be nothing but water, he guessed. Soon, Kale was pawing at the woman with such persistence that she rose and pulled him up. "See you later." He winked at Wilbur.

The wall-eyed woman took Wilbur past the bar, down a long dim hallway, and into a small room furnished with a bed and a washbasin on a stand. The walls were a deep blue.

"Momentito." The women pinched the air with her thumb and index finger and vanished through the curtain into the hallway.

He sat on the bed, then, feeling beat, lay back with his feet on the floor. The plaster in the yellow ceiling was cracked like baked creek mud. What was Kale doing? A stinking hypocrite, keeping his daughter locked up as if her virginity were a precious treasure to be hoarded then slipping off down here as soon as his wife's not watching. Fellow told him about this place? Yes, well I'm looking behind the veil of illusion, Meester Jones. He's indignant and all choked up because some Indian looked twice at his grandmother, thinks that they're all going to take a grab at his daughter; it's pretty clear how he excuses his murders. Getting even. And how did anybody know that grandmother was raped? Maybe the grandmother only yelled rape, maybe she and the Indian got caught, and nobody in the family would admit that their precious virgin white women would want an Indian's affection or attention. God only knows what happened to that poor redskin.

So the hate goes on. Kale had carried it into his generation, thinking of getting even, but that was just a lame excuse for his own savagery and greed. No wonder he was concerned about that daughter, what with him swindling and murdering any Indian in Wetoka County who had the misfortune to become rich.

The daughter was how the Indians could get even with him.

You want to know my philosophy of life, Mr. Kale? It's imagining the most satisfying way to torture you.

Maybe I've found it.

Restless, he sat up. Music and laughter came from the patio. Shadows flitted along the wall from moving lights outside the small high window in the room. Spanish. He could smell piss and something sweet but acrid, like sugar burning. He was bleary from the drinks he'd consumed; anger had kept him propped up and alert, but now he sagged as exhaustion and sadness sank down on him like a damp weight. He'd thought his grief would kill him when Bobette died, but he'd kept himself alive for Pearl and to bring to justice whoever had killed Bobette. He hadn't bargained on descending into a hell such as this to get it done. But there seemed no way back. And the sooner Kale was brought to justice, the sooner Wilbur could find a way out of this life.

The woman came back and tossed the towel she was carrying onto the bed. A crucifix was mounted over the bedstead, and, facing it, she discreetly genuflected.

"Why are you praying?"

The women, startled, turned to look at him. "No babies."

"Not for sin?"

"Sí, that too."

"It helps?"

She shrugged, smiled. "I have four babies."

"No, for sin, I meant. It helps to feel better? Clean?"

The wall-eyed women sat on the bed. "I don't know. I have always done it. When I don't do it, then I will know, maybe."

The interview seemed to have thrown off her rhythm; when Wilbur let a silence stand between them, she leered and pulled the elastic top of her blouse down to her waist.

"You like my teetees?"

Wilbur nodded; the woman rose and glided toward him with her arms out.

"Wait."

"You don't want to fock?"

"No."

"What do you want, señor?"

"I want to watch Mr. Jones."

The women gave him a look of bemusement but didn't move. He flushed and thought of saying that he had no interest in Mr. Jones's sexual practices, but he owed the woman no explanation. And why did he want to watch? It was hard to define. Know thine enemy.

He took out his wallet, removed a $10 bill and gave it to her. She inspected it briefly, then said, "My friend, she get mad if she knows I do this." He added a $5 bill, and, satisfied, she led him out of the room.

Going down the dark hall he slipped his hand into his coat pocket and wrapped his hand around the razor's cold shaft. He should have gotten a gun a long time ago. Something you could protect yourself with if somebody jumped you. Be hard to get the razor out of his pocket.

The woman led him into a dark room and through an archway on the far side of it, into another hallway, through still another room, once stopping to peek through a cracked door and shaking her head, then they eventually arrived in another dark room, where she stopped abruptly, and he bumped into her. A curtain on a doorway on the far side of the room was outlined by a reddish light. The woman held a finger to her mouth, then used it to point toward the doorway.

He crept to the curtain. He felt self-conscious to be spying, but when he turned around, his guide had vanished. Behind the curtain he heard breathing, the comic squeak of bedsprings. With his finger, Wilbur edged the curtain away from the doorframe. The room was suffused with a red light from candles in crimson glasses. Wavering shadows were flung onto the wall facing him. From his position behind the curtain, he couldn't see the bed or its occupants, only their silhouettes. Someone was grunting in a steady rhythm. The semaphor of shadows was hard to read. The woman must be on her hands and knees. The other, reared at her behind. Slap slap. Wet smack like shoes lifting out of mud. Grunt. Ahhss!—sharp intake, an audible wince—the woman hurt. On the wall the man's head had projections like horns. Huff huff huff. When Wilbur drew the curtain farther aside, the foot of the bed came into view. They must be faced to the far wall. He gripped the razor and bent forward to see more. Shoe soles, pointed toes pointed down, together, like hooves. Still shod. All he had to do was unfold the razor, take two steps into the room and bring it down over the neck like a guillotine. Everything would be over. His pain would find its equal weight in Kale's blood, the scales balanced. Just a little more now.

He glimpsed a ruddy haunch like a baboon's rear with a deep black crack between the cheeks like a tail folded into it. A hog squeal. His nape prickled and his scalp burned; fear zipped up and down his spine and jolted in his skull. He turned away. The image of the hooves and tail burned in the darkness. Kale looked like some devil, billygoating the woman so that her head banged against the wall.

Holding his breath, he put a trembling finger back to the curtain but didn't move it. The sounds were unearthly to his ears. The flickering bloody light on the rim of the curtain. He felt a little dizzy. Mind playing tricks. No, it must be just a human man taking his pleasure, not the Devil. Only primitives. He never believed there was one; is this the moment he discovers otherwise? Look behind the veil. He walks the earth in the form of man named Kale. He was chilled all over; he was sweating. He couldn't breathe without fear of being discovered. The darkness surrounding him turned malign and he was glowing in it. His enemy and he were far from the law; they were in another dimension now. Where he could get no help.

He fled.

▣   ▣   ▣

On Wednesday after the trip to Juarez, Wilbur came back from lunch to find Kale's Chrysler Six parked at the curb. Jo Kale, dressed in a gray suit that highlighted her pale pink jowls, got out of the car and carried a flat department store box into the bank. Seated on the passenger side was Kale's daughter. Her head was bent down; she was flipping through a magazine. He stepped to her open window and leaned with a palm on the roof.

"Hello."

Startled, she looked up. On her forehead was a thick

smudge of charcoal or ash shaped like a cross. She had high cheekbones, crow-colored hair and bold dark eyes, but her face was narrow and her thin nose looked like the blade of an instrument. The cute kid on the pony had vanished. That photographer had sure known which side his bread was buttered on.

"Oh, hi. I know you." She slapped the magazine shut and turned it face down in her lap.

"You do?"

"Sure. You work in there."

He grinned. "Okay, Smarty. What do I do?"

"You work for Daddy."

"Well, I work with him."

"Do you tell him what to do?"

"No."

"Does he tell you what to do?"

"I guess."

"You guess?" She snorted. "That's funny, everybody else in the world who has to take his orders knows it for sure, I can tell you that." She glanced toward the bank, puffed her cheeks and blew out a breath. Temporarily at a loss, Wilbur said, "Well, I've seen your pictures on his desk. Just wanted to say hello, that's all." He pushed away from the car.

"Oh, I'm sorry I'm being so ungracious," she said quickly. "I'm just mad, and you're in the line of fire."

"It's okay."

She smiled by pulling up one corner of her wide mouth. "Are you a frontiersman?" When he looked blank, she rubbed her chin.

The gesture was as infectious as a yawn; he rubbed his chin, the mat of wiry curls. He couldn't meet her eye.

"Aw, no. Razor rash. Skin condition."

"I think beards make men look wise and kind of rugged."

"Maybe I'll keep it then." He caught her gaze, and she colored.

"I meant in general, you know." The dark pupils of her large eyes darted to and fro in panic. "Oh, not that I don't like yours, I mean."

Her gaze cut to the bank; Wilbur turned, saw Jo Kale now holding the door open while talking to someone inside. He murmured, "Nice to meet you" to the girl and moved away from the car. Coming out, her mother passed him without recognition. She had that same ash smudge on her forehead that made Wilbur think of firing squad victims.

Later in his room, Wilbur mulled over this exchange with the girl. Everybody else in the world has to take his orders. She sure wasn't happy about it. What was behind that?

Didn't Kale's calendar have him off to some Chamber of Commerce do tonight? He located the home number and asked the operator to connect him. The girl answered after two rings.

"Hello, again. This is the fellow you met this afternoon. Is your father in?"

"Will Hunter?"

"Yes." Had he told her that name?

"No, they're out for the evening. Should I tell him you called?"

"Uh, no, thanks anyway. It's nothing important. I was just wondering, maybe he could give me some ideas about something. But, say, maybe you can help. Do you have a minute?"

"Sure."

"I'm not interrupting anything, am I?"

"I was studying."

"Oh, what were you studying?"

"Latin, geography, calculus. You can write that down."

Bobette saying Only college kids. "Calculus?"

"C-a-l-c-u-l-u-s."

Say, that's pretty tough stuff."

"I like it."

"You must be a smart cookie."

A lull fell. She wasn't helping him much. "What's your favorite subject?"

"Why do you want to know?"

"Just curious, I guess."

"Don't you want to know what I'm going to do when I finish studying?"

"Sure, if you want to tell me."

"You could say I'm going to sleep."

"Okay, that sounds reasonable."

She scoffed. "Want me to spell it for you?"

Did she have him confused with someone else? "You sound like you're still mad."

"Yeah. You can write that down, too."

"Okay, but where am I going to write all this down?"

"In your report."

"What report?"

"You work for my Daddy, don't you?"

"Holy cow, kid! You think I'm a spy or something?"

"Maybe. Are you?"

He laughed; the idea was genuinely funny. "Gosh, no. Actually, I was kind of hoping you wouldn't let him know we were talking."

"Really? Why not?"

"I guess because he's so particular about who strikes up a conversation with you."

"Stop the presses."

His chuckling vibrated over the wire and she giggled, as if pleased with herself. "Hold it. This chair—" A grunt, a rustle, then her voice was closer in his ear. "So what was your question?"

"My question? Oh, well, I'm new in town, and I was wondering what a single fellow might do for entertainment."

"You were going to ask him that? That's rich!"

"Why?"

"He'd say head for Whore—ez."

He laughed. "Juarez?"

"Yeah. So what's keeping you?"

"I guess I didn't have that kind of thing in mind. Actually, to be honest, I wasn't really thinking of asking him. I thought maybe somebody like you might know."

"Me, I never get to go anywhere."

"Well, since the two of us are pretty new to having fun around here, maybe we could find something together."

There was a long pause. Wilbur tried to imagine, as he often did when talking with Pearl, where the girl was sitting.

"Are you sure he doesn't know you're making this call?"

"Yes."

"Well, Will Hunter, it sounds like a good idea, but there's just no chance. Haven't you read the rule book?"

"No."

"It says Sissy Kale will not go out with older men; it says Sissy Kale will not date anyone who doesn't go to our church and whose parents are not known to him; it says Sissy Kale will not go on any dates anywhere that he is not present as a chaperone, and that pretty well limits it to Sunday afternoon socials and highly supervised tea dances; it says in effect that Sissy Kale is under house arrest."

"That's pretty strict. What are you, seventeen?"

"I'll be eighteen in two weeks and two days, thank God!"

"You suppose maybe I could talk to him and—"

"No! Don't!" Her voice shook. As if to explain her panic, she added, "It's, well, there's a history to all this. Don't bring it up. Please."

He guessed his plans were scotched, but she said, after a moment, "He can't know."

"Then you'll go out with me anyway?"

"Yes."

"How come?" He worried that being put on the spot might embarrass her, so he added, "Never mind."

"No, that's okay. I guess I'll go because you asked. You're talking to a girl with an empty dance card."

She said she could meet him Saturday at one o'clock in San Jacinto Plaza. He waited by the alligator pit at the appointed time and was about to give up on her at 1:30 when she stepped from the Chrysler in the middle of Oregon, blew a kiss to the driver—her mother?— and, on seeing him, waved and came across the plaza. She was wearing a flapper's cloche hat and a dress with a short hem and a dropped waistline, and when she approached where he stood leaning on the parapet over the dozing alligators, he was astonished to realize that she was over six feet tall. Her long straight arms had no muscle; they were like tubes on hinges. She was a goofy-looking kid. Her flat-heeled black shoes were shaped like long canoes.

She came close, but just out of arm's length she sank down on a bench with her back to the parapet, halving her height.

"Sorry I'm late. We had trouble getting away."

"Who was it brought you?"

"Mother."

He looked about but the Chrysler had vanished. "Did you tell her—"

"I said I was meeting a friend to go to a movie."

"Is that what you want to do?"

"Sure." She shrugged. "I guess. That's fine."

"I checked the paper. *Modern Marriage* is on at the Sphinx Club."

"Ugh!"

He laughed. Across the street, on Oregon, at the Plaza Theatre, a line was forming for the 2 o'clock show. "There's the Plaza."

She twisted about and squinted at the distant marquee. "What's it say?"

She was too vain to wear her glasses, he guessed. "Something called *Dangerous Paradise*."

Later, when they came out into the strong spring sunlight, the park was full of people enjoying the balmy afternoon, and they strolled about for awhile, slowly, ceremonially, in step. He had the feeling she wanted him to take her hand. Once the back of hers brushed the back of his as their arms swung. She'd seemed indifferent about going to the picture, but once inside she'd bent forward and frowned earnestly at the screen and never once glanced at him or whispered or moved in any way that suggested she wanted what boys were supposed to do in a dark theatre. The picture had a Valentino lookalike playing a sheik who rescues an English girl from an Arab bent on selling her into slavery. Bobette would have loved it; she went for farfetched romantic stuff.

This girl didn't want anybody to take her for a sucker, however.

"Movie bunk sometimes makes me mad."

"How come?"

"Because they try to make you think it's real. I don't believe that most men would go to all that trouble for a girl, you know risk their lives, and all she's done is wiggle around and scream her head off when the villain gets within ten feet of her."

"Heroes aren't most men; most men aren't heroes."

"Well, that's true, for certain. I don't know any heroes."

"Neither does anybody else—that's why we like them in the pictures, I guess. Somebody to look up to."

The phrase was like a cue for him to turn his head and catch her glance above his own, and, worried that she'd think he'd made a pun on her height, he suggested that they sit, though the way she colored slightly as they did made him worry that he'd only made things worse. They sat in an awkward silence. A group of soldiers strolled by with girls on their arms. From a man pushing a cart he bought two candied apples on sticks; he soon abandoned his because the caramel coating flaked and stuck in his beard, but Sissy worked on hers with a determined relish and never glanced his way—she ate it seeds and all until the pointed stick it had been impaled upon was slick as freshly whittled wood and damp from her saliva.

"Would you do that for a girl?"

"What?" His mind clicked like a ratchet, then—"Oh, you mean rescue her?"

"Risk your life."

He thought of the handsome sheik, tried to fit himself into that place. He laughed. "I'm no hero. I told you that."

"What if she was special?"

He shrugged. "I guess I would, then, if she was special enough." What was she driving at? The question seemed only academic until she said, doggedly, "Has there ever been anyone special enough for you to do that?"

"No." He looked away. His face burned. Lying about it seemed a betrayal; yes, I would've traded places with Bobette had I been given the choice, and gladly. And I'd do it for my own daughter. He wished he felt free to say this aloud where Bobette might hear it were her spirit hovering about.

"See. The pictures aren't real life."

"I never said they were. They're just stuff people wish."

"They're not about what I wish."

He looked at her, his interest piqued. "And what's that?"

"Lots of stuff." She nodded toward the walk. "You see them?" A Mexican mother was passing, a baby wrapped in a shawl at her breast, trailed by a son, a daughter about Pearl's age, and two niños clad in their Sunday best strung behind like ducklings. "I wish I would have been born into that family."

"Why?"

"All those kids. You could be in the middle, not the oldest or the youngest. You could kind of soak up the family feeling and still not be noticed too much."

Pearl always wanted brothers and sisters. "You don't like being an only child?"

"You kidding? People think you're really spoiled, but there's a lot of responsibility to it. You have to keep everybody happy, and that's really hard to do when they make you take sides, and you go from one side to the other and wish you could just get out of the way. I think that's why I really like school so much — it's got nothing to do with either of them, it's mine alone."

"Whose side are you usually on?"

She shrugged. "Mother's, I guess, but that's because she at least talks to me. She wants to be my friend. Too much so, sometimes I think. She tells me stuff I don't always want to hear. She nicknamed me Sissy because that's what she called her own sister." She laughed suddenly, struck by a new thought. "I guess it's like we're both daughters, the way he lords it over us."

"What do they fight about?"

"Nothing in particular. It's more the way he treats us. He rules with an iron fist and he doesn't mind using it." She sighed. "I guess I shouldn't air the dirty family linen. Especially...."

When she didn't continue, he said, "You can talk to me about your problems, Sissy. I was an only child, too, and I sure don't know a soul here in town to gossip with."

"No, it's really nothing. I guess I shouldn't gripe." Besides—" She gave him a quick sidelong glance. "It's probably not very becoming for a girl to sound troubled."

The lefthanded confession that she wanted to be attractive charmed him. He smiled. "Oh, I don't think you sound troubled, Sissy. You're sure a frank person, though."

"I am?" She sounded genuinely surprised.

"Sure, you don't seem to worry about people knowing what's on your mind."

A tattered net of pigeons was flung over them and onto the walk. Broken out of formation, the birds strutted like aimless windup toys, beaks pecking air. Sissy bent over, retrieved something small and white from the ground and tossed it into the flock, but they failed to notice. Wilbur wondered what to say. Sissy's candor invited something reciprocal, perhaps even obliged it, but such would be impossible. They might have a thousand dates and still he could never tell her more than she knew right now. He couldn't even tell her he knew her when she was just a kid, let alone that her father could count his own mother among his conquests. This girl would never know him. By his second date with Bobette, he'd told her about his mother and the way she went with men and Atlas and his life in the boarding house, and only after he'd already revealed these things did he realize that the girl who had been a total stranger a week before was now the repository of his life's history. Bobette had become the only other person alive on the planet who knew both where he was and where he'd come from. If she were here, Bobette would be jabbering about that stupid picture. Her pleasure would ring through her voice, and listening to her talk about it would be like hearing cheerful music. She would be sitting here chattering away, and he'd slip his arm about her shoulders and bask in the moment like sunbathing. Pearl rushing up to tell or show them something....

Dabs of shit glistened like oil paint on the walk. The birds stepped in it. Their incessant busy meandering dizzied him. He closed his eyes, leaned his head back, saw spots. He clenched his jaw. What was he doing here with this girl? The other night in Juarez, that weird hallucination of Kale as the Devil. Wilbur had only been worked up, half drunk, sure. But something he'd seen in that room had repelled him, roughly shoved his gaze around like a magnet reversed. The two of them had crossed a line. He'd meant to strike but started shaking. Then he'd held back because to kill Kale was to relinquish the opportunity to make him suffer. This girl—he wanted a closer look at whatever Kale valued highly.

"The thing is, Will, I guess I'm not that way with everybody."

"What?"

"I said—"

"Oh, I know. Sorry."

"You see, I can't talk to Mother about herself and I can't talk to Daddy about himself, and I can't talk to Mother about Daddy without her feeling I'm taking sides, and I can't talk to him about her for the same reason."

Shut up! Shut up! His gut was churning; he swallowed. I don't want to hear about Daddy.

"And I can't talk to either one about me." She presented him with a smile of gratitude as if it were a gift, and he had to blink and turn away.

"How about a teacher, a minister, maybe a girl-friend?"

"They're not good listeners the way you are."

He bolted up from the bench and jammed his fists into his trouser pockets. Off in the gazebo, an orchestra was setting up. A horn went blat, something squealed. His calves quivered.

"Maybe you shouldn't tell people too much."

"Why not?" She was speaking to his back.

"I dunno. You might get hurt, maybe."

"It's a chance you take, I guess."

Well, he'd given her fair warning. He turned, passed her as much of a smile as he could muster; she returned it, her swollen black pupils a quivering, glistening jelly. She recorded his slightest movements with a studious devotion that unnerved him.

"Don't you have to be somewhere?"

"I'm supposed to meet Mother at Popular Dry Goods at closing time."

"I don't want you to get into trouble on my account—I guess you better go."

Sissy rose slowly and stuck out her hand for him to shake. She had long fingers and a firm grip.

"Thank you very much, Mr. Will Hunter, for taking me to see *Dangerous Paradise* even though I complained about it. I hope I haven't scared you off by being such a whiner."

He scanned her face for playful irony but found none. It was a speech one might give a neighbor for doing one a favor of some sacrifice. He couldn't suppress his grin; he'd give her one thing—she could be winning. "Well, you're quite welcome, Sissy."

"So we can meet again?"

"Sure!"

"Good. You know, I just figured out why I like it that you're older."

"Why's that?"

"It makes you as tall as me."

He laughed. "If you say so."

"I do. And, also, will you do me a favor?"

"What's that?"

"Could you walk away first? I can't stand the idea of you standing here watching my back while I'm going. It makes me die of embarrassment just to think about it."

"Okay. But you're a goofy kid, you know that?"

She shrugged. She stood waiting with her hands clasped over her waist, and it dawned on him for the first time that she wasn't carrying a purse.

"Bye." He turned and walked toward the side of the

Plaza opposite from his hotel. Her eyes burned into his back.

▣ ▣ ▣

Sissy called Wilbur at the bank Monday afternoon; she'd just learned from her mother that her father would be out of town Tuesday and Wednesday nights. Wilbur was surprised that Kale hadn't mentioned this, but he confirmed it by sneaking a look Kale's calendar—entries for Tuesday, Wednesday and Thursday had been erased. What did that mean?

He called her back. "What would you like to do?"

"We can't really go anywhere, but you can meet me? Soon as it's dark, come and park behind the auditorium at my school. There's a play going on, and I'm supposed to be working on the stage crew, but they don't really need me, and I can come out and find you. Don't you think that's a swell plan?"

She had the air of a child plotting an adventure, and he smiled. How did a monster like Kale produce a child so charming and innocent?

The moon, half full, cast shadows with its ivory light; he parked under an elm on the street behind the Episcopal church and school complex, where the rear auditorium door—a windowless rectangle darker than its surrounding brick—was clearly visible. The orange tips of his cigarettes were metronomic in their arcs to and from his mouth; the glow was oddly comforting, a smidgeon of fire in the chilly darkness.

Eventually she emerged, wearing her hair pinned up, a pair of men's trousers and a man's white shirt with the tails of it knotted at her waistline. The car door squawked when she got in.

"Oh, I'm so glad you came by! I just knew you wouldn't!"

"Why wouldn't I?"

"Oh, because. I should keep my trap shut. It sounds too pitiful. What've you been doing?"

"Working." He urged himself on. "Missing you."

"Oh, you didn't."

"Yes, I did."

"What did you miss?"

"Talking to somebody. You know, feeling like I had a friend. Like I told you, I'm new in town."

"How about California, where you came from, don't you have friends there?"

Had he said he was from there? "Sure, I had friends. But they're not here. I got the feeling after we were together on Saturday that you could be a new friend."

"Gee, I'd like that, too."

"Well, that's settled then." He stuck out his hand and she shook it. "Didn't you say your father's going to be out of town tomorrow night, too?"

"Yes."

"Where'd he go, anyway?"

"He went to Wetoka—it's a little town in Oklahoma where we came from."

Wilbur's heart thundered once in the hollow of his chest. "What—business? Pleasure?"

"I dunno. Who cares?"

"Only curious. So what have you been doing?"

She talked nonstop for a time about her school. Chums, classes, teachers, the scratchy wool skirts they had to wear, the stupid play she had to work in to get credit for Drama, an essay she had to write about proper home hygiene. She sounded very young to him tonight. She had an only child's total absorption with herself, and he drifted off. What was her father doing in Wetoka? Since Wilbur had secretly pried into Kale's files at the bank looking for incriminating evidence and had found none, he wondered if Kale kept any documents in his home office. Maybe since Kale was gone, Sissy would sneak him into it. But on what pretext?

She brought him back by leaning over him to roll down his window and toss her gum out. The cranking motions of her arm made her breasts brush against him. She smelled of something floral mingled with turpentine.

"She wants me to go to Stephens College in Missouri. That's where she went. But he keeps saying junk like, 'Don't push the girl out of her house. She doesn't have to go anywhere until she's ready.' And of course he knows damn good and well how ready I am! But I don't know for sure what I want to be."

She frowned at the windshield. "Maybe a doctor. I think about that sometimes."

"Not a nurse?"

"No. Like in deepest Africa, wearing khaki and one of those pith helmets. Helping natives. Maybe I would study abnormalities."

"Most girls would think about having a family."

She shrugged. "Oh, sure. Maybe. But not unless the father wanted a whole lot of children. Not just one."

"What if you married somebody who didn't want any?"

"I wouldn't. I mean, I really don't want to get married to anybody."

"Really? Why not? It's the most wonderful thing that can happen to a person. I guess."

"Maybe because I'm not prettier than my mother, and look what happened to her—a man only married her because her family had land and money."

"Now how do you know that?"

"She told me."

"Why does she stay with him?"

"Maybe it took her too long to figure it out. And then because they had me, and I'm the best thing that ever happened to her."

It sounded like a slogan. "You're a lot prettier than she is, you know. Some man will marry you for yourself."

He'd said it to soften her up, thinking she'd roll over to have her belly scratched on hearing it—or else deny it to hear it repeated. But she said, "Yeah, I guess I know that, most days. I am too tall, but I have good eyes, good cheekbones, and I got Daddy's hair. It's just like yours—thick and black. I'm also a lot smarter than she, even if she did go to Stephens College in Missouri. I wouldn't let anybody take me unawares."

The auditorium door banged open against the wall, and several members of the stage crew came out and stood stretching. "Guess I better go." She opened the noisy door. "Will you take me some place grown-up tomorrow night?"

"Sure. Where?"

"You think of it, okay?"

◘　◘　◘

The urge to take her to Juarez prodded him with an insistence strong as the creature need to migrate. He kept fighting it because she was too innocent for such

a sordid setting. But why protect her? He rejected playing an overprotective brother and instead relished
exposing Kale's child to something seamy. Any way he
could harm the man, he would.

Sissy was thrilled. "Oh, let's, let's!" she yelped over
the phone. "Let's celebrate! Tomorrow we may die!"

He was worried that she might be recognized by an
acquaintance of her father's in Kale's favorite restaurant, so he chose another. It was a barny place with
black and white tile floor, potted palms, an orchestra.
She had three glasses of champagne in quick succes-
sion despite his warnings, and color rose up her long
neck like the plumage on a tropical bird. She grinned
woozily at him, her chin propped in her palms, elbows
and arms two sides to a bony triangle. He coaxed her to
eat her steak.

"Tell me about Cal - eye - forn - ya here I come. I
want to hear about movie stars. Did you know any
movie stars?"

Copperfield. Copperfield's witch-wife Laura and the
would-be "director" the woman shacked up with
behind the Indian's back. Sissy's father's co-conspirator.
What a bunch! Dopers. Scum. Murderers.

"Yeah. Nobody you'd know, though. I guess they
weren't stars. Actors and actresses, more like it. Extras,
you know."

"I thought movie stars were all over out there, like
orange trees and sunshine and the ocean."

"Sure—ask the Chamber of Commerce."

"I wish I lived out there instead of here." She sighed,
looked dreamy. "I wished I lived about anywhere but
here."

"What's wrong with here?"

She made a face. "It's not here. It's who." She rolled

her chin onto one palm and raised crossed fingers in the air. "But soon I'll be eighteen."

"And then?"

"Whatever I want, that's what."

"What's that?"

"Haven't decided."

"You think that's what it means to be grown up? You get to do whatever you want?" He meant to chide gently, but her innocence, her self-absorption with her own future, and her well-being—her golden, unspoiled health—suddenly plunged his soul in gall.

If she caught the biting undertone, she ignored it. "Yes and no. Some grown-ups I know do, some don't. I give you my father to exemplumfy the former and my mother the lat - ter." She went morose for a moment, then said, "Oh, hell, Will, let's dance!"

He wasn't much good at it, but fortunately it only required using himself to prop the girl upright and shuffling about in time to the music. She hung her chin over his shoulder but cocked her head and her warm breath huffed in his ear. One arm roped all the way around his back to his opposite shoulder and pulled him close. The material of her dress was thin. Her body felt warm, her palm damp. She hummed off-key to the music. Her slender legs kept brushing across his loins. He swallowed.

"Are you sure you want to dance?"

"Oh gosh, yes! Don't you?"

"I was afraid maybe you were getting dizzy from the champagne."

"Yes, yes, I am!" She bent back to look at him. "It's wonderful."

She snared him with that long arm again and clung to him. She laughed in his ear. "I was thinking of all the tea-dances where I've had to dance with silly little boys and I'd be about a foot taller, you know? I always about died of embarrassment. But now I know there was some reason. I was practicing for this." She pushed her long lean form snugly against his belly and his chest.

They danced two more numbers, then she went off to the powder room. He sat at the table and thought of Kale's taking him to the donkey show and the whorehouse. Kale winking, nudging him with an elbow. Mr. Jones, they called him. A regular. Sissy, I've heard about a show down here in "Whore-ez," they say it's a dandy. Like a circus act. Might be worth seeing.

Sissy came back to the table flushed and bright-eyed. "Will, some women in the girls' room were talking about going to a gambling casino. Couldn't we go there?"

"Aw, Sissy, they're just gyp joints for tourists."

"Can we go somewhere else?"

Maybe she'd like to see the room where her father took the whore on her hands and knees? Maybe she'd like to sit at the table where her father watched a woman screw a donkey?

But he didn't have it in him to take her there. Not at the moment.

"I'm feeling kind of beat, kiddo. I had a hard day at work. And tomorrow's school for you."

"Okay." Her eyes fell.

"I'm sorry to funk out on you."

She raised her eyes. "I understand. I'm just afraid, you know?"

"Of what?"

"That this will be the only night we'll have."

"How about when you turn 18?"

"Oh, sure. It's not rational. But I never can argue with my fears, they won't listen. Promise me this won't be the last night we ever have any fun?"

"Cross my heart and hope to die."

He had picked her up in front of her school, but on their way back to El Paso she told him to drop her off at her house.

"Won't your mother know you were with me?"

"Nah. She'll be asleep."

"Aren't you afraid she'll wake up?"

Sissy shrugged. "When she's asleep not even dynamite will wake her."

Kale's office. Dropping Sissy off at home suddenly posed the chance for taking a look. He parked just down the street and turned off the motor. The moon waxed three-quarters full, a sliver more than last night, and in this treeless suburb the car was exposed under its glow. On the barren ground laid out before them boulders stood in puddles of shadow and made the landscape appear lunar.

"I'd like to see your room sometime."

"Really? Oooo! That would be fun, Will."

He laughed. Her responses were unpredictable. "Well, it would help to satisfy my curiosity, anyway."

"About what?"

"I can't put my finger on it exactly. Being in it would make me know a little more about you."

"So you want to, huh? That's a good sign. When?"

"Sometime."

"Why not tonight?"

"Tonight? But how about your mother?"

"I said don't worry about her. She won't wake up. Even if she does, like I told you, she wants to be my friend. Come on!"

She led him over the barren lighted lot in mock tip-toeing, one raised finger to her lips, her brows miming secrecy like a silent picture actress. They went along the perimeter of the brick fence, through a back gate, and when they reached the rear entry to the house, she reached above the header, produced a hidden key with a magician's flourish, and opened the door.

In the first dim room they encountered, she bent close, bumped into him, grabbed his arm to right herself, and whispered, "This is the kitchen." She pressed a hand to her mouth to stifle a giggle, kept the other clutched about his forearm. She tugged at him, so he let her lead him along like a blind man's guide. They passed under an arch. Light filtering through the drapes outlined a large table; the high rounded chairs pressed to it looked in the gloom like heads on torsos, a board meeting of mummies.

"Nobody really eats here," Sissy said.

A closed door led off the dining room. He jerked his head toward it.

"Daddy's study."

"Can you show it to me?" He worried that his trembling would communicate through his flesh to her guiding hand and invite suspicion, but she merely nodded. She released him, stepped to a sideboard, slid open a drawer, fished in the back of it, then led him to the door. It was locked. The latch clacked when she turned the key, and he jumped.

The door eased open without a sound. They crept in and she shut it behind them. It was pitch dark.

"I can't see a thing."

"Wait." She left him. He heard her shuffling, bumping into something, giggling. A scratching sound. Tink.

A light sprang up. Sissy was bent over the desk to

reach a lamp. Greedily, he noted a bookshelf behind the desk, two file cabinets, then caught her grin as she stood upright and pointed to the wall on his right.

"Look."

Heads, mounted. In the shadows their features were indistinct. A lion. Sissy came close, clutched his bicep with both hands and dropped her cheek against his shoulder.

"When I was little I gave them names. Ronald Rhino." She tittered. "That's Andy the Antelope."

He stood gawking, eagerly making mental notes, but she yanked him toward the desk.

"Looky." She turned a latch on the top desk drawer, slid it open and pulled out a pistol. She brought it into the shower of light pouring from the desk lamp. She held it with one hand and stroked the blue-steel barrel with her finger.

"Feel it, Will!" she whispered.

"It might be loaded, Sissy."

"It is."

He passed his hand along the oiled metal cylinder and Sissy then put the pistol back into the drawer.

"Come on!"

Then she'd turned the light off and was pulling him out of the study. In the dining room, she stepped to the sideboard to replace the key.

"You didn't lock it back," he whispered.

"Oh!" She went back to the door, inserted the key; it set with the same loud clack.

"Shh!" Sissy said, then smothered another giggle. Coming back to the sideboard, she bumped into the table; it squealed against the floor, and Sissy was struck by a fit of choked-back laughter. She doubled over silently, shaking. Then she straightened up, gasped for breath. She read the look of alarm on his face.

"I can't help it. Come on, let's go to my room."

She reached across for his hand, but footsteps thumped on the second floor and a light turned on upstairs was rushed down the stairwell onto the landing outside the dining room. Sissy grabbed him; he looked quickly at her face for a cue, but she was not frightened.

"Sissy?"

Sissy squiggled her eyebrows comically, cleared her throat. "Yes, mother?"

"Is that you?"

"Yes, mother."

"Who were you talking to?"

"I was on the phone."

"Oh, well, go to bed now, dear."

"Yes, mother."

The light stayed on, but they traced the steps across the ceiling, then a door closed. Wilbur let out a breath. He wanted to leave, but Sissy held them both frozen for a long moment. Then she stepped toward the landing, grabbing his elbow.

"Come on."

"Where?"

"Upstairs to my room."

"No! You're nuts!" he hissed. "She'll hear us. I'm going to go before I get you into trouble."

He retraced his path to the rear entry, and she tagged behind. At the back door, she held out her hand for him to shake.

"Thanks again, Will Hunter. Now I'm going to go gush to my diary. I feel more like a grown woman after tonight."

A flicker of fear zipped down his spine. "I hope nobody ever reads it but you."

"Of course not. That's what diaries are for—I'd be mortified."

He tried to break her grip to leave, but she hung on. "I'm not doing anything on Saturday but shopping downtown with Mother."

He smiled. "What a coincidence. I was planning on being in the plaza about one o'clock."

"Oh, great! I didn't ask you for a date, did I?"

"No."

"Whew! I'm glad. I worry sometimes that I'm too impulsive. I sure don't want to be one of those girls who wears her heart on her sleeve."

▣   ▣   ▣

The glimpse of Kale's lair in the half light only inflamed Wilbur's desire to tear the room apart. The set of mental photographs he'd quickly snapped there didn't yield much, but he kept them close by for study in his idle moments. The heads shrouded in the dimness, the file cabinets, the empty desk top, the pistol. What was he looking for? Kale's guilt was certain. The motives? Greed, racial madness, blood lust. Yet it was hard to conceive of one human performing such monstrous acts then going about his business of shuffling papers, arriving home for dinner, chatting with his wife, being a father. Between Kale the citizen and Kale the murderer lay a chasm whose depth was an enigma to Wilbur. Circumstantial evidence assured him Kale had murdered Copperfield on purpose and Bobette by accident—she'd merely been crushed underfoot as the beast lumbered along on its way to a feeding. Wilbur's grief and rage told him the worst conceiveable punishment would be just; yet he held back from setting a plan into motion. Though he kept picturing himself rifling through Kale's files, coming upon some document (a power of attorney with Copperfield's forged signature, say), the fantasy would soon slip away, unanchored: no document could make Kale any more guilty than Wilbur already believed him to be.

Saturday afternoon, Sissy arrived at 1:45 and surprised him by coming from behind and easing beside him on the bench where he sat watching the street for Kale's Chrysler.

"Sorry I'm late. It was my father. God, I hate him!"

"What'd he do?"

"Every time he comes back from being in Wetoka he's in an uproar. It gets him all stirred up."

Wilbur held a breath and counted silently to three. "What about?"

Sissy's bony shoulders jerked under her dress. "I dunno. But he takes it out on me. He makes me feel like I'm in jail. He starts watching me real close."

"You think we should be sitting here?"

She twisted about, looked around. "I guess. He's playing golf out at Fort Bliss. I had to wait until he left. He's probably got spies everywhere, though."

"Maybe we should go to a picture or something."

"No, I'm not in the mood. I'm in the mood to just sit here so that somebody can really get an snootful." She gave him a look with her bold black eyes he couldn't decipher. She smiled thinly. "I'm going to get close—" she scooted to his side "—and put your arm around my shoulder."

She lifted his arm and draped it about her neck and lay her cheek against his chest.

"Now let them take a picture."

"Sissy, if he finds out, he might stop you from seeing me, you know."

She straightened up, and he lifted his arm away from her neck. "Oh, I know. But he makes me so mad! I don't know why he has to be so strict. Well, I guess I do know. But, anyway, oh, never mind!"

Spies. He felt watched. He rose from the bench and took her hand.

"Come on, let's get out of here."

They walked up Main toward the Santa Fe yard, Sissy taking a look behind them every few yards, until, blocks later, she slumped visibly and heaved a breath.

"I'm okay, now. Boy, I was pretty worked up, I guess."

"Yeah."

"What do you want to do?"

"I don't know. Hey, is your mother at home?"

"Yeah. Why?"

"I thought maybe I could see your room."

Sissy cracked a grin. "You're strange, you know that? Why don't you show me yours first?"

"Mine?" His scalp prickled. He looked ahead; from the rail yard a low rumbling vibrated under their feet, tons of metal creaking.

"Yeah, don't be such a man of mystery. I don't even know if you live in a house or an apartment or what."

"It's a . . . hotel."

"Oh, that's swell! I always wanted to live in a hotel."

When he failed to respond, Sissy stopped on the walk. "What—you don't want me to know where you live?"

"No, it's just that there's not much to it, kiddo. You know, a bureau, a bed, a desk, a chair."

"Show me."

An instinct urged him to resist, but he could think of

no good reason to. He led her back to San Jacinto Plaza and across the street to his hotel.

"Golly, you mean it was right here all along? You're a sneaky fellow, Will."

"I didn't think to mention it."

He made her wait in the lobby while he went upstairs "to tidy up." The maid had already been through the room, as he knew, and the bed linens were taut, crease-less, the waste basket empty, the floor clean. He closed his valise and shoved it under the bed, then stepped to the desk. The hinged, gold-framed triptych of photos of Bobette and Pearl. Book of his life. Folding it, he thought of the images embracing. He held his breath and slid the book into his desk drawer, shoved it closed. Forgive me. He'd call Pearl later.

When Sissy stood beside the bed, she turned in a cir-cle, clearly disappointed. "Gee, it's so simple."

"I told you."

"But it looks like nobody lives here, Will. Are you sure this is your room?"

He laughed. "Of course. What'd you expect—knick-knacks and a pipe stand?"

"Okay if I sit on the bed?"

"Sure."

She eased down gingerly onto the bed, and he drew out the desk chair and rode it, arms draped over the back. Sissy sniffed the air. "How long have you been here?"

"Since January."

"How come you didn't rent an apartment or a house?"

"I wasn't sure how long I was going to stay. I didn't want to have to take care of anything, cook meals, stuff like that."

She looked at him for a long moment, mischievously, her mouth curved into a smile. "And how long are you staying?"

"A lot longer now I know you."

She clapped and giggled, bounced once on the bed. "Smart fellow!"

He watched her; she kept looking about the way a cat does on coming into a strange room.

"Is that the phone you call me from?"

"Sometimes."

"Can I use it?"

He nodded, rose from the desk chair, and she bolted up and took his seat. He lay back on the bed, staring at the ceiling. She gave the operator her own phone number.

"Hello, mother? Are you okay?" She listened for a moment. "Don't worry. I didn't run off again. I'm with my 'friend' I told you about."

Wilbur's gaze cut to Sissy. Sissy winked at him. She turned back to the wall and listened again, then she drummed her long fingers on the desk. "Okay, okay, I said. I'll get back before he gets there, golly!"

She hung up without saying good-bye. She stood at the desk, her mouth puckered sourly.

"What's the matter?"

"I get so tired of her not standing up to him."

"Does she know about me?"

Sissy laughed, skipped to the bed, sat on it, then lay across it on her side, leaning on her elbow and facing him. "You scared?"

"Just wondered."

"I didn't give her your real name. But she knows I've got a fellow. That's why she's so hysterical."

"It's pretty natural for a girl to have a fellow, you know."

"Yeah. But I told you there was a history."

When she didn't go on, he said, "Now you're being mysterious."

She winked. "That makes a woman more appealing, I hear." She was absently swinging her leg and the bed moved up and down. "Would you care if I did tell her your name and who you were?"

He fought back his panic by making a show of stretching and yawning. "Oh, I don't suppose so. I'm sure not ashamed of being seen with you, I can tell you that." He winked at her. "But I'll leave it to you to decide if that's a good idea or not. You know to trust her or not."

"Thanks, but I don't."

"Okay, it's settled then." He watched her hips rock back and forth with the arc of her leg. She was tracing a design on the bedspread with a fingernail.

"Did you have a good time with me the other night in Juarez?" she asked.

"Sure."

She glanced up at him from under her brows. "Did you like dancing with me?"

"Yeah."

"What'd you like best about it?"

He felt his face go hot. "Oh, I don't know, the music, it's fun, you know, to dance."

"I liked how it made me feel normal."

"Normal?"

"Well, like other girls. I worry about it sometimes."

"Why?"

"I guess because I'm so tall. Did I seem okay to you when we danced?"

"Heck, yes, Sissy."

She flopped onto her back, her knees bent at the

edge of the bed, feet on the floor. She raised her long arms toward the ceiling and let her wrists go limp, flapped her hands loosely, idly turning and inspecting them like a bored child.

"I liked how you held me."

"Yeah, that was fun, I liked that too."

"I hope I am normal."

"You are."

"How can you tell?"

"Well—"

"See, it's only a guess. I know what!" She sprang upright and moved close to him. "Let's experiment, okay?"

"How?"

"Well, you can kiss me and tell me if it's like kissing normal girls."

He studied her face, trying to read her mood. Was she only being coy, playful? Did she think she was fooling him? Was she only fooling herself? She looked earnest but also eager and cheerful, a ten-year-old with a plan.

"I don't know if that's a good idea or not. I'm sure that kissing you would be like kissing normal girls, Sissy."

"What would it hurt? Please? I have to know."

To get through it quickly as possible, he bent toward her, and, seeing him coming, she closed her eyes and canted her face toward his. Her lips were soft, her mouth slightly open. He kept pushing back the image of the triptych in the drawer, Bobette's face. He tried to break away, but Sissy squealed in protest in her throat and wrapped her long fingers about the back of his head to restrain him. She smelled of soap, flowers. Her breath went down his throat. He struggled to conjure up the photos in the book. Finally, Sissy dropped her hand.

"Well?" She was breathing in quick shallow scoops.

"You're exactly like other girls."

"You're sure? Okay, never mind. Thanks. And that's the way they do it, too?"

"Yeah."

"Can you do me another favor?"

"What?"

She sat forward, palm up in her lap as if to cup water. "Would you, well, examine me?"

"Examine you?"

"Uh-huh." She looked away. "Like a doctor or something. To check, make sure I'm okay."

"Holy cow, Sissy. Maybe you ought to see one, you know, I'm not a medical expert."

"I'd be too embarrassed. I trust you."

Her eyes pleaded; he sighed and sat up. She unbuttoned her blouse. Then she dropped her head back with her face to the ceiling. She closed her eyes. Her palms were flat on the bed behind her, and she was propped up by her long arms, elbows locked.

She waited. For Christ's sake, he knew what she wanted. He made a pretense of inspection by massaging the muscle joining her neck to her shoulder, then went down over her collarbone. He slid his hand under the loosened lapels, saw the lacey edge of the camisole top. He cleared his throat. His legs were crossed and he swung the free one.

"Looks okay, Sissy."

"Uhn." Her mouth was parted. She was breathing through it.

For Christ's sake, he knew exactly what she wanted! Her skin was soft, she smelled good. Months. He'd for-

gotten. His hands started to shake. Since before
Bobette was killed. By this girl's father. Their shoulders
were touching, hers was warm. His fingertips stroked
her flesh below her collarbone; her skin was so smooth!
He held back, eyes shut, teeth clenched, his whole
attention on his palm and fingers, moving over the silk,
her breast was small, nipple tickling his palm, he shuddered as heat scorched his lap.

He jumped up and went to the window, stiff, aching.

"Golly, Will! What's wrong? Did you find something
strange?"

He collapsed onto the other side of the bed in laughter. He kept trying to control it so he could explain that
he wasn't laughing at something grotesque in her he'd
discovered, but every time he looked at her panic-
stricken face the irony struck him anew.

"No, Sissy, not at all! Don't worry. You're normal,
believe me!"

Her gaze traced the distance between them on the
bed. "Then why—"

"Because you are like other girls."

He sent her home in a taxi. He unearthed the triptych from the drawer, set it on the desk again, avoiding
the gazes of the woman and the child as he unfolded
the wings. Then he paced the room, but he kept inter-
cepting Sissy's scent the way currents of warm water are
encountered while swimming in cold. The framed
panels on the desk were like windows into another
world through which he was being observed. He closed
the wings but left the triptych upright, then curled on
the bed, hands thrust between his knees. Silk under his
fingers. Breath in his ear, in his throat. The rosy flush
on her high cheek bones, her closed eyes, mouth parted as she absorbed his touch.

He tried not to think of the girl, but the tension shoved its way back into his groin, and he rocked. He groaned. Desire swept over him with a transforming power he'd forgotten, and it was like feeling hungry for the first time after being sick. Yet he was afraid of it. The world now had a hard stick stuck between his legs to grab and shake him by.

He lay floating in a light sleep through the night, jarred awake often by squealing tires, hollering drunks, sirens. Much later the noise died off and he woke up in a dark forest. A gargantuan black snake reared up in his path and chased him; he thrashed about wildly in the darkness to escape, branches whipping his face and arms as he ran through the trees, at last tumbling into a moon-struck clearing; feeling he'd eluded the beast, he stopped, panting, looked around, relieved, then realized he was looking out its mouth.

He writhed his way into hot daylight. He was drenched in sweat. His room was slathered in a buttery heat. A church bell pealed somewhere near. His heart was thundering and he lay for a time staring at the ceiling.

The phone's jangle jolted him upright; he was so stunned he made no move for the receiver. Only Mildred ever called, only she had the number. Something happened to Pearl!

He leaped from the bed and grabbed the phone.

"Yes!" he shouted.

A girl giggled. "Boy, are you awake!"

His head spun. He was about to say wrong number, then, trembling, he eased down onto the chair.

"What are you doing calling?"

"Golly, don't you want to hear from me?"

"I meant I'm surprised, that's all."

"Mother and Dad are in the back yard having coffee. I was thinking of you and wanted you to know that. I really appreciate what you did for me yesterday afternoon, when you kissed me and the other."

"It was nothing, Sissy."

"Little things mean a lot to a girl."

"Sissy, listen, the maid wants to get into my room...."

"They're coming back inside, anyway." She was whispering. "Bye bye."

The receiver rattled when he dropped it back in its cradle with a shaking hand. He sat a long moment and rubbed his face, coaxing his pulse to slow. An invisible giant had yanked him from sleep and out of bed to pummel then release him. The terrifying dream, the shock of the phone—

Thank God nothing had happened to Pearl!

He shook off his uneasiness by going down the hall to bathe and shave. He was the last this morning and the water was only tepid. He went out, bought a paper, strolled in the Plaza, ate breakfast slowly, and read the *El Paso Times* word for word. He was waiting for the clock in Mildred's kitchen to crawl forward so that those out there in another time zone would be ready to hear from him. He and Mildred and Pearl exchanged letters, but often he missed her too much to tolerate the post, and today, imagining some harm to his child, he decided to ignore the expense of another call.

At noon he called California. Pearl, however, had gone to church with the family next door. Mildred said, "Pearl's doing fine, but she does miss you, you know." He could have uttered this sentence in unison; she always opened her letters with it, and it always inspired relief, regret, and guilt. And what is always his answer? *I miss her, too.*

Today Mildred described in detail how she and Pei-Ling took Pearl to a dentist, and Wilbur hungrily absorbed the conjured pictures of Pearl reading a magazine, in a chair in a white dress and black shoes, a red ribbon holding her hair back, chin cupped by her palm, knocking her toes together idly, then, when the drill passed her pale lips, he winced.

"Please tell her I called and I miss her something terrible."

"How much longer will you be there? You know I'm not about to complain about taking care of my own granddaughter, Wilbur, because she is such a delight, and God knows she's good for Pei-Ling. But she does miss her father, any child would."

So you said! "Not long. I'll be home soon."

As soon as he hung up, the phone rang. Thinking Mildred had forgotten something urgent or that Pearl had come back inside, he scooped up the receiver.

"It's me again!"

"Oh." Behind the girl's voice he heard clattering, crowd noises.

"We went out to eat. I'm in the cloakroom. I was trying to call you, and the operator said the line was busy. Who were you talking to?"

He clenched a fist. "Wrong number."

"Oh. I know I'm being a pest, but I can't stop thinking of you, Will. I'm going to say one thing and you don't have to say anything back, and then I'll hang up. Okay? Here it is—nobody has ever treated me as nice as you do, and it really really means a lot to me. Bye."

He stood at the window. His Ford was parked across

the street under the trees; the trunk was visible. Go open it, load it, right now! Get back to Pearl now, while you can, before this gets too messy!

Or at least change hotels. On a whim Sissy could ring his bell now, jerk the leash. Place had too many bugs, Sissy. New one's named uh I forget. Boarding house, very strict landlady, won't allow lady visitors in my room. No phone. If you call me one more time today you stupid little.

Well, she was stuck on him. He'd been playing with fire. He'd only meant to befriend her to learn what he could about her father. Spending too much time with her, getting her so involved in him, he was running the risk of heading down a side road and coming to a dead end. If he wasn't careful, the girl might do something unexpected and cause needless complications, ruin his plans.

But he had no "plans." And the longer he waited to act, the more he risked losing his resolve, having events cheat him of his chance. Twice already with Kale he'd almost exploded from rage. The chance to hack him up in the Juarez whorehouse—that was like a window stuck open on an opportunity, seconds and even minutes of time ticking by while he stood imagining it. Nobody had known they had gone to Juarez together; it was Mexico, he could've slipped away either deeper south or back across the border, putting the bureaucratic machinery of two nations between himself and getting caught.

What was he waiting for now, anyway? Was he just yellow? When you got right down to it, wasn't it just a matter of walking up to the front door, ringing the bell, and when he answered it, blowing his brains out?

You, you're Kale, you're sitting down to dinner, the doorbell rings, you go to answer it, there's a young man who works for you at the bank there with a shotgun, and he says, Here! This is for Bobette! and before you can gather your wits an explosion rips your face off.

But see, the man would have no idea. He needs more information to absorb the implications of his predicament. More information to get the full impact of why he's being executed, not what the crime was—sure, he knows the crime—but which victim is striking back, chalking up a score. So there should be a few words to announce the verdict and to pronounce the sentence before carrying it out. What words? How many? And if the sentence is carried out immediately, then the interim between his knowledge of what's to happen and its happening is so short that his agony—the fear of being executed—is much too mercifully brief. A longer speech, then? And will the man merely stand in the doorway holding his napkin and swallowing the last morsel of roast beef while you explain why he's about to die? Who's at the door, dear?

That was the crux of his indecision. The instant Kale's head exploded like a gourd from the blast, Wilbur's ability to make him suffer would instantly end. He wanted to stretch it out. Just taking Kale's life was not eye for eye, tooth for tooth: a dozen Kales might not equal one Bobette. And he could not kill Kale a dozen times. So he had to find a way to make Kale die a dozen deaths. Standing on his doorstep and interrupting his Sunday dinner with a shotgun blast wasn't good enough—Kale deserved far worse.

Mid-morning on Monday while distributing the mail, Wilbur was astonished to hear Sissy shouting at Kale from behind the man's closed office door, and the man shouting back. She was sobbing, furious, speaking in a wail that made her words indistinguishable but for the general drift: I want, I will, you can't stop me and her father's No, no, no you won't, can't, yes I can stop you.

When he saw the knob turning and the door opening, he darted out of sight. He wasn't surprised when, moments later, he was called to the telephone in the back office where four accountants shared a bull-pen. The girl was weeping into the phone.

"Oh, Will, I'm so mad! Please help me, please?"

"What's the matter?" One accountant made a show of turning up his cuffs to have an excuse to look his way. Wilbur met his gaze and the man turned back to his work.

"Oh, Daddy! I could kill him!"

"How can I help?"

"Oh, I need to talk to somebody. Can you meet me tonight?"

"Yeah. Where?"

"School. Same as before, okay?"

She didn't sound childishly excited now, only unhappy. "Sure."

When he arrived, the school was dark. He parked behind the auditorium in the empty lot. A shutter of drifting overcast closed slowly over the light of the three-quarter moon, then when it lifted like a dream-struck blink, Sissy was emerging out of the darkness from, apparently, the front of the building. He'd heard no car, seen no lights.

"How'd you get here?"

"A friend. Let's go somewhere else. Dark schools give me the creeps."

He drove. She slumped in her seat with her knees against the dash and chewed on a hangnail.

"Thanks for coming. I really don't deserve it. I'm

starting to get worried that I'm going to be too much trouble for you and you're not going to like me any more."

"If we're going to be friends, Sissy, we're going to be friends. To me that means I do whatever you need to ask me to do, and vice versa."

"Oh, Will!" She draped her long fingers over the inner crook of his elbow. "That's so nice! God, you're so swell!"

"So what's the trouble?"

She sighed, drew in a long breath, sighed again. "I came to a decision. I told my mother that I wasn't going to live at home after Friday—that's my 18th birthday, you know. She kind of went crazy. She told him. I couldn't believe she did that! She plain outright betrayed me!"

"He was going to know anyway, wasn't he?"

"Yeah, but not until I was ready for him to know. After I was already gone."

"Where were you going?"

"I wanted my own little room. Like yours. Not a hotel, like yours though, maybe a room in some nice lady's house. I was going to ask him to let me work at the bank so I could support myself and so I'd be right where he could see me every day. I thought maybe that would pacify him. I thought he'd be happy to hear I wasn't going to run off again and that I was going to stay close by but be a little independent." She sat up. The muscle in her jaw pulsed. "I thought he'd appreciate my willingness to compromise, but no, not him! Golly, what a . . . bastard!"

"I'm sure he has your best interests at heart, Sissy!"

"God!" she wailed. "You're not going to take his side, are you?"

"No, not at all. I can really understand why you'd want to be out from under his thumb, kiddo. And everybody deserves freedom. It's your life, not his." He had the distressing sensation of being propelled willy nilly into a complicated mess where the principals were all in violent, unpredictable motion and were threatening to collide and crush him. These Kales would not sit still long enough for him to fix his ideas about their lives together; they were an unstable compound.

"That's what I was doing at the bank this morning. I told mother at breakfast and she immediately got on the phone and told him, and then he told me to come down there right that instant before I even went to school. I told him I wanted to live somewhere else but I also wanted to work right at the bank where he could watch me."

"What'd he say?"

"He said there's no point in discussing it until after I'm eighteen. He said he'd see. That was just putting me off."

The idea of Sissy's working at the bank disconcerted him. "What would you want to do there?"

"Anything. I can add, spell, type, file. I'm not dumb. I make good grades. I could be a stenographer."

"You might get bored."

"Not as long as you were working there."

"But I might get fired or have to move."

She shrugged and looked away. After a moment, the dash lights glinted on her cheek. "I don't have all the answers, Will. I'm so dreadfully unhappy, that's all I know for sure. Sometimes I think about getting on a train without even a bag and travel a long way it doesn't matter where, then I get off the train in a strange city where nobody knows me and I go check into a hotel and go up to a room and sit down on the bed and slit my wrists. I might just fling my life upon the winds. Nobody would know the corpse was mine. Mother and Daddy would sit here waiting to hear something and never would. That's what I think of doing this time."

"Don't talk nonsense."

She wiped her eyes with the heels of her hands.

"What'd you mean—this time?" he asked.

"I meant do that instead of running away again."

"How'd they catch you before?"

"I didn't get very far. Daddy found out I was going."

"What did he do?"

"He fixed it so I wouldn't want to run away again."

"How?"

Her sigh opened into a groan. "He has a man who works for him in Wetoka, he was the foreman of our ranch. Real ugly man, with a big ugly scar on his cheek. I think Daddy had him scare away this friend who was going to help me. I knew if I tried very hard to run away that Mr. Shingle might hurt my friend. Daddy told me this morning that Mr. Shingle lives here now and still works for him. It was like he was saying you better do what I tell you to do and don't get any ideas about running away again or I'll sic my watchdog on you!"

The hair rose on Wilbur's neck. "Surely he wouldn't have this fellow who works for him harm you."

"Oh, no. Daddy meant in case I was thinking of having somebody help. He doesn't believe I could possibly do it on my own. That's where I might surprise him!"

Wilbur went cold all over. Boxes, closets, a jail cell. Everywhere he turned, doors were closing. The kid runs off, the parents investigate, wouldn't be too hard to discover she'd been seeing him, then he'd be blamed no matter what he'd actually done. He'd be up to his ears in their lives before he even had a chance to put anything into motion.

"Don't do anything foolish, Sissy. And don't be hasty. Promise me that. You've got a long life ahead of you, and you don't want to do something you'd regret."

"You're so wise, Will."

He eventually drove her back to her school after making a long loop up toward Fort Bliss and back down to the international bridge. As he was pulling up before the black-windowed building, it seemed odd that she'd managed to get away from the house tonight given the turmoil it was presently in.

"You say a friend dropped you off."

"Yeah. She's coming back at 10. What time is it?"

"A little before. How'd you get away, anyhow?"

"I turned on my radio and locked my door and went out the window." She grinned with pride. She pointed ahead. "Pull on down there." He eased the car in gear and drove it down the block to where she'd pointed under a large elm overhanging the street. They sat for a moment with Sissy twisted in the seat and looking through the back window, until, after a few minutes, headlamps from an auto flickered across his rearview mirror.

"There she is! Bye!" She leaned over quickly and gave him a quick kiss then bolted from the car. He watched her silhouette shrink in the rearview mirror, outlined against the illuminated headlamps. He couldn't tell the make of the other car. A door slammed, the car backed away from the intersection, pulled ahead in the opposite direction before he could see anything. Who was that? What did "she" know about him? Shingle lived here? Under his own name?

These unanswered questions were like invisible ropes about to be tossed about him. A spring trap hidden under the leaves on a path. Everyone seemed to be hatching plots and cross plots, and he was only on the periphery of their story. A pawn. Pawns never knew what the player had planned for them, but generally the master's strategy was to protect the king.

It made him nervous not to know everything.

▣   ▣   ▣

Sissy's confusion and impetuousness alarmed him. He'd never considered that coping with her would call for more than merely drawing information from her. Now she seemed volatile, unpredictable. He was already involved with her too deeply to stand safely aside while the conflict between her and her father played itself out, because he suspected he was no small part of the reason she wanted to be "a little independent." No doubt she imagined a comfy little room where she could entertain him without worrying about her parents, maybe even a cozy little cottage for them both? Sooner or later, his name would pop up in an argument with her father: one age-old way for headstrong daughters to leave their fathers was on the arm of a husband. She might even threaten her father with marriage to his clerk to get her way.

Sometime during the night, while mulling this over, an idea crept upon him: he should facilitate what he could not prevent. He grinned in the darkness. He could outwit Kale, take advantage of their quarrelling, put it to his own use.

After school on Wednesday afternoon, he called the Kale home from the drug store near the bank while

Sissy's father was in a meeting. When she answered, he said, "Hi, can you talk?"

"Oh, hi, Melanie. Have you finished your French yet?" Sissy said glibly.

"Okay. Well, listen to me for a minute. I've got an idea I want to try out on you. But I need to meet you. Is there any way you could get away tonight?"

"I don't know for sure. Is your mother going to be there if I come over to study with you tonight?"

"Are you saying you don't know if your father is going to be home?"

"Yes. Are you sure your Daddy won't mind if I come?"

"Why don't you say, 'I'll ask my Mom if I can come over to your house' and then ask her."

"Okay. I'll ask my Mom if I can come over to your house and then ask her."

He was confused; a beat of silence passed, and Sissy burst into laughter. "Boy, I had you going!"

"Your mother's not there?"

"Out back. Her garden, you know. It's spring."

"You're a stinker."

"I'm sorry. I couldn't resist fooling you!"

"Well, can you meet me?"

"I'll try. Where?"

"You tell me."

"You know where the library is?"

He shuddered. "The library?"

"Yes. I'll tell mother I have to do research. It's on Oregon and Missouri. We walked by it—"

"Yes, I know. Is there any place else—"

"Melanie! Can't you ever do your own homework?" Her voice was suddenly loud and bright. Then muffled. "Mother, Melanie wants to know if I can help her at the library tonight?" He didn't hear Jo Kale's answer, but suddenly Sissy was in his ear: "About seven, okay, see you then!"

Just before seven he stood inside the library's doors with his back to the checkout desk waiting for her to arrive so he could intercept her to steer her instantly back outside. Her mother's car pulled to the curb, Sissy stepped out, books under her arm, and mounted the steps, but as she came up, his panic soared and he strode outside and turned her around.

"Let's go to a cafe."

"Okay." She held out her books for him to take. He tucked them under his arm, then he was disconcerted by they way people seemed to presume he was a beau, carrying them. In the cafe, he requested a table away from the windows. He ordered coffee only, but Sissy took a menu then told the waitress to bring her a veal cutlet, mashed potatoes, pinto beans, bread, apple pie and milk. She seemed uninterested in the reason for the meeting and chatted awhile about school. Then, after her food was served, she asked, "So what's the big news?"

"I told you I've got an idea."

"Yeah?"

Sissy cut into the meat and squinted at it. He wondered if he had her full attention. "You wanted me to help with your problem."

"My problem?"

"Sissy! You don't remember being so upset and yelling at your father about wanting to be on your own when you—"

"Oh, yeah, sure, Will!"

"Okay." Now his solution seemed oddly out of proportion to the problem. He plunged ahead, nevertheless. "You'll be eighteen on Friday, right?"

"Well, actually 12:03 on Saturday."

He toyed with the salt shaker, wondering how best to sell his idea. "I've been thinking about moving on, Sissy."

Her fork dropped to her plate. Her eyes went big. He bent forward quickly. "Don't worry! There's more to this, okay? Just hear me out."

She fell back in her chair, looking at him.

"You remember saying you wanted to go places? Like California?"

"Yeah?"

"Well, how about this—when you're eighteen, let's you and me go together."

She grinned, quickly and easily. "That's a great idea, Will!" She leaned forward, picked up her knife and fork again and cut her meat.

"It'll be a great opportunity for you." He felt vaguely perplexed, as if he had to defend the plan, even though she'd expressed enthusiasm. "There's lots of banks to work at out there, and you won't have to answer to any-body, you'll be completely on your own."

"I won't have you?"

"Oh, sure, Sissy! I mean I wouldn't boss you around. We'd be, well, partners!"

"Partners? Like in a business?"

"Yeah. Two friends, buddies, travelling around together."

"That sounds so swell, Will!"

They walked slowly back toward the library, and Sissy was hanging on his arm, chattering gaily, at last showing the excitement that he'd expected. She want-ed to live in one of those Hollywood bungalows! She wanted to see a movie set! Maybe she could work in the movies, who knows! And she could learn to cook so they could save money.

"Sissy, we don't have to live together out there, you know. I don't want you to think I'm going to take advantage of your situation—"

"Oh, Will, I don't care! You can live with me, and you don't have to marry me. I don't care about that! It's like you said—we'll be partners."

He left her on the steps just before her mother was to pick her up, but he'd hardly reached his hotel room when his phone was ringing and Sissy was on the other end.

"Oh, God, Will! I never dreamed I'd be leaving home by eloping! I just can't wait until this Friday night!"

Eloping? He could imagine her voice booming in the house.

"Be careful not to give it away, all right? Act normal. Act like you're still mad at him but don't bait him or provoke an argument, all right? In fact, act like you're going to do exactly as he says but you're not happy about it."

"Okay." She fell silent for a moment, then she said, "Are you going to walk right up to my door and ring the bell and come inside and carry me off? Boy, I can't wait to see the looks on their faces!"

"Do you think that's really a good idea? I mean, maybe your father would call the police or maybe they'd try to keep us from going, you see? I'm not yellow, you know, but maybe we shouldn't ask for trouble. You won't really be eighteen until after midnight—"

"And we don't want you to violate the Mann Act! Okay, so I'll leave a note."

They each, in silence, composed a note. His began, If you ever want to see her alive again.

"Should we say where we're going?"

"No, but after we get there, you can call."

"Yes, that's good. I don't want them to worry too much, Will."

"Sure, I know."

Thursday Wilbur poked about in Kale's files and located a telephone number for Shingle, who was now calling himself "John Bliss." He called the man and suggested a mutual friend had urged the contact because "Bliss" knew "how to get things done." He arranged for "Bliss" to meet him at his hotel room on Friday after work.

Friday, as soon as he had come back to the hotel after gassing up his car, he called California. When Mildred answered, he tried to sound calm. Pearl was doing fine, but of course she was very sad at night. She did miss her Daddy.

"Mildred, I should be through here next couple of days. Look for me along about next Wednesday or Thursday."

"Well, that's good news. I know Pearl will be thrilled to see you. And to tell the truth, we're going to be a mite crowded around here soon."

Some sniggering giggly hitch in her voice gave away her news even before she could add, "My Little Harold's about to become a daddy!"

"Wonderful," uttered Wilbur from between clenched teeth. Then he thought—why begrudge poor pitiful Little Harold this? It's not his fault.

Mildred put the receiver down to call Pearl in from the yard. The phone, like an eavesdropping ear, gave him Mildred's voice calling his daughter, the child's voice answering, then Mildred saying it's your Daddy, the child yelping, then a slap of a screendoor, footsteps, and his heart lifted as he pictured her running into the house.

"Daddy!"

"Hello, sweetie!"

"We were playing Swing the Statues."

"That's good." He imagined her frozen into a pose, arms akimbo. "That's fun. Did you do well in school today?"

"Yes."

She sounded uncertain—perhaps she was fibbing—but he didn't want to embarrass her.

"How is old Miss Moustache?"

She giggled. "Fine. But she's mean to everybody now."

"Oh? Well, maybe she has something on her mind. Just try to behave and forgive her."

"Mumbles had babies."

"Really? How many?"

"Seven."

She told him the kittens were born in the closet on an old sweater during the night. She'd gone into the closet in the morning to get dressed and there they were.

He let her words wash over him, trying to hear her subtones, using the telephone like a stethoscope to measure the strength of her heartbeat. Is she all right? She paused, and he asked, "What colors are they?"

"Four black, two white, and one black with white stockings. Daddy, can I keep him?"

He almost said, "Yes, of course," then realized that this kitten might already be a bone of contention between Pearl and his mother-in-law. Being unable to give her this made his heart ache.

"It's up to Gramma."

"Oh." After a pause, she asked, "Daddy, when are you coming home?"

"Soon, sweetie. Next week, I promise."

"My birthday is pretty soon."

"Yes, I know. You don't think I could forget your birthday, do you?"

"I guess not."

"I won't. I know you miss me. And I miss you."

Shouts in the background, footfalls, children laughing. The other kids had come inside.

"Gramma's going to give us some cake now."

Hearing her restlessness, he said, "All right. I'll talk to you soon, sweetie. I love you."

"Love you, Daddy."

Then clunk went the receiver and he sat for a long minute with his hand on his telephone looking out the window into the hard blue sky over Mexico. He'd wanted to say something special—if anything happens, remember...—but knew anything like that would alarm her. He should have at least mentioned Bobette—it worried him that he didn't encourage Pearl to talk about her grief to him.

He longed to be home with Pearl in that golden world and in that golden time when they three were together. Looking off to the mountains, he remembered that he and Bobette had always planned to take a second honeymoon down in Acapulco, maybe. Too late now.

But it wasn't too late to be Pearl's father. Her voice in his ear, a soothing melody. Made him ache to be there. Just get in his car and go West, forget Kale. Not forgive him, no, but just try to forget he's still walking about alive.

By going on with this, isn't he risking the future he

and Pearl can have? Suppose Shingle or Kale gets the best of him? There's no law says he has to win.

All at once he felt distraught and lonely. Isn't he being a terrible fool to pursue this revenge when it could cost his daughter her father? It's only been six months since she lost her mother. When he left home and came here to do this, he felt compelled by a force far stronger than he. He felt he had no choice; he wouldn't be able to spend the rest of his life knowing that Bobette's and Copperfield's killer was walking freely about unpunished. Leaving Kale to an impotent and ineffectual law hadn't seemed a choice he could live with, then.

Now, with his Pearl's voice fresh in his memory, he could picture a future in which this moment was when he turned his back on all this. He could cut loose here, go back to rebuild his life with Pearl and Bobette's family. It was hard to imagine now, but it was possible that some day he might remarry. The future might hold many different things for a man who allowed himself to open all its doors of possibility.

If he hadn't come to El Paso, he might have learned to endure living on the same Earth with Kale and his evil. If he left now, he might still.

This pursuit had kept him continually soaring in a manic rage or plummeting in melancholy. His rage was baffling; it was like some second person inside him who kept prodding him, urging him, insisting on the necessity of killing Kale. It was like a monster conceived by the killer and the avenger in unholy buggery and had outgrown both its parents. This beast would not be satisfied by legal justice, would not be satisfied to hear that Kale had dropped dead from a heart attack or had been run down by a truck; this beast seemed to embody a rage that was only somehow inspired by Kale but could not precisely be said to be caused by him. The beast inside kept pointing to Kale as the reason for its own existence, but there was the perplexing sense that Kale's crimes were created by the rage and not vice versa: yes, Kale had conspired to have Copperfield killed and was thus guilty of Bobette's death — but the rage wasn't content with only these monstrous murders; it obsessively gathered into its burgeoning sense of injury even the most petty idiosyncrasies of character. The rage insisted on "justice," but to gratify itself completely, it seemed to withhold defining justice in order to include under that rubric whatever cruelty it could conceive.

Sometimes he lay awake all night hating Kale, and in the morning he'd feel so exhausted and weepy that his condition was one more grievance to lay at Kale's doorstep. It had transformed him, this hatred. He had begun to see that carrying out his revenge would make it difficult to step back into his old life as if nothing had happened. What will he say to Pearl about this when she's grown? At the least, until then he'll bear the wretched secret of it; that alone will make him a very different man.

What he was doing, what he was about to do tonight, would alter him permanently.

His plans were vague — he saw himself and Sissy running away, holing up or cruising aimlessly around the West, and he could torture Kale by dribbling bits of macabre information until it was time to lure him someplace and kill him.

After that, what? He'd considered running off to Mexico, but now he wondered how that squared against a future life with Pearl. Was he going to return for her and take her down there to live like a fugitive? If he killed Shingle, then Kale, would normal life be possible?

But would normal life be possible again even if he turned his back on Kale and walked away? Bobette's death had convinced him that, even with Pearl, he would never be utterly whole and happy again. Kale had killed that part of him, too. Nothing he can do will bring Bobette back!

He rose and stood at the window, feeling as if he were at a crossroads. He should give up this sickening pursuit before it was too late. He turned from the window, then fell to his knees by the bed to drag his suitcase out from under it. He tugged it up and laid it like an open book upon the bed. Let the Feds catch Kale, if they can. Or will.

He had just folded the triptych of photos from his desk when someone knocked on his door. He froze, electrified. He checked his watch—6:30. Must be Bliss.

He sat on the bed with the book of photos on his knees. He could swear he could hear the man breathing—alive!—on the other side of the door.

Wilbur swallowed back a spasm of bile. He was shaking all over. He set the photos on a stack of shirts in the suitcase and closed it.

Bliss knocked again. Don't answer! he thought, but he said, "Who is it?"

"John Bliss."

"Just a minute."

That only a thin sheet of wood separated him from Shingle made him think of a fireman's axe slamming right through it and into the man's head, halving it like a melon. Ram a corkscrew through his eyes. Hammer screwdrivers into his ears. Rip off his balls with pliers. No, none of that would bring her back, either.

But neither would getting on the train right now and never returning to this hell. His rage was a room without a door. He'd been given no choice in getting to this point. Fate had put him on a line that intersected with Kale's: leaving the farm in Wetoka where his stepfather had gone bust, Wilbur had believed they were going to Dallas for a new start only to discover that Kale's money had allowed his mother to abandon his stepfather; going to California and becoming Copperfield's assistant, he'd dreamed he'd cut himself free, escaped them all.

Now it seemed to Wilbur that he'd spent his life running toward this place and this event to come. He'd lost his will to choose and his confidence in outwitting whatever the future had in store. His life was hopelssly entangled with Kale's. They were now a knot that no one could unravel.

Thinking deep in his bones the cock crows three times, go down for the third time, he awaited the summons of the final impatient rap on his door.

6

HE AND SISSY both took slugs from
the bottle of Scotch. Then he started the
engine. When the lights shot on, bushes
and boulders sprang at them.

"One more kiss," Sissy breathed in
his ear.

"Sissy, we can have all night once
we get to where we're going."

"I want to kiss you because you're
going to be mad at me."

"Why will I be mad?"

"Because I need to go back for something."

"Don't be ridiculous!"

"See—I knew you'd be mad!" She scooted away and hid her face from him.

"You're an excellent judge of human nature."

"How can you be sarcastic when you haven't even given me a chance to explain? That's not fair!"

He cut the lights but not the engine. The vibrations gave him the uneasy sensation of being in motion through the surrounding darkness. He put his foot on the brake.

"Okay."

"Oh, gosh, thanks Will! You—"

"I meant okay start explaining."

"Well, we left in such a hurry and I've been so excited that I haven't hardly had a chance to get my breath, and now that we've been sitting here I started thinking about things I really need or forgot. I left all my money at home, Will! And—don't laugh!—my bear. He's been sleeping on my bed since I was four years old, and I know that I couldn't live without him! Also, I'm afraid maybe I said some things in those notes to Daddy that will make him too furious to ever forgive us, and I can't remember if I tore them all up or threw them all away where they won't be found. There's nothing to worry about, it's only a little ways from here, it won't take me five minutes, I promise! It's not much to ask, is it, considering what I—oh, never mind! I mean, it's the last time we'll be here, and it's not really out of the way from here, you know? And you don't have to worry about Daddy coming back—they'll be out past midnight, and, anyway, I'll be eighteen then."

"I'm not afraid of your father."

"Okay."

What was this all about? Money, the bear, the torn-up notes—not a single good reason for going back, only excuses. Why not tell him the real reason? Maybe she was afraid of leaving home. Both because she'd been sheltered from the world and because of that business with Shingle before. He could reassure her about that, but telling her anything would be telling too much. She probably didn't want him to know she was afraid, too—she wanted him to think she was "mature," as she'd put it. Considering the ugly surprise that eventually lay ahead, it couldn't hurt to play along, wean her away from home.

"All right. Five minutes!"

"Thanks! I'll make it up to you."

When he pulled into Kale's driveway, Sissy hopped out of the car, dashed to the house and through the front entrance, leaving the door yawning open. Her shoe soles beat a brief tatoo on the terra cotta foyer. The image of her red dress burned in his retinas. A breeze huffed up out of the north; the porch light swung, casting shadows that moved like a ghostly metronome across the face of the house.

He waited five minutes—it was 11:40—then another five. He drank another couple of shots. He thought of honking but the neighborhood was too silent. At 11:50, he sighed in irritation, got out of the car, and went into the house. In the foyer, he stood listening. He thought maybe Sissy had gone to the kitchen to fix something to drink or eat, but she'd not turned on any lamps, and the mute darkness in the house was spooky. What? Did she want to play Hide and Seek now?

"Sissy?"

No answer. He blew out a breath, licked his dry lips,

and stepped into the salon. In the semi-darkness her cloche hat lay on the floor like half an eggshell, open side up, empty. Whatever hatched had fled.

Maybe she'd decided to change again and had flung off the hat in her hurry. He passed through the kitchen—on the table her rope of black beads lay heaped like a sleeping snake in a square of bony light streaming through the window. The can of corn on the drainboard had toppled and rolled into the sink. The glass he used earlier glinted as he lifted it; he filled it until water splashed across his knuckles, then drank the contents down at once. He shivered, sweat along his hairline cold, like a metal band.

Her shoes were at the foot of the staircase, but, to his surprise, they stood side by side, a matched set in a display. She obviously hadn't kicked them off. It was as if she'd vaporized out of them. They pointed upstairs. Was this her idea of being clever—Hansel and Gretel?

"Sissy!" he yelled.

Putta putt putt, child's feet. The sound overhead brought bile up his throat, and he swallowed hard.

"Come on! Let's go! Don't play games!"

When she didn't answer, he went up the shadow-dappled staircase. On the second-floor landing, it seemed more light was available, as if a big orange harvest moon had come out, and, reaching into the house, had infiltrated the second story. But, no—a lamp on a table in the hall had been left burning. Above it a black window gave him back a faint reflection of himself. When he moved, his image burgeoned on a distorted wave in the glass like the flourish of a dark cape.

"Sissy?"

A suppressed giggle behind a nearby door sounded like a squeak. He stepped to the door and opened it. The room was dark, but light from the hall stood on the floor at the end of a canopy bed like a trunk. He felt along the door frame and flicked the light switch. The wall he faced was adorned with colored satin rosettes and ribbons from riding competitions. Under them, a kidney-shaped desk, on it a bottle of Scotch.

"You found me."

She was lying in the bed with the spread pulled to her chin. He was afraid that she was nude under it.

"Jesus, Sissy! What're you doing? Let's go!"

"I came up here to get my bear." She nodded toward the corner, where a huge white bear, propped against the wall, was sagging like a man who'd been slipped a Mickey. "I wanted you to come find me here because I spent so many hours lying in this bed dreaming of having you in it with me, can you believe that? I wish we could take it with us, I've always loved my bed."

"Sissy, get up and get your clothes on."

"Heyyy!" She looked hurt. She grabbed a corner of the spread and flung it off her body. She was fully clothed except for the hat, the beads, the shoes. "You think I'm a tramp or something?"

"No, I'm sorry. But please get up."

"Okay. Just one thing, okay?"

"What?"

She held out her arms to him. "One kiss in my child-hood bed, that would be like a fairy tale, and you'd be like a fairy tale hero who has come to kiss a princess awake after a long sleep."

"Thought you didn't believe in heroes."

"Humor me."

He knelt one knee on the bed and bent to peck her cheek, but she grabbed him around the neck and pulled him down so that he lay between her legs.

"What are you doing?"

She grabbed him around the neck like a drowning swimmer and panted in his ear. "Take me here, Will, right in my childhood bed!"

"We might get caught."

"I don't care!" she hissed in his ear. "Do me, Will!"

She jabbed at his mouth with her tongue and squirmed wildly under him. Her "passion" was too out-sized to be authentic.

He held her and kissed her to gain time to think. His stomach felt weighted with lead. A realization came crawling over him like a giant slug—she'd been working ever since they left the house to bring him right back here. She didn't really want to run away.

She wanted to see her father's face when he realized she could leave.

He pushed himself off of the girl and sat up. "Sissy, we've got to go. You don't want your parents to come home and find us here, do you?"

"Will, I've been thinking. It seems unfair to sneak off like we're ashamed. Maybe it's best to face them. I think I owe it to them."

"Sissy, is this what happened before?"

"What do you mean?"

"When you and that 'friend' in Wetoka ran away, did you even get out of the house?"

"I told you we got caught."

He lay down beside the girl on his elbow and slid his palm onto her stomach. She closed her eyes. She seemed to calm down the instant he appeared to change his mind about rushing off.

He got the picture now. She's walking down the street in Wetoka, a boy—a Creek, likely—looks her way and she gives him a come-on. Boy, will this make Daddy have a fit!

Say she made sure Daddy caught them with their pants down. But the boy is no match for Kale and Shingle. Next time she'll pick somebody older, stronger. Say the whole point of this deal here is not to run off at all. Say the whole point is for him and her father to fight over who will have her while she stands by watching. Cheering on the suitor? The father? The victor? Why couldn't he see this all along? The conniving little bitch was only using him.

They weren't going to get away from here unless he dragged her. Though his plans had been vague, they were based on his and Sissy's being elsewhere. And on Sissy's ignorance of his motives. His idea of cruising the West like honeymooners while he secretly tormented her father before eventually killing the scum—this imagined revenge was no longer so simple; it was getting tangled in the actual. How would he torment Kale if they were all here in the house at once? He might threaten to torture Sissy, yes, but could he actually do it?

He shivered. Back when Sissy had been only an extension of Kale's vulnerability or the memory of a haughty little rich girl on a pony, he could imagine using her any way to get back at Kale. But he hadn't believed torturing her would be necessary—he'd planned only let Kale think he was. He hadn't known that his rage might lead him here to this hellish pass. Now it would be harder. He would have to prepare himself, steel himself to hurt her.

Sissy had lured him into the center of this web. She would have to pay the price.

"Aren't you going to make love to me?"

"You really want me to?"

"Yes."

"Okay."

"Bring me a drink first." She pointed to the desk. He got up, grabbed the bottle by its neck, returned with it and sat near her head. He saw now that she'd cleared the bed of all her stuffed animals. They were heaped ass-to-elbow on the floor at the feet of the giant white bear. He held the bottle and she scooted up on her elbows to take a swallow as if she were in a sickbed. When she finished, he took a long pull.

She said, "Maybe I should go ahead and get drunk. You know those movies where the soldier boy has to have the arrow cut out of his leg and his buddies have to hold him down and make him drink whiskey?"

He handed her the bottle. She drank again. Then she gave it back, lay down and pulled the bedspread over her face. "I hope you realize this will make you very special to me."

He tried to look out of the window, but it was too black outside. The valance of the canopy hung in the glass, reflected. He wondered if she'd go on. He didn't want to hear another syllable on behalf of her maidenhead.

"Sissy, you don't have to go through with this, you know."

"Why don't you just say I'm special to you, too?" She sounded hurt.

"You are special. Maybe you don't know how special. I always have admired you. I admired you when you were only a little girl."

She threw the cover off and leaned up to kiss him, a quick smack. "You're silly. I wasn't a little girl."

"You once were, and I used to watch you ride."

"Where?"

"Back in Oklahoma."

"You're kidding me!"

236

"No, you remember that brown pony with the patch on his nose?"

Sissy's eyes got wide. "Jester!"

"I don't know what you called him. But then sometimes I'd see you sitting on your porch, too, in that white rocking chair."

"Really? My God! Yes, I did."

"Uh-huh."

"But I don't remember you."

"Oh, I was just a scruffy barefoot boy living in a dugout down the road."

"Huh! You lived near me? How come you never told me this?"

He shrugged. "Guess I thought you'd recognize me and look down your nose. I thought you were awfully conceited then."

"God, Will! I was only a kid." She laughed. "Boy, isn't it a small world? What a coincidence!" Her smile drifted away for a moment while she stared at the underside of the canopy. "Isn't fate strange, Will? I mean, how it brought you to me." She wriggled close to him and smiled woozily. "How can you resist the pull of kismet, my darling?"

"It wasn't a coincidence. I came here from California because I wanted to go to work for your father, and I knew who he was, where you had lived."

"Did he know you from then?"

"Nah. Like I say, I was just a boy in overalls. He knew my mother, though."

"Huh! Does he know now that you're from then?"

"No."

"Really? Why not?"

"Same reason, I guess. I'll probably tell him tonight."

She considered this then gave him a crafty smile. "That Scotch warmed me up."

He kissed her throat, and her knees rose like a slow drawbridge. Her hands went to his hair, his cheeks. Her dress was all of a piece, came to her neck and buttoned in the back. He passed his palm across her breasts, and she shivered.

"Let's play cowgirls and Indians," she said.

"What's that?"

"Just a game."

"Game?"

"Yeah. Right here, in bed."

He shrugged.

"First you take my stockings off, okay?"

She pulled the hem of her dress above her stocking tops. He bent close to her loins and smelled bath powder, put his trembling fingers around each stocking roll and tugged them off.

"Here, let me show you," she said. She raised up and bent over her left leg like a ballet dancer and, using the freed stocking, tied her ankle to the bedpost. "You do the other."

He tied her right ankle to the bedpost with the stocking from that leg.

"What're we doing?"

"I'm a white slave captive."

She stretched her arms toward the posts on the headboard; she met his gaze.

"Third drawer of my bureau."

He found two more stockings there and quickly moved to bind her wrists to the posts. Then he sat on the bed and drank from the bottle again.

"Give me more firewater, chief."

He held the bottle to her lips.

"You better not touch me or my father will come out with his calvary. He's buggy on the subject of Indians. I am a pure white maiden and I will perish of shame before I will submit to being ra-ra-ravaged!—" Sissy broke into peals of drunken laughter that turned into hiccups. Then, her eyes closed, she said, "You might be planning to put your nasty old redskin hands on me merely because I cannot protect myself."

She was slow to realize that his mood wasn't playful. She opened her eyes. They were silent. She observed while he looked at his watch.

"What's wrong? Are you worried about Daddy?"

"No, not really. I have some things to say and I don't quite know how to say them."

She waited, and when he didn't continue, she said, "Will, my wrist hurts."

He heard in her voice that she was afraid now of admitting her fear. "No, it doesn't, and you know it. You don't trust me and you want me to let you go."

"Yes, I do trust you. But I don't like this any more. Untie me, now."

"I'm sorry. This was your idea. You wanted to fix it so that when they came home you'd be this way, so that's the way you're going to be. Now be quiet for a minute. And listen." He offered the bottle to her but she shook her head. He drank from it. "Here's the deal. I've been, well, lying to you about some things."

"Like what things?"

"Like our running away. To make a long story short, I've got an old score to settle with your father, and I guess we've come down to the part where I have to do it."

"An old score? Will, what's this about?"

"I can't explain it to you."

She twisted her arms and jerked her legs. "Will! Come on! This isn't fun. You're acting queer. If you don't let me go, I'll scream!"

"If you scream, I'll gag you, Sissy."

She struggled fiercely for a moment, grunting and hissing between her teeth, but the bonds held. Then she lay silent, panting.

"Will?" Her voice was soft.

"Yes."

"You can stop joking now. I get the point. Untie me and I promise we'll walk right out of this house. I won't even pick up Bear."

They could leave, yes, he could drag her off and they could dash away from the house and get back on the road, but his adrenaline had been pumping since early in the evening and now he could feel the ragged edge of a letdown. Las Cruces was far, far away. His original plan now seemed hopelessly remote, far-fetched. And at the end of that road they'd be at exactly the same place: he'd have to tell her that her only use to him was to hurt her father.

"Don't you want me to prove to your daddy I'm strong enough to take you away?"

"Let's just go. That'll show him."

Her eyes would not meet his. She was so transparent! "Sissy, I'm sorry it has to be this way now. But it's your fault. I didn't want to come back here. But now we're here, and your parents will be home soon."

"We could leave right now!"

"Too late, Sissy. Your daddy and I have some . . . business—" his nostrils flared and he clenched his fists to squelch the rage that washed over him.

"Please tell me you're kidding about all this! Don't you love me?"

"You're a nice kid, and I didn't want to hurt you."

"What are you going to do?"

"I told you—settle an old score."

"Won't you at least tell me what it's about?"

"It goes back to another time and place, Sissy."

"Will, if you don't let me go, I'll scream, I swear!"

He held up a wad of the bedspread in his fist. "Open your mouth!"

"No, Will! Don't do that!"

"Don't cause trouble, then. And don't try to get free!"

"Let me go, Will! Right now!"

"Shut up, Sissy!"

"You know what? You're a bastard! When my daddy gets home and sees what you've done to me, he's going to rip your balls off!"

Wilbur scrambled down the stairs three at a time, took the last bunch in one leap and landed hard on the floor. He scurried into the dining room, hit the over-head light, then yanked open the sideboard drawer and ransacked it for the key to Kale's study. He upended the drawer and poured its contents onto the dining room table, sent his hands skimming through the jumble of papers and pencils and playing cards but found no key. He flung the drawer onto the floor.

He darted to Kale's study door and bumped it with his shoulder, but it didn't budge. The unyielding door was a reproach, as if Kale were thwarting him; the room on the other side of the door held itself tauntingly beyond arm's length. He stood back and kicked the door several times, but nothing gave. In a fury, he grabbed a dining chair and slung it against the door; it slammed with a crack against the facing but fell away in pieces still fastened like gristled bones.

Cursing, he strode into the kitchen, searched the

drawers, yanked out a cleaver, then he used it to chop at the frame around the lock, only half aware of the tremendous thundering whacks reverberating in the dining room. At last, the wood splintered, the lock gave, and the door swung open.

The cleaver thunked to the floor, and he stepped inside Kale's study. Light from the dining room lay across the carpet, and he stepped to the desk and turned on the gooseneck lamp curved like a drowsy cobra over the ink blotter. Then he jumped, startled by the heads. He'd forgotten them. The uproar had brought them to alert attention. A gazelle, an elk, a lion, their eyes watchful, expectant. They were spectators, he a creature penned in a corral. A new head poked its way through the wall since the night he and Sissy had been here: zebra. For an instant, it confused him; he juxtaposed a carousel against the wall, then thought, No, that's nuts! A rhino too had joined the group, its tumescent horn a gray stake against the white wall.

He circled the desk, yanked the chair out of its cubby and threw it aside, hooked the lip of the flat top drawer with his fingers and pulled it open. The ease with which it slid out set him off balance. Kale thought the lock on the door security enough. The tray was messy: scattered pen nibs, paper clips, a button, two pennies, papers spread liked a tossed deck of cards, the bawdy photos from Juarez.

He found the pistol, held it up, checked the full cylinders, shoved the drawer shut and opened the larger drawer to the right of the cubby. Files, alphabetized. His fingers spidered quickly across the labels. He had nothing particular to look for now; nothing he found would change his mind about anything. It was as if the edges of the files were Kale's ribs and he was probing them with his fingers to find the softest spot where a knife or a bullet could enter the easiest. Here in Kale's study he was on a rampage in the man's own private lair, and brandishing Kale's pistol he felt an exultant relish of triumph and vandalism.

He slammed the top drawer shut, yanked the second drawer open, but then, outside the study window, a car pulled into the driveway. The engine gasped and died, a door opened, was slammed shut; frozen, he heard steps on the concrete, then another car door opening, a murmur. He dashed out of the study and into the darkened parlor off the foyer, where he slipped behind a wall.

Rough shhh like sandpaper, their soles on the drive. His calves were jelly; he felt the butt of the gun against his belly, pulled the weapon out and held it. In his left coat pocket the razor was still secure; he patted it. He licked his lips. He was trembling. What if things went wrong? Any second now Sissy might start hollering and alert them. Maybe he should just say This is for Bobette! when they came in and yank the trigger.

The lock clicked, hinges squeaked, and someone passed into the foyer, talking. A sudden draft curled around his ankles. The woman's heels clacked on the tile.

"Shadow," she murmured. "Kitty." Then, loudly, "I'm hungry. You want something?"

Kale answered "Yeah" from the porch. The woman came to the archway connecting the foyer to the salon and stood silhouetted for a moment. Sissy began yelling just as Kale's wife flicked the wall switch to the overhead light, and Wilbur sprang up and pointed the gun at her.

She screamed. Her handbag dropped to the floor, her palms clapped her cheeks, her eyes rolled and she collapsed as if struck in the skull by a pipe. Kale came bounding in behind her, saw her, started to bend over.

"Don't move!" Wilbur shouted.

Kale, startled, raised up.

"What are you doing here?"

"You'll find out, you fucking bug!" He pointed the gun at Kale.

"Whoa. Calm down, son. I don't know what—"

"Shut up!" His legs were shaking and a wild energy made him dance in place; he kept pacing, one step up, one step back, aiming the gun at Kale. His eyes stung; his breath was ragged, and he was afraid he was going to burst into sobs.

Kale stood very still. "Why don't we—"

"I said shut the fuck up!"

The woman on the floor stirred, then moaned. Kale looked down at her. He gestured toward his wife and cocked an eyebrow.

"Put her on the couch," said Wilbur. "When she wakes up maybe I'm going to blow her brains out while you watch."

Kale hooked his wife under her arms, pulled her up and over to the divan and laid her supine on it. The folds of her ivory silk dress slid and fell over the side of the divan. Wilbur stepped closer, jabbing the pistol at Kale, and Kale stumbled backward until he was against the wall. Wilbur jammed the muzzle under Kale's jaw, gritted his teeth, shoved his own face close to Kale's.

"I'm going to kill you but not until you're begging me to do it!"

Kale's wife moaned, then she hoisted herself upright by grabbing the backrest of the divan. Wilbur shoved the pistol harder into Kale's throat.

"Tell her not to move."

"Jo, don't move!"

"Bill?" Her voice broke.

"It's all right, just do as I say," said Kale.

"Yes, it's all right," said Wilbur. "Just do as he says." He was flooded with such rage that he almost pulled the trigger, but he blinked, swallowed, and took a ragged breath.

"Bill, who is this?" she said angrily.

"Shut up," said Kale. "I don't know what he's after."

"You shut up!" said Wilbur. "I'll tell you what I'm after. You killed Bobette, and I'm here to get even."

"Who's Bobette?"

"She was my wife. She was on Copperfield's boat when your man Shingle rigged it to explode. Any of this coming back to you now?"

He pressed the muzzle against Kale's jugular; the woman sat frozen, watching in horror. Kale was not moving. Wilbur heard his own breathing. Upstairs, Sissy was screaming for them, crying hysterically. He couldn't see how to get from this moment to making Kale's life a long and living hell. He yearned to pull the trigger but it would be much, much too easy for the man.

"I don't know what you're talking about, son."

"I'm not going to argue about it."

"Bill, what—"

"Be quiet, please," said Wilbur. The woman was a nuisance and an unexpected obstacle. "Right now let's all go to the kitchen."

He followed them into the kitchen with the gun at their backs. He went to the pantry door and opened it.

"Get in here and sit down."

The woman edged slowly into the closet, cleared a place on the floor and sat down among the brooms and mops. Her pale face hung in the darkness like a plain luncheon plate.

"You stay in here. If you do, you'll live through this. You understand? Just keep telling yourself that, no matter what you hear going on out here. Do you understand?"

The woman's jaw was trembling and her irises were refracted like underwater stones. "Why is he torturing us?" the woman said to Kale.

"You don't have any idea what torture is, Mrs. Kale. I loved my wife, and I saw her blown to bits, right before my eyes, and it was your husband's doing. Torture is what he's done to me."

"Bill, what—"

"Just shut your mouth and don't pay any attention to him."

Wilbur laughed. "Yeah, don't try to see behind the veil of illusion, Mrs. Kale."

"This is all your fault, Bill, I just know it!" She turned to Wilbur. "Young man, I have a lot of money hidden here in the house, and I'll get it all for you—"

Wilbur slammed the door in her face.

Kale shifted his weight from one foot to the other. Wilbur poked at his back with the gun. Kale raised his hands as if he were being held up.

"Let's talk about this," said Kale.

"We will." He shoved Kale forward back into the parlor, where he made Kale sit on the floor.

"Daaadddddy! Helllp me!" they heard Sissy wail. Kale's head snapped toward her voice, and he glanced quickly at Wilbur.

Wilbur said, "Don't you want to know how Sissy is, Mr. Jones?"

"I imagine you'll tell me."

"Can't you guess?"

When Kale didn't answer, Wilbur said, "You should have been here earlier, Meester Jones. I had my fun. You hear me? She about bucked me off. My partner's up there right now going at it like sixty, got her in the doggy way, that's why she's yelling bloody murder." He eagerly watched Kale's face; Kale looked keenly attentive but not worried.

"What is it you want?"

"Just some good clean fun, Meester Jones. Before I blow your fucking brains out."

"I'm afraid I don't know what this is about."

"I told you."

"I still don't know." When Sissy screamed again, Kale stroked his cheek in a gesture meant to convey casual consideration, then he said, "Whatever it is, my daughter has nothing to do with it. She's done nothing to harm anyone."

"It's good to see you care, Mr. Kale, you know that? Bobette hadn't harmed anyone, either. You forced me to see my wife blasted into bloody pieces, so I'm going to return the favor with your daughter." Wilbur pulled the straight razor from his coat pocket. "You know what happened to Shingle earlier tonight?" Wilbur drew his finger across his own throat. "I'm going to take more time with Sissy, though, and you're going to sit and watch. Who knows, we may have some more fun, too. You should see what I've already done. I'm afraid it's not a pretty sight."

Kale said coolly, "You're making a mistake, son. I had no idea you were in California or that you worked for Copperfield. To tell the truth, when you showed up here I thought you'd come to learn from me, you know, take whatever I could pass on, like father and son. Whatever Shingle did, it was on his own account."

"Then why were you and the grieving widow going to carve up the pie?"

Kale shrugged. "Business."

"You're the father of lies, Meester Jones. Get up!"

Wilbur kicked him hard in his ham. Kale winced from the blow and struggled to his feet. "Move!" Wilbur jabbed the pistol into Kale's ribs and shoved him toward the staircase. The fury rose again, and he slapped Kale's ear with his left hand and felt pain shoot through his thumb. Kale winced "Ooo!" when the slap struck his ear, then he covered his head with both hands.

"We're going upstairs. Move!"

As they took the stairs, there was a muted thump from above, then Sissy yelled, "Daddddyyy!"

"Daddy's coming!" Wilbur yelled.

Wilbur prodded Kale down the hall then shoved him through the door to Sissy's room. Sissy had thrashed about so violently that the mattress had slipped half out from under her, and her flailing had scooted the heavy bedframe several inches from the wall. Her feet had worked loose from the bedposts but her hands were still bound. When they burst into the room, her gaze swung to him, and she looked terrified to see the pistol in his hand.

"Daddy! Oh, Daddy!"

Kale look as if he might bolt to Sissy's side.

"Don't move! You so much as blink and I'll shoot her, you understand? Sit down, right there!"

Keeping his eyes on the pistol, Kale felt behind him for the desk chair, then eased into it.

"Will, untie me!" Sissy bawled.

"Calm down, Sissy," Kale said. He gave Wilbur a strange smile from one side of his mouth as if to tsk and say, children! It enraged Wilbur that Kale pretended not to care and tried to slick him into a league of men against a "silly" girl. Kale could see Sissy wasn't hurt, so maybe now he thought that Wilbur lacked the stomach for it.

"You didn't think I'd hurt her while you weren't here to watch, do you?"

Sissy writhed to pull herself free. "Daddy, make him let me go!"

Kale didn't move. "Well, 'Daddy'?" said Wilbur. "Aren't you going to make me let her go?"

Kale half smiled and crossed his legs. "Well, you obviously have the royal flush here."

"Do you think I'm not serious? You don't seem to be taking me seriously, you fucking bug!" Wilbur brought out the razor again, unfolded it and held it up.

"Look, Wilbur, maybe there are things here you don't know. You wouldn't want to make a bad mistake, would you?"

"There's no mistake." Wilbur moved to the bed and sat on it. Sissy's eyes followed him, and she squirmed and squealed when he moved the razor toward her face.

"Look here, I'll swear to you that I didn't kill your wife," Kale said. He cleared his throat. "I didn't know her, I had no reason to do anything to her."

"I know that!"

"Sometimes mistakes happen."

"Mistakes??"

"Well, that fellow Shingle. He's crazy."

Wilbur gently touched the edge of the razor to the girl's cheek. His sorrow welled up, and he fought it down.

"Don't move, Sissy." He looked at Kale. "Now I want you to watch this mistake. I can make them, too!"

He turned to Sissy and was determined to cut her cheek, but her eyes were flooding with tears and she was looking at him like a wounded pup. His own eyes stung.

"Will, please don't hurt me. I loved you."

Kale bent forward in the desk chair. "I'm asking you, don't hurt this girl. She's innocent, she's done nothing—"

"Tell you what, Mr. Kale. It's you or her, what do you think?"

"Well, then, of course, take me."

"I was kidding. Or maybe I wasn't. I could take you, then I could do as I pleased, no?"

Wilbur looked into Sissy's swollen eyes. "I'm sorry it turned out this way."

They all fell silent and still as if waiting for instructions to arrive. Wilbur stared at Sissy. Her beakish nose, gaunt cheeks, her owl's wide eyes—she looked extraterrestrial to him now. Sissy was holding her breath, her long form rigor-mortis stiff the way you freeze when faced by a coiled rattler. Wilbur was hesitating yet knew his hesitation was dangerous. The moment moved forward but made no progress as if time itself were marking time, and they had arrived at their own small Las Cruces here in the bedroom: they could not stay put; he had to make things happen or give over control, surrender in defeat. Bobette! Bobette! he chanted to himself, purposely wringing his own wretchedness from her name, using her name as an incantation to fuel his rage.

He took a deep breath. He pressed the tip of the razor to Sissy's neck and she winced. Kale lurched but froze when Wilbur aimed the pistol at his eyes. Wilbur's gaze swung back to the square inch of flesh where the triangle of steel pressed its apex. A prick of blood. A pearl of it growing at the tip.

"Will, that hurt!" Sissy cried.

Wilbur jammed his elbow across her brow to hold her steady and clenched his teeth. It'll be over soon! he thought to say, and felt suddenly as if he were removing a splinter, feeling that squeamish discomfort of hurting someone, and you just keep digging, digging as quickly as you can, holding your breath while you try to get it out—he was faltering; with every second that passed his energy and ability to concentrate sagged in spurts. Just count one! two! three! then slice her goddamn throat and get it over with, don't torture the child, Daddy it hurts! just hold on a second, sweetie, and Daddy'll have the splinter out!

He stiffened himself, gathering every ounce of his being into a weapon, an inanimate thing with a trigger hooked only to his will.

One.

Two.

Three.

He blew out his breath, gasped. Drew back the razor. Kale slumped. They were all relieved.

He pointed the pistol at Kale but sat frozen. Kale's eyes showed that the man was busy making plans now; Wilbur's failure was a window of opportunity.

"It's a very good thing that you couldn't do that, Wilbur, do you know that?" Kale said quietly. He might have been speaking to a six-year-old. "You shouldn't feel bad about it. You and Sissy have a very special relationship, you see—"

"Shut the fuck up!" Wilbur leaped from the bed to the desk chair and slammed the pistol across Kale's forehead. Sissy screamed, Kale slumped, howling, in the chair, rocking back and forth, holding his palm over the bloody gash. Wilbur moved behind him, planted the muzzle of the pistol against the back of his skull.

"I'm tired of you and your lies. Say goodbye, Mr. Kale."

When his hand tightened, Sissy went wild on the bed, flailing about.

"Will, please please please don't shoot him!"

Wilbur longed to pull the trigger but could already anticipate the emptiness that lay on the other side of that act.

But that he lacked the grit to execute Kale himself was a torment he couldn't endure. This time when he counted he would pull the trigger and kill Kale or turn the gun on himself.

Then he heard the front door open and the woman was screaming from the porch, "Help us! Help us! Police!"

Her cry alarmed and rattled Wilbur, and he darted through the door, remembered Kale and Sissy, leaped back inside the bedroom.

"Don't move!" he shouted to them, then he sprinted down the staircase and swung off the newel post, sliding across the foyer and through the open front door onto the porch, saw nothing, then cursed his own stupidity for having left Kale, rushed back inside, slammed the front door, and scrambled back up the stairs.

The door was closed and no light showed beneath it. Cursing, he kicked open the door, reached inside and felt for the light switch, then when the light splashed his wrist, he bounded into the room.

"Hold it!" Wilbur screamed. Kale froze by the bed, and Wilbur spun to see Sissy crouched behind the door.

"Get up!"

She held her hands in the air and crabbed to her father's side, where she embraced him.

"Don't hurt Daddy!"

He tossed the razor aside, brandished the pistol, grabbed the girl and tried to wrench her out of Kale's embrace with his free hand, and the three of them went hobbling about the room for a moment in a drunken dance.

"Get out of the way, Sissy! I'm going to shoot this fuck!"

He flung the girl aside, raised the pistol and stuck the muzzle in Kale's face. From the corner of his eye, he caught a black motion hurling toward him; he whirled and yanked the trigger.

"Shadow!" screamed Sissy.

The blast hurt his ears; the smoke choked him. He squinted against the acrid sting and saw that his bullet had hit something black and furry, a small animal, and slammed it against the wall. It was heaped in a bloody mess. Sissy was screaming; he half-turned to look at her and saw Kale's arm coming down, and he leaped aside but something hard struck his wrist and the pistol fell to the floor. Kale sailed over the desk chair, scrambled to his hands and knees, and Wilbur dived for the pistol. They both grabbed it and struggled fiercely, Wilbur windmilling with his elbows and knees, Kale grunting, clenching his teeth. Kale's finger was on the trigger, but Wilbur had his hands wrapped about Kale's. Kale butted his head with his own, then slammed Wilbur's head against the desk with his free hand. Wilbur felt his left hand giving, and the muzzle of the pistol swung toward his face, but he averted it and the blast seared his forehead and brows.

"Sissy!" Kale choked out as they wrestled on the

floor. In a burst of effort, Wilbur suddenly rolled over onto Kale, pried his trigger finger loose, bent the pistol back toward Kale's chest, crammed two fingers through the hole and jerked the trigger.

The blast lifted them both off the floor. Kale instantly fell still with a groan. Wilbur raised up onto his knees, gasping for breath, staring at Kale's fluttering eyelids. Suddenly he felt a hot sting like a lash from a whip across his neck. He slapped at his neck with his right palm and felt the hot pulsing spray of blood against his hand.

Sissy stood by the door holding the razor in one fist. Her other fist was against her cheek. Her mouth was open.

"Oh, Will!" she gasped.

He staggered to his feet. His neck and shoulder were soaking wet, and the dampness felt slick. He pressed his fingers to the side of his throat. When he stepped toward her, she spun and bolted from the room.

Dizzy, he pursued her, but she was too nimble. He went down the stairs and ran into the salon, his hand pressed to his neck. She wasn't there. He heard a noise on the second floor, so he rushed back up the stairs, kicked every door open and went through all the rooms. In her bathroom, he paused to look into the mirror. His hand and the right side of his body were competely saturated with his own blood. She'd made a long deep cut from front to back, and no matter how hard he pressed, the blood spurted from his jugular around the edges of his hand.

He stumbled back downstairs. The front door was open again. She'd run out of it, he guessed. He felt dizzy and leaned against the frame. He peered into the yard. No sign of her, but in the distance a mewling carried on the breeze. Dizzy, he sank to a hunker in the doorway. Little had gone as planned. He shouldn't have answered Shingle's knock on his door.

The woman came tiptoeing out of the darkness. She sniffed the air like a timid jackal. When she reached the edge of the porch, she squinted. He opened his mouth; he meant to call out "help!" but could only groan.

"Now I see who you are. I always knew sooner or later you'd come around and you'd be exactly like him. I hope you're both happy."

Then she stepped back into the darkness. He kept trying to spy her and the girl out beyond the perimeter of the yard, where he could imagine Sissy squatting behind a shrub and weeping, but his vision was fading to an undeveloped photograph. In the sky over Mexico, a crescent moon hung like a tipped cup and poured libations of light onto a dark and arid landscape.